FIVE AGAINST ONE

ROSS ALEXANDER

For A, A & E

AUTHOR'S NOTE

This is a work of fiction. Names and characters are the product of the author's imagination and any resemblance to actual persons, living or dead, is entirely coincidental. Whitebank is a fictional village, as are the pub and village store contained within the story.

PROLOGUE

Day 1 - 06:34 - Whitebank Village, West Lothian

Whitebank is a small village on the outskirts of Edinburgh, a village which is famous for nothing more than being a village on the outskirts of Edinburgh. Made up of a handful of small housing estates, it had thus far avoided the rapid expansion of fellow commuter areas. A lack of local amenities being the main reason, boasting only one newsagent/grocer shop and a seldom used pub.

All that was about to change.

With the village being located away from the main roads into Edinburgh, the dark figure moved unnoticed towards the rear of the semi detached bungalow and crouched down behind the garden shed. He had been watching the area for a while and knew the adjoining property was empty. The property he was interested in was solely occupied, by the person he had come to kill.

From the rear garden, he could see that the bedroom light was still off, the homeowner would still be sound asleep. His alarm would not go off for a further twenty five minutes or so. Plenty of time to complete the task that lay ahead.

Access to the house had been carefully planned. The rear door was locked by a single key, which the occupier kept in the lock overnight. Rookie mistake. There was a small single glazed window next to the door which would assist with gaining entry. The figure crept low from his hiding place and approached the door.

Extracting a self adhesive sheet from his rucksack, he carefully removed the backing and pressed it against the window pane. He then brought out a rubber mallet and gently tapped the glass which shattered easily, remaining stuck to the adhesive sheet. Pushing at the side, he was able to reach his arm through silently and turned the key in the lock. He sprayed the hinges with lubricant and entered the house.

Leaving his rucksack inside the doorway, he headed towards the bedroom door, gun with silencer in hand. He had dreamt of this moment for a long time, playing the scenario in his mind over and over. He had considered various obstacles that could have prevented the completion of the assassination, already many of these had not materialised. There were not many left that could prevent his goal.

Once more he reached gently with his gloved hand, a matter of seconds remaining. No need to lubricate the hinges of this door, he wanted the sleeping figure to wake. Noise would be kept to a minimum, however, no need to take additional risks. The door squeaked softly and the gloved hand threw on the light switch.

The man in the bed bolted upright, blinking ferociously to adjust his eyes to the blinding light. It did not take long for him to make out the gun pointed directly at his forehead. Troubled eyes met the assassin's, showing shock, fear and confusion. He managed to speak just one word before the bullet snapped his head back, spraying blood up the wall behind him.

'Why?'

PART ONE - GO

CHAPTER ONE

The Chain is the most notorious serial killer in Edinburgh. He named himself after his choice of murder weapon, a bicycle chain used to strangle his victims. Detective Inspector Joanne Christie and Detective Sergeant Mike Lyle had finally caught him and seen him sent to prison with three life sentences. It was with unspeakable horror that they both witnessed his escape whilst attending his father's funeral.

They were back trying to catch him once more, although now they knew exactly who they were looking for. It had been three months since the escape and Kevin Curtis had managed to remain underground. A man of great intelligence, wealth and resources, they had a full team working the case. Christie and Lyle felt a sense of blame for the escape, regardless of the reassurances of the senior officers. Despite having an impressive case resolution record, both knew their careers could be jeopardised if his killing spree restarted. Fortunately, he had not attacked since his escape, but a feeling of apprehension for what horrors may yet come was never far away from either of their thoughts.

Christie had been at her desk for over two hours already. She had been racking up the hours lately, not expecting to be paid overtime even if it was available. The escape had hit her hard and she knew that Detective Chief Inspector Fergus Montgomery would be celebrating her error. He had never taken to Christie, being an 'Old School' cop that believed promotion was based on hours served rather than talent and potential. Christie had accelerated through the ranks quicker than expected and Montgomery had held a grudge since the day she reached the rank of DI. Detective Chief

Superintendent Alex Hepburn, however, had been a mentor and supporter from early in her career, although Christie was aware that that could change at any time. If The Chain was not caught soon, it may happen before much longer.

DS Lyle gently placed a cup of coffee on Christie's desk with a comforting smile. He too was affected by the escape and was trying to contain his own frustrations. Where Christie was methodical and patient, Lyle was a man of action. His skill lay in dealing with people, interviewing suspects and witnesses.

Christie lifted the coffee to her mouth, pausing before tasting.

'I assume this is fresh from the best cafe in Edinburgh?' she asked with a smirk

'Only the best for you ma'am.'

Lyle was the co-owner of The Classic Crock Cafe, specialising in fine coffee and classic rock music. Christie was addicted to the first and getting more accustomed to the latter. Being strictly tee total, and one of best drivers in Police Scotland, Lyle had been subjecting Christie to much of his personal back catalogue in his immaculate Golf GTI.

'Any news?' he asked.

'Nothing yet. We've been keeping tabs on his various bank accounts but he has not used any of his cards. Of course, he is worth a small fortune so I assume he's stashed a pile of cash away that has since been accessed. The question is, how long can he remain underground?'

Bitterness flowed through Christie's words as she spoke. Lyle could do little but nod and flick through the file on Christie's desk. He paused at a section in the file and leaned in closer.

'Can I take this bit from you? I've a little thought that's developing.'

Christie nodded as she looked at the section in question. It was a report on the motorbike used in The Chain's escape.

Lyle wandered off towards his desk, re-reading the report. The bike concerned had used a false registration plate and had been reported stolen from just outside Glasgow a week before the escape. Lyle picked up his car keys and waved them towards Christie. Christie knew that he was on to something and decided it was time to get out for some air.

'LET'S GO,' Christie shouted over to him.

She picked up her coffee and led Lyle out the room just as Montgomery arrived.

'Off chasing ghosts again DI Christie?', he asked scornfully. Christie stopped in her tracks and faced him

'Just following up on another lead, sir. Have you got anything you need me for?'

The question was asked in such a way that she was challenging what he had brought to the investigation. It caught him off guard and Lyle had to pass quickly, stifling a laugh. Montgomery remained silent, allowing his facial expression to do the talking for him.

'Didn't think so.' Christie replied as she exited behind Lyle.

Day 1 - 09:15 - Calder Road, Edinburgh

Lyle had been explaining his theory to Christie, even switching off the music to emphasise his points.

'So the theft of the motorbike was done outside Glasgow, not in Edinburgh. I believe that the bike was stolen to order and not necessarily by the rider. The bike was specific to the task, powerful and easily ridden off road if required.' Lyle punched the steering wheel in a mixture of frustration and excitement. He knew he should have thought of this sooner.

Christie nodded her head knowing now what he was thinking and where he was headed.

'Bad Boy' Billy Broon had grown up with a life of petty crime. For the past two years, however, he had established a successful burger van business. As well as keeping his nose clean, his new life away from crime was now allowing him access to his young son. The last time they visited him, he was hopeful of a reunion with the boy's mother.

The GTI pulled to a stop in front of Bad Boy's Wester Hailes flat and Christie and Lyle jumped out. A young boy in scruffy clothing ran towards the car.

'Nice motor, mister.' he shouted with wide eyes.

'Aye it is, wee man.' Lyle smiled at the boy. 'And I'll tell you what. If it is still this nice a car, when I get back in about ten minutes, I'll give you a fiver.'

The boy's eyes lit up and he nodded excitedly, words failing him.

Christie gave Lyle a look of surprise as they headed for the main door of the flats.

'Are you really going to give that wee boy a fiver?' she asked in disbelief.

'The trick to these areas is to link in with the locals. He's been given a job and he will not let anyone near the car if there's reward at the end. Years on patrol have taught me that ma'am.'

Christie could do nothing but shake her head in astonishment.

'And', he continued. 'It's still cheaper than parking on George Street.'

The main door was ajar and the officers headed up the stairs to Bad Boy's flat. Lyle gave the door a good thump with his fist. The door shot open to reveal a girl in her late twenties staring through them.

'What's he done now?'

Although there was some anger in her voice, the overriding emotion to come through was disappointment. She never gave them a chance to answer the first question.

'I knew it would just be a matter of time before the police would be at this door. Two months!' She gave a dramatic tut. 'Two months I've been here witnessing the so called 'Reformed William', just waiting for this day.'

She turned on her heals, leaving the door open. Christie and Lyle heard his name being screamed out, before a bashful Bad Boy came out the bedroom.

'It's okay Maria, it's just Mr Lyle. I told you, I've changed. Mr Lyle, unless I'm very much mistaken, will just be wanting a wee bit help.' Bad Boy was putting a reassuring hand on her shoulder.

'Good job the bairn's at school.' Her voice had softened, but the retort was sharp enough to convey that she still needed convincing. Christie spoke directly to Maria.

'William is correct. We just want to ask him a few questions and then we will be on our way. I promise, there is nothing that you should be concerned about.'

Maria gave an appreciative smile and headed to the kitchen to boil the kettle. Bad boy escorted the pair into the living room. Once more, the immaculate nature of the room came as a surprise, despite them having been in the room a number of times before. A recently taken photograph of the whole family was framed and proudly displayed. An indication of a life turned round. Lyle walked over to the photograph.

'So, how are things going with you two?'

Bad Boy stood beside Lyle, picked up the frame and gave it a polish with the sleeve of his jumper.

'Still early days, Mr Lyle, but they have been going well. Maria wants some stability in Michael's life.'

'Michael?' Lyle asked. 'Good name.'

'After Maria's grandfather, not you Mr Lyle.'

Bad Boy let out a small chuckle at Lyle's mocked hurt expression.

'The business is picking up and I'm hoping soon we will have enough for a deposit for our own home. Won't be in Edinburgh unfortunately, but maybe West or East Lothian. We're not looking for much, just somewhere nice to bring the wee man up and a place we can call our own.'

'Nice the hear, Bad Boy.' Lyle was using his nickname for impact. A reminder that his past couldn't be changed, the choices that had been made. A reminder also that they were here on business. 'I assume, however, that you still keep an ear to the ground?'

Bad Boy was slightly rattled, but was keeping his emotions in check. There was, however, a glint in his eye. A warning to Lyle not to push too far.

'I promise that I've put all that behind me, Mr Lyle.' The latter part of his reply was spat out. 'I do still have some associates that are not so squeaky clean and share some of the goings on in their circles. But I promise, that's all it is.'

Christie decided to take over. Lyle had been supportive of the changes Bad Boy had made to his life, but the two also had history. The information Bad Boy had shared with them in recent times had proven useful and Christie didn't want egos turning off that particular tap.

'We didn't suspect otherwise, William, and we didn't come here to drag up any previous misdemeanours. We're just looking for some information that could assist with a line of enquiry we're working on related to a major case.'

Bad Boy's eyes lit up, Christie immediately realising her error of stating 'a major case'.

'The Chain? You're here about The Chain?'

Christie could do nothing but nod in confirmation.

'One sick bastard. An intelligent sick bastard, but sick bastard none the less.'

'Tell us what you know.' Lyle asked the question firmly but without aggression.

'Well, obviously I've read what the newspapers have posted online. There's also been a lot of chat going around, mainly about how he got away. Not your finest hour, Mr Lyle.' Lyle ignored the remark. 'Obviously a resourceful man, but his cash was not offered in any of the underground circles I'm aware of.'

Maria appeared from the kitchen offering tea or coffee, but Christie politely refused. She offered a smile and returned to the kitchen. Christie's eyes wandered around the room, taking in the minimal furniture and excessive cleanliness.

'So you have no idea of who helped him escape?'

'None whatsoever, but if you ask me it would be someone from Glasgow or Lanarkshire. Edinburgh's underground tend to work their own patch, the city and the Lothians. At a push, they venture into Fife, but never Motherwell.'

Bad Boy smiled at the shocked expression on his guests faces. There was no news about the motorbike being stolen from Motherwell in any of the press reports.

'My acquaintances still have one or two bent coppers to spill the beans. Pity Mr Lyle here is not one of them or I could've made a killing back in the day.'

William walked over to the window and looked out across a housing area that had seen better days and desperately needed investment.

'Tell you what though. Since you have both been straight with me these last couple of years, I'll see what I can find out. If you text me the full details of the bike, I may know someone who knows someone who knows something.'

'Very public spirited of you', Lyle mocked. Christie threw him a warning look.

'We'd appreciate anything you can find out, William.'

'I'll see what I can do, but I need to let you know one thing first. I won't put my family at risk. First sign of trouble, you're on your own. These people are not stupid and I've seen first hand what they do to a grass.'

'Thanks William,' Christie said gratefully.

Lyle gave him a pat on the back and mumbled a thanks. An expert reader of people, he knew the boy was genuine. He also knew he was useful and would bet a substantial share of his vinyl collection that he would bring them something worthwhile. Christie had popped into the kitchen to speak with Maria.

'For what it's worth, Maria', Christie started softly. 'I truly believe he means what he says. Now that might not be worth much, but my partner can read anyone like a book and he feels the same. Let me give you two pieces of advice.'

'Go on then.' Maria's interest had piqued.

'Firstly, give William a chance. For your sake as well as your son's. He's made mistakes, but there is no dirt on him now. Believe me, I've checked. On the few occasions that I've met him, he's always spoken about you and Michael. It's obvious where his priorities lie now'

Christie smiled and put a hand on Maria's arm before turning to exit the room.

'What's the second?' she called after her. Christie turned with a grin.

'Never play poker with DS Lyle.'

Day 1 - 11:55 - The Classic Crock Cafe, Edinburgh

Given Christie's early start and lack of breakfast, she was in desperate need of an early lunch. With Christie not concerned over where to stop, Lyle inevitably drove to the cafe he co-owned with his best friend, Frank. He had made some excuse about needing to see Frank, but Christie was happy to go regardless of the lame excuse. As well as the best coffee in Edinburgh, they had started a range of handmade artisan sandwiches.

'I still can't believe you gave that wee boy a fiver,' she said as they got out the car.

'Look at her, not a scratch. Worth every penny.'

They walked into the cafe and Lyle greeted Frank with a hug and an instruction to get something decent on the sound system. Pearl Jam's 'Alive' started.

'Now ma'am', Lyle began. 'The grunge movement of the late eighties and early nineties gave rock music the same kick up the arse that punk did in the late seventies.' Christie rolled her eyes, knowing he was on another of his infamous musical rants. 'Like it or not, it made other bands up their game. Now Frank and I, as per usual, disagree on one major factor. For me, Pearl Jam were the best grunge band. Songwriting, musicianship and one for the best rock vocalists of all time. Frank is a champion of Nirvana, arguing they were closer to the grunge vibe and for the deep lyrical context.'

Frank appeared with a tray containing two coffees and sandwiches. He mirrored Christie's eye roll.

'The only thing you need to know, ma'am', Lyle went on. 'Is that I am right.'

Frank left them to it, knowing that police business was about to be discussed. The grunge argument would wait for another day. They sat at a table in the corner of the cafe that would offer them privacy. There were only a few other customers around, mainly students on laptop computers and noise cancelling headphones. Most of the lunchtime trade would be take away.

'Do you think he will turn up with anything useful?' Christie asked.

'Difficult to say, he's always been a good source of information and usually it's pretty accurate. Depends how much his new clean lifestyle is isolating him from that information.'

'Do you think he's genuine?'

Lyle took a sip of his coffee and shook his head.

'Who knows. For his sake, I hope so. The stuff about his family is genuine, of that I have no doubt. It's not easy leaving the old life behind and moving on. Personally, I think he's like a drug addict that has gone cold turkey, the draw to go back is always there but they can see the benefits of persevering.'

Christie and Lyle finished off their lunch mainly in silence. Lyle spent a bit of time chatting to some of the regulars and having good natured debate with Frank. Time was passing and they knew that they had better head back to the station. The last thing she needed was for someone to walk in and accuse two detectives of slacking on the job.

Montgomery would have a field day…

CHAPTER TWO

<u>Day 1 - 18:54 - Whitebank Village, West Lothian</u>

Barbara Stewart had lived in Whitebank village for over fifty years and had seen firsthand the many changes that had happened to the place. When she had first moved in as a newly married twenty year old, there had only been a small number of streets and houses. There had been a post office, butchers, newsagent and separate grocers as well as a popular public house. One by one they had closed, demolished for property redevelopment with only the pub and newsagent surviving.

With her husband now dead ten years, she lived an isolated life. Some family came at the weekends for a visit, but most of her days were spent reading, watching television and drinking copious amounts of tea. One thing she did do every morning and evening, regardless of the weather, was to take a walk around the village. This kept her active ensuring she remained physically and mentally fit. Most days, it was a wander round the housing estates as the tarmac made it easy to get round. Only on longer spells of milder weather would she venture to the surrounding woodlands, where the dry paths could be navigated safely.

This week, the weather had been kind and she had enjoyed a walk through the woodland, listening to the birds and the sounds of the leaves gently blowing in the wind. She had a sturdy pair of walking boots that had seen her tackle some of Scotland's Munros in her early sixties and, although she was past that level of adventure now, the boots still served her well.

She decided to walk round the village this evening and headed out a bit earlier than usual. There was a new Agatha Christie adaptation on the television later and she wanted to be home and settled in for that.

The main street was quiet as usual. A young couple were heading into the pub, no doubt grabbing an evening meal. Barbara didn't recognise them, perhaps they were Livingston residents popping in on their way home from work in the city. The food was excellent in the pub, probably the reason why it was still open.

The newsagent/grocer was still open and Barbara decided that she would invest on some biscuits for an evening treat. She popped into the empty shop and selected a packet of Hob Nobs, determined to make this packet last at least a week. The owner of the shop was a lady of similar ages to herself but, at this time in the evening, her son looked after things for her.

They had a brief conversation before Barbara exited to continue her walk. She turned into one of the housing estates that backed onto the woodland and had a wander round. She liked to have a subtle peek into the houses, often remarking to herself about the furniture or decor. One of the houses in her rounds caught her attention.

The owner's car was still in the driveway, even though she knew he worked late most weekdays. Also, the living room curtains were drawn and at this time of day they were always open. Something felt wrong and Barbara was not one to ignore such things.

The neighbouring houses were quiet, with people getting on with their lives behind closed doors. Barbara didn't think it would be too much if she was just to have a quick look round the back. Of course the occupant could be ill or just arranged a day off work and stayed in bed, but it was worth having a quick peek just in case.

She squeezed past the four by four car to reach the top of the driveway, where a gate and six foot fence enclosed the rear garden. She reached for the handle and gave it a tug but the gate remained closed. She noticed a dead bolt on the other side and was able to glide her thin hand through a gap in the slats and unlock the bolt. The bottom of the gate stayed in place as she pushed open, wedged to the concrete path. With a swift kick of her right foot, her trusty walking boots did the job and the gate flew open.

Tentatively, Barbara walked round to the back door and noticed immediately the smashed window. Suspecting a burglary, she entered the house cautiously and walked through the kitchen and into the living room. Nothing appeared to have been taken and the large television, DVD player and computer laying untouched.

Barbara retreated back towards the hallway and made her way towards a room at the back of the house. The bedroom door was closed and Barbara opened it gently with her foot. The horror of the scene in front of her filled her senses. The dead body, slumped upright on the bed, an array of blood splatter and tissue covering the walls.

Barbara let out a scream and collapsed to the floor.

Day 1 - 19:24 - Corstorphine Police Station, Edinburgh

The call had come in just as Christie was calling it a day. She had already clocked over thirteen hours and was starting to feel the effects. She had planned on an early night and a refreshing swim in the morning. She and her partner, Tom, had a triathlon booked next month and she needed to keep up her training.

With the report of a dead body coming in, that would have to wait.

Lyle had headed to the cafe to help out for a couple of hours and Christie felt bad dragging him away, but she needed him. Hepburn had asked Christie to go especially, leaving Montgomery to stay on The Chain case.

Lyle arrived in the GTI and they headed out towards Whitebank. Lyle had put on Pink Floyd's 'The Division Bell' album and skipped to a mellow instrumental track called 'Marooned'. Christie could tell that he was distracted, his mind somewhere else, but she didn't question at this point. She shut her eyes and listened to the soft sounds, working out her strategy of what to do at the scene of the crime.

When the track ended Lyle played it again, something he never did in Christie's company. He was always playing different songs, sharing strange facts, recalling concerts and festivals attended. Something was seriously wrong. Christie couldn't leave it any longer.

'Do you want to talk about it?'

Lyle kept his eyes on the road and shook his head.

'An old case, nothing more.'

'What's triggered it?' Christie wasn't pushing, she needed to know if anything could jeopardise the case. She would rather proceed without her best officer that risk the case. Too much was riding on it to let personal feelings get in the way. Lyle's or Christie's.

'Whitebank. It's a place I never drive through or go anywhere near. I'll tell you all about it one day. Let's just see who and what we have waiting for us.'

Lyle pulled into village and could see the blue flashing lights of an ambulance in one of the housing estates.

'A bit late for that is it not? I thought the guy was shot dead.'

Christie and Lyle got out the car and headed towards the ambulance to find out more. An elderly lady in some distress was being treated by one of the two paramedics. The other approached the officers who were both holding out their warrant cards for inspection.

'The lady that found him,' she stated in way of confirmation. 'We've confirmed the occupant is deceased and disturbed as little as possible.'

'Is she able to talk to us?' Christie asked.

'We're going to take her to St John's for a thorough check up. She's in no fit state to talk at the moment, but you should be able to ask a few questions once the doctor has seen her.

Christie thanked her and headed towards the house. The forensic team had arrived as they were talking to the paramedic and were in the process of protecting the scene. Lyle handed Christie a forensic suit and shoe covers.

'Do we have an ID on the victim?' Christie asked one of the forensic officers. She shrugged her shoulders in reply and continued her work.

Christie and Lyle were only given limited access until the forensic team gave the go ahead. They were able to view the body from the doorway. The bullet had penetrated the man's head which had sent it backwards from where the body sat. From their angle they were unable to see the face.

Or what was left of it.

'Lyle, I spotted a woman lurking around the front of the ambulance. Go grab a word with her and see if you can find out anything. I'll call in a check on the property and vehicle parked outside, make sure they match.'

Lyle headed off as Christie had a look round the hallway and kitchen. A forensic officer was giving her a stare and she knew she was over staying her welcome, for now. She took the hint and headed outside, pulling out her phone to make the call.

Lyle was looking animated as he spoke to the lady by the ambulance. The lady was crying, shock obvious on her face as Lyle was writing notes frantically in his book. As Christie was getting confirmation of the homeowner and vehicle registration details Dr Arthur James, the police pathologist, arrived on the scene. He exited his car wearing a dinner suit and black tie.

'Good Evening DI Christie, how's the training going?'

Dr James was a man with an unrivalled reputation. On top of his expertise, experience and both academic and professional qualifications, he was also an incredibly nice person.

'It would be going better if the job didn't keep getting in the way. What have we disturbed you from this evening?'

Dr James gave a chuckle.

'Doing me a favour, truth be told. Was heading to Glasgow University for an evening of dull speeches and inadequate dining. Not a touch on Edinburgh University events. Just don't tell anyone I said so.'

He gave a wink and headed towards the house.

'Don't worry Doc, your secret is safe with me.'

Dr James gave a thumbs up as he continued walking, stopping to get the initial details from one of the forensic officers. Christie decided to join Lyle to find out more about the mysterious lady. As she arrived beside the pair, she began to get a little concerned for Lyle.

Lyle introduced the woman as Mary, the deceased man's next door neighbour. A tall lady whom Christie guessed to be in her late forties. She had stopped crying and looked more composed, with only the redness in her eyes indicating her previous distress. Lyle let the woman speak for herself as she repeated her story for Christie's benefit.

'Dave has lived here for over twenty years, I think, nice guy who kept himself to himself. I've only been here five years, moved in with my daughter when my divorce was finalised. Only really knew him to say hello to, but you don't expect that to happen right next door to you, do you?'

Christie shook her head sympathetically. Something she said startled Lyle.

'Is your daughter at home now?' he asked her.

'No, she's with her dad tonight. No doubt she'll come back tomorrow with constipation and reeking of fast food.'

Christie was slightly concerned about Lyle's question, but carried on.

'When was the last time you saw your neighbour?'

Mary thought for a while, then shook her head.

'No idea, a few weeks back perhaps. He was out pottering in his garden, but didn't say anything except for a quick hello.'

'Did you see anything suspicious, either today or in the last few weeks?'

Mary gave the question some thought, something was stirring in her. Lyle could sense it and tried to reassure her.

'Anything at all, Mary, regardless how silly it may seem.'

'Well, a couple of weeks back I spotted a guy wandering around the street in a high visibility jacket. Nothing unusual in that, but I remember that he didn't have a van with him. He passed the house a few times then disappeared round the corner. I'm sure it could have been genuine.'

Christie pounced on the information.

'Could you give a description of this individual?'

'Definitely a white male with dark hair. Never caught a good look at his face. His jeans were clean, I remember that now. I remember thinking the state some workies get their jeans in, but his were new. As was the jacket come to think about it. He looked more management than labourer.'

Christie thanked Mary for her time and handed over her card, should she have any more information she wanted to share. She also asked her to make a formal statement.

By the time they had finished, the ambulance had taken the patient away. Christie suggested they head to the hospital in the hope of getting to ask questions quicker. Hanging about pestering medical staff was one of

Lyle's strengths, and usually resulted in submission. He was an exceptional people's person, both dealing with and the reading of them.

Lyle started the car, switched on the stereo and skipped through the songs until he reached Metallica's 'Kill 'Em All' album. He selected 'Seek & Destroy' and Christie felt the heavy, fast paced song had meaning to the story he was about to tell. She raised the subject sensitivity.

'So I assume that the name David Stafford means something to you? The reason you avoid Whitebank?'

Lyle was a seasoned cop that rarely showed emotion. For the first time, Christie could see some of that emotion leak.

'They say that there is always one case that never leaves you. The case against David Stafford was that case for me.'

Christie knew the full story would come eventually, so didn't push.

'The one part of this job that gets to me ma'am, is that we treat victims equally. Just like doctors must do with their patients, we have to treat everyone the same...'

The singer was screaming out the song title as Lyle spoke.

'...even suspected murderers.'

PART TWO - ANIMAL

CHAPTER THREE

Day 1 - 21:37 - St John's Hospital, Livingston, West Lothian

Christie and Lyle remained mainly silent as they were kept waiting by the medical staff. They had ascertained her personal details and knew they had to speak with her quickly. The doctor was not keen, but after an hour of waiting, she finally relented. They were allowed five minutes, not a second longer.

Barbara was propped up on the bed by a number of pillows, but looked like she longed for sleep. She had been changed into a hospital issue gown and her complexion was as white as the snow topped mountains she once climbed. The doctor has confirmed to them that she had been given a mild sedative and they planned to keep her in overnight for observation. It looked like the sedative was starting to work, they had little time to waste.

Christie introduced herself and Lyle, choosing to sit on a chair close to the bed. Lyle preferred to stand and observe.

'I'm sorry that we need to ask you questions so soon after such a shock', Christie began softly. 'I can only imagine was you experienced this evening.'

Barbara gave a slight nod of her head, appreciating the sentiment and giving her agreement to continue.

'Did you know the victim?'

Barbara cleared her throat and spoke with equal degrees of difficulty and determination. She had an educated local accent.

'I've lived in Whitebank for over 50 years. One does not live in a place that long without knowing the goings on of a village, especially of such a size as Whitebank. I knew of Mr Stafford, albeit he was a reserved

26

man and not one for meaningful and deep conversation. He had his reasons for being the way he was.'

Barbara's eyes flickers and she took a deep breath, Christie's mind was racing but continued with the most obvious of questions.

'Do you know of anyone who would want to harm Mr Stafford?'

Barbara's eyes opened once more and met Lyle's for the first time. She answered Christie's question whilst maintaining eye contact with her sergeant.

'My dear, if his past were to come back and haunt him, a great number of people would want to harm him. I believed he was innocent of what he was accused of.'

'Accused of?' Christie asked, her tone sharping.

Barbara's eyelids drooped once more as a mixture of exhaustion and medication started to take control. She managed one more sentence, pointing weakly at Lyle, before she drifted off completely.

'Your colleague over there will fill you in...'

Day 1 - 23:27 - M8 Motorway, Eastbound approaching Edinburgh

It had been a long day and Christie was not sure if she was ready for the full story. Lyle was not quite ready to rely it anyway.

'Ma'am, if you will permit, I would like to review the case notes in the morning and then I will be happy to tell you everything. I'm too emotionally attached right now and I would only be telling you my feelings rather than all the facts.'

Christie trusted Lyle more than any other colleague and knew that he wouldn't ask for such understanding if it was not imperative. She knew she would have to make a judgement call, would he be able to assist with the case? Had it been any other officer, she would probably would have dismissed them from the case already. Lyle was different and she knew that they trusted each other enough that he would be the first to admit to her if he was unsuitable for the case.

'Okay Lyle. Drop me off and go get some sleep. Get the case files in the morning and meet me at my desk at eleven o'clock.'

'Thank you, ma'am.'

Lyle continued to drive in silence, old memories coming back to him. The thoughts were hurting him, like old forgotten wounds being reopened. He often wondered if this day would come, the day that his underlying vulnerability would be exposed. He was not ashamed of that, but hoped that Christie would not think less of him...

...given the mistakes made over twenty years before.

Day 2 - 11:00 - Corstorphine Police Station, Edinburgh

Christie had slept better than expected, but woke early with thoughts of the dead man flooding back to her. Her first thought would be to try and establish the motive for the murder. Lyle seemed convinced that it related to the previous case that he had worked on, even though she had still to find out the details. She had become slightly frustrated at Lyle when she returned home, but had enough trust in him to let him play it out in his own way. Other superior officers would not be so patient or understanding, but Christie knew that Lyle was worth more to her than the rest of her team combined.

With her bedside clock showing 06:25, she decided to change quickly and cycle to the Commonwealth Pool to get an hour's swim in. Swimming was her favourite part of her triathlon training and she loved getting to the pool early to get her laps in, surrounded by fellow endurance and competitive swimmers. Although she did not take the sport too

28

seriously, she cared enough that she was as best prepared for any race that she could be. As well as maintaining her high level of fitness, the gentle rhythm of the swim allowed her thoughts to flow and often she considered a key element to a case in the middle of such a swim. Today, however, she just focused on her strokes and breathing, allowing her mind time to empty and recover. The start of any case was the time that Christie felt at her most vulnerable, worrying if she would be able to solve the case. Once she got going, though, her confidence would rise and she would become the natural leader required to get a result.

She headed into the station around 10 o'clock and spotted Lyle at his desk going through a pile of old files. She decided to leave him in peace and headed to her own desk. She spent the next hour typing up some notes and initial thoughts. She put a call into Dr James and he agreed that she and Lyle could visit him later in the afternoon.

DCI Montgomery appeared at her desk sipping from an old and chipped Heart of Midlothian FC mug that probably dated from the 1980's. Christie never witnessed him making the tea himself, he would always send one of the junior ranked officers off to make it, shouting 'lots of milk and two big fucking sugars'. The whole station knew how he took his tea, but he always insisted on bellowing out his order.

'I hear you've got a new body on your hands,' he commented unemotionally.

Christie kept her eyes on the computer screen as she continued to type away on the keyboard.

'Yes, we've just picked it up from Whitebank, early days, not much to report as yet, sir.'

'Whitebank?' Montgomery's expression changed instantly, he was now interested. 'Who was it?'

Christie lifted her head to make eye contact, looking for a sign in him that she may find useful later in the case.

'David Stafford.'

'Fuck, that's a name I remember from back in the day. He was mixed up in some business, something with a missing kid. Can't remember the full details, but I know that it was proven that he had nothing to do with it. Wrong place at the wrong time. Your pal, Lyle, will no doubt remember more.'

He looked over and spotted Lyle going through the files.

'Looks like he's already doing his study.'

Christie just nodded, interested in the softer stance Montgomery was taking with her. Was it her earlier outburst that changed him, or did he get a talking to from DCS Hepburn? Christie expected the latter. His parting comment surprised her even more.

'Why don't you take your two DC's back, I've enough of my guys working on The Chain case and I'm sure we will crack it soon enough.'

With that he drained his cup, belched loudly and headed back to his desk.

DC Anna Miles and DC Raj Chowdhury had worked on a number of cases with Christie before and she was glad to get them on her team. Miles was in her mid twenties and destined for great things. Christie seen many of her own positive traits in Miles and they worked together well. As well as having her as her mentor, Christie had also solved a case involving her partner, Fiona, and Miles felt forever in her superior officer's debt. Christie had treated solving the case just like any other, but deep down she had felt an increased sense of relief at getting the result, very probably saving the girl's life.

Chowdhury was in his early thirties and had not been in the team that long. He joined Police Scotland from the Metropolitan Police in London. Christie knew that there was an incident that led to him moving to Edinburgh, but as yet she was unaware of the details. Regardless of his reasons, she was delighted to have him on her team. His attention to detail was incredible, his patience never wavered and he was an expert in reading CCTV, having worked for 3 years as a CCTV Operator before joining the Met.

Christie called Miles and Chowdhury over to her desk.

'Welcome to the Whitebank murder case,' she began, the two junior detectives listening intently. 'David Stafford, 59 years old, found shot dead in his own home in the village of Whitebank. From what we have gathered from the locals, he lived a quiet life, lived alone and kept himself to himself. He was also a suspect in a case that Lyle was involved in many years ago. Lyle is currently reviewing the case files and we will be having a meeting shortly to discuss this further.'

Christie looked over towards Lyle who was keeping his head down, glued to the pages in front of him. Christie gave a slight nod of her head to instruct the pair to come closer to her.

'This previous case,' she whispered so that only the two could hear. 'It was one that got to Lyle, so I fully expect you treat this sensitively. We all know how important it is that we have him on this case and I will not jeopardise the outcome in any way, understood?'

'Yes, ma'am,' they replied in unison.

'Right, Miles, I will want you to do some door to door enquiries and report back anything interesting directly to me. Chowdhury, I want you to do full background on Stafford. Lyle and I will go and see Dr James this afternoon and get his preliminary report.'

The couple headed back to their desks to start their own files and Christie returned to her own notes. She wanted to make sure that she prepared herself for Lyle's briefing on the old case. It was imperative that she kept an open mind, which would not be easy giving her connection with Lyle. Although she had received a lot of credit for the results she had already achieved as a Detective Inspector, many of these would not have been obtained without the support and input of Lyle. Another of Lyle's strengths was his ability to distance himself from a case. He was methodical in his dealings with suspects, witnesses and friends or family of the victims. She never once witnessed him losing his composure and had learned more in the first month observing his approach than she had in the years working through the ranks.

Christie for once felt like Lyle often did, ready for action and frustrated to be stuck in the office. Lyle's pacing of the station floors was legendary and often a sign that it was time to get out and speak with people. In more cases than most, that was the key to a breakthrough and Lyle was better than most when it came to getting a witness to give the critical piece of information that would open up a case. Christie was now longing to return the favour.

Getting up from her chair, she headed to the kitchen area to make a cup of coffee. It would be weak, instant coffee lacking in flavour but she needed the caffeine now. She was craving her favourite Classic Crock latte, but this would have to suffice for now. Returning to her desk, she spotted Lyle rising to meet her.

'Okay ma'am, I've got what I need to start.'

His voice was solemn, lacking in its usual chirpiness and humour. Christie nodded softly.

'I've booked Meeting Room 2, Miles and Chowdhury will be joining us. Montgomery has let me have them on the case.'

Lyle just nodded and headed towards the meeting room. There would be no powerpoint presentation, graphs, charts or technology. Lyle would stick to the facts of the case and give time for the others to take notes and ask any questions. Christie indicated to Miles and Chowdhury to follow them and they made their way to the meeting room.

The room itself was cold and felt damp. The decor was now dated and could use a lick of paint, but none of that mattered at the end of the day. It was the discussions, the thoughts and the joint sharing of theories that was the most important element of such rooms.

Lyle sat at the top of the table and spread out some notes in front of him. His audience all opened their respective notepads and waited for him to begin.

'The 17th of August, 1992 is a date that is ingrained in my head. It was the date in which David Stafford was acquitted of having any involvement in the kidnapping and probable murder of 16 year old Samantha Kerr.' Lyle paused for a moment, ensuring that the recollection would not get the better of him.

'Samantha, known as Sammy to her friends, was a bright, outgoing girl who loved life and lived it to the full. She was also exceptionally intelligent and had a bright future ahead of her. She had a baby brother, Nicholas, and her parents were both devoted to the family. They set strict boundaries for Samantha, but were also keen not to be too restrictive on her social and personal life.'

The other three listened intently, scribbling notes quickly into their books. Lyle continued.

'Samatha was reported missing on the 2nd of January of the same year, having failed to return from a sleepover with her best friend, Morag. They had both attended a Hogmanay party with friends from school in the local area and had returned to Morag's house, somewhat worse for wear, around 4 o'clock in the morning of the 1st. They spent the day recovering in Morag's bedroom before Samatha headed home, making the ten minute walk on foot. She never reached her home and was never seen again.

'Where did all this take place?' asked Chowdhury.

'Both houses were in Kirknewton. Morag had offered to walk her part of the way back, but she insisted in going alone. It was around 8 o'clock in the evening and was dark. I interviewed Morag at the time...'

Lyle took a moment to compose himself, the recollection of his own involvement in the case was starting to hurt.

'She blamed herself for Samantha's disappearance and no amount of reassurance from Samantha's family, her own family or from me would make her change her mind. She was admitted to hospital a few months after the event with an eating disorder, but fortunately she managed to pull through.'

Christie looked up from her notes.

'Did she provide any useful information or insights during the interviews?' She asked cautiously, not wanting to sound either patronising or critical.

'Mostly not, however, there was one thing she did say that I could not get out of my head. She said that she thought that Samatha may be meeting somebody and that she thought that somebody was a man. Now, nothing much unusual about that for a sixteen year old girl. It was not even unusual not to confide in her best friend as Morag said that Samantha kept

34

boyfriends secret until she was sure they were officially dating. The thing that struck me was that she said 'man', not 'boy'.'

Miles leaned back in her chair.

'So, you think she was dating someone older,' she stated.

'Not only someone older, but I think it may have been David Stafford who was in his early 30's at that time.'

'Fucking animal,' commented Chowdhury. The others looked round at him, he was not one who was known to swear.

'My thoughts exactly,' confirmed Lyle.

CHAPTER FOUR

Day 2 - 13:03 - Classic Crock Cafe, Edinburgh

Christie had called a halt to the meeting shortly after Chowdhury's outburst. There would be more details to be shared about the old case, but Christie wanted to get started on the current case. She had sent Miles out with a PC who had recently been assigned to the team for role experience, although most people didn't think he was cut out for CID. Chowdhury was doing his background work, taking the files from Lyle in the process. After the work he had put in during the course of the morning, Christie decided to treat Lyle to lunch at his own cafe. Within minutes of entering the premises, he was back to his usual self.

'Right Frank,' he bellowed and he strolled towards the music system. 'Let's get some decent tunes on here and turn it up to eleven.'

The music system screamed out 'Ah-ow' as Layne Staley of Alice in Chains started 'Them Bones'. Christie recognised the voice, having heard one of their songs before in Lyle's car.

'Yes, Big Guy', affirmed Frank, impressed by his partner's choice. He had prepared a couple of sandwiches which he brought over to the Pink Floyd table that Lyle preferred when eating. Christie braced herself for her latest musical education.

'Now, as you may recall, Frank and I disagree profusely about the greatest grunge band. What we do agree on, however, is that the most underrated grunge band was the mighty Alice in Chains. The Dirt album is up there as one of the best rock albums of all time.'

'Amen', confirmed Frank as he returned to counter to serve some lunch time customers who were waiting in line.

Christie and Lyle ate their lunch with the music becoming background noise as they made small talk to fill any awkward silences. As Christie drained the last of her coffee, she asked the question that had been burning inside her since Lyle had given his speech.

'Do you think Stafford was involved?'

Lyle twirled the remains of his coffee round in his cup. It was not a question that he needed to prepare an answer, the question had been in his head for over 25 years.

'The honest answer is that I don't know. The evidence that we had at the time suggested that he was involved. To be fair to him, he didn't deny knowing Samantha but stopped short in confirming if they were in some sort of relationship. My people reading skills were not as honed back then as they are now. Looking back at the file, the case should never had gone to court. We had very little evidence and most of what we had was circumstantial.'

Christie let the answer sink in, letting her eyes wander around the room at the various rock posters, album covers, concert tickets and other memorabilia attached to the walls.

'And there was no body either', she commented, causing Lyle to nod his head at the relevance of the statement.

'We had no chance of prosecuting for murder without a body, not in those days and not with the evidence we had. We had to go for kidnapping, but the main evidence was Samantha's diary which made some reference to Stafford. Also there was an eye witness, however, she was elderly and had poor eyesight. Given how dark it was at the time of the sighting, the defence lawyer had no trouble getting over that particular hurdle.'

Lyle excused himself from the table and wandered over to help Frank at the counter. Christie could tell that the memory of the case was playing on his mind and he was obviously trying to hide the fact. Although she neither had Lyle's knowledge or years of service, she could somewhat relate to him. She had experienced a recurring nightmare from when she had been investigating the Songbird case.

Songbird was the nickname given to DS Miles' partner, Fiona. Fiona is an incredible singer who was subjected to a poisoning plot that Christie had managed to solve. The nightmares had her dreaming that due to a mistake she made, Fiona had been killed and Miles had turned against her and blamed her for the death. She always woke up just as Miles was about the physically attack her. The nightmares served to remind her of two things. Firstly, how important Miles was to her both professionally and as a friend. Secondly, it brought home how dangerous the job was and how important it was to do it right. Her thoughts were disturbed by Lyle's return to the table, having cleared the lunchtime rush.

'Sorry about that ma'am. I'm sure that after The Chain attacked me in this place, the sales went through the roof. Everyday I'm in here a customer brings it up. I just hope we can catch him again, as I don't fancy going through that again.

Lyle unconsciously rubbed at his throat, a reminder of how close he came to being another victim.

'I would rather forget about him for the time being and focus on other things, ma'am.'

'Which brings us back to the current case,' Christie responded. 'I have two burning questions. Firstly, is his murder related to this case or are there other secrets lurking in Stafford's life? Secondly, if it is related why did the perpetrator wait nearly thirty years to act?'

Lyle stared into space, stumped by both questions.

Day 2 - 15:53 - The Office of Dr Arthur James, Edinburgh

Dr James welcomed Christie and Lyle in his usual positive matter and led them through to his office. He always referred to the lab that he performs his autopsies at as 'The Office' and he also occupies a small room beside it that he welcomes his visitors, usually with a choice of coffees from his self funded, top of the range capsule machine.

Dr James is a tall, slim man with broad shoulders from his rugby playing university days. He is always immaculately dressed in handmade suits and is never without a tie. Incredibly fond of both Christie and Lyle, he is considerably more welcoming than many in his profession. He does, however, remain profoundly professional and only releases information to them when he is comfortable doing so. He was waving to them to take a seat as he headed towards the coffee machine.

'Right, you fine people need wee a shot of caffeine before we go into the limited details I am going to give you. I have a beautiful sample for you from Indonesia, not too strong so that it allows the flavour to come through. Biscuits are on the side table over there if you fancy a dunk.'

Lyle grabbed a couple of packets of the caramel coffee biscuits, passing one to Christie. Dr James placed the cups on the table in front of them, waiting for their consumption before getting down to business.

'The victim died of a gunshot wound to the head, however, you don't need my decades of experience to have worked that out. The bullet has been recovered from the scene and is currently undergoing analysis. I have not finished my full report, or investigation, thus far, however, I can furnish you with a couple of early observations.'

Both Christie and Lyle shifted forward in their seats.

'I think the killer was not a professional killer and I think they got lucky. Thoughts DI Christie?'

39

Christie sat back in her chair taking in the question, the answer to the first part coming quickly.

'They only shot once. You said that they recovered the bullet, not bullets. A professional killer would fire multiple times to ensure the job is done. Often they would shoot at the head and chest.'

'Very good,' he looked at Lyle. 'She'll go far.' He was mocking, however, it was said affectionately. Lyle could not help but smile at the remark.

'You said he was lucky?' He asked.

Christie was stumped too, so Dr James let them out of their misery.

'You would not believe the amount of people who survive shots to the head. Real life is not like the movies and it takes a very precise shot to do the damage. Often the bullet can graze the skull or partial penetration of the bullet can cause brain damage or the victim to go into a vegetive state. Your man, or woman, hit the exact mark. Death would have been instantaneous.'

The vision that Dr James had painted remained in the mind of Christie and Lyle and they were excused and headed back out to the car.

Day 2 - 23:14 - Undisclosed Location, West Lothian

For a first time killer, he felt relatively relaxed as he contemplated his work. He had impressed himself on how calm he had remained throughout the process, and he put that down to the meticulous planning that he had undertaken years before the actual day had arrived. His studying of his subject left no stone unturned, learning everything there was to know about David Stafford.

He wandered around the small flat that he bought recently, feeling the location was perfect. It was near enough to Whitebank for his purposes but far away enough as not to get too close to police interest. He had lived all his life in West Lothian and knew that he would never leave the familiar territory. Everything that he needed was in West Lothian and the next few weeks would require him to stay close to his flat. After he was finished, he may go abroad for a while, take a belated gap year. He had always fancied visiting Australia and New Zealand, perhaps he could work there for a while. He was physically fit and knew a bit about the construction industry so he could easily get a job as a general labourer.

With that thought in his mind, he opened his wardrobe admiring the high visibility jacket that he had used during one of his reconnaissance missions. It amused him that a high visibility jacket was actually a really good disguise. They were commonly seen around and people tended not to notice them. In fact, their eyes would be drawn to the jacket rather than the face of the person who was wearing it.

He heard his kettle boil and moved through to the kitchen to make himself a coffee. He always took the time to hand grind his coffee beans and prepare his drink in a proper cafetière. Placing the exact spoon measures in, he slowly poured the boiled water over the grinds watching the steam rise gently towards the ceiling. The fresh aroma of the Costa Rican roast filled his nostrils to his full satisfaction. No milk or sugar was added, a crime to good coffee in his option.

Wrapping his hands round the mug, he walked through to the spare bedroom and looked admiringly at the wall chart he had created. It had all the information that he had gathered over the preceding decade. This mission that he was on was personal and now that he had began, he was not going to stop until it was completed. He knew that his handiwork would have to be destroyed as soon as he was finished with it. In truth, he didn't actually need it now, all the information that was showing on the board was ingrained into his memory. It served another purpose, however, that of inspiration. Every time he viewed the display it edged him onwards with his mission, his destiny.

Satisfied with the drug like hit he had obtained from standing in his spare room, he made his way back through to the living room. He sat down on his preferred chair and picked up the local newspaper he had bought earlier in the day. He had already scanned the pages for any news of the killing, but had not found it yet. It may have made the online reports by now, but he would check that later as there was an article that he was interested in reading in the pages in front of him.

The Chain was an impressive killer, having successfully dispatched three in a relatively short period of time. He had, however, made some mistakes and was currently underground in hiding according to this particular report.

The killer allowed himself a smile as he drained his coffee before he spoke his next thought aloud.

'Which is nothing, when I'm planning to kill another four in the next fortnight.'

PART THREE - DAUGHTER

CHAPTER FIVE

Day 3 - 09:27 - Corstorphine Police Station, Edinburgh

It was a call that Lyle was expecting, but was not sure how ready he was to hear it. DC Chowdhury had taken the call and was standing at Lyle's desk unsure what to do. Of course Lyle would speak with the caller, he just had to give himself a minute to prepare himself. Head bowed, he took a few deep breaths and then looked up once more.

'Patch her through, Chowdhury.'

Chowdhury jogged back to his desk, spoke briefly with the caller and transferred her over to Lyle's phone extension. Lyle lifted it with some trepidation. The caller spoke straight away.

'Is it true, Sergeant Lyle, is Stafford deid?'

'It's true, Mrs Kerr,' Lyle's voice was apologetic in preparation for his next line. 'I was planning to call you today, we were not expecting his name to have been leaked to the press so quickly.'

'You have nothing to apologise for, Sergeant,' continued Margaret Kerr. 'You were they only officer that appeared to care and you ken I appreciate you still taking ma calls after all these years. I suppose that you will want to speak with me on a more formal basis, and my ex too?'

'A matter of routine, Mrs Kerr, but yes myself and DI Christie will see you at some point today. How is Mr Kerr?'

'He keeps in touch now and again. Some couples that were married as long as Patrick and I, what near thirty years was it? Aye, some couples canny stand the sight of each other when they get a divorce. Paddy and I are no' stupid. We ken that it was the tragedy that broke our marriage. We still love each other, in oor own way, but after what happened we were never the same again. He is looking after himself though, been off the drink now for years, not that he was a heavy drinker mind, but you ken how some men get after something like this.'

Lyle knew exactly. Strictly teetotal himself, he had witnessed first hand the damage that alcohol could do to people and to their families. There was a pause in the conversation, Lyle knew he had to get on but was reluctant to end the call until Mrs Kerr was ready. He needed these calls as much as she did and they never last so long as to cause an issue. Mrs Kerr's next remark caught Lyle somewhat off guard.

'I didn't kill him,' she said solemnly.

'It's just routine,' Lyle responded, unsure why he chose those words. They sounded clumsy, like what an inexperienced police officer would say. He regretted them as soon as he said them. Fortunately, Mrs Kerr didn't seem to notice and continued.

'I look forward to seeing you again, Sergeant. I'm still in the same hoose, so you ken where to find me. I will also get a chance to meet your new boss finally.' Margaret considered asking what she was like and what Lyle thought of her, but considered that it was probably inappropriate.

'We'll come round this afternoon, if that's convenient for you?'

'I'll have the kettle on,' and with that she said her goodbyes and hung up the phone.

Day 3 - 10:12 - Cycle Path near Murrayfield Stadium, Edinburgh

Christie had decided on a later start, considering that today would be a long day and she needed to catch up on some sleep. Between work and triathlon training, she had been neglecting the much needed rest period of looking after herself. She had managed to grab some dinner with her partner, Tom, before he headed back to own apartment shortly afterwards. He had a conference today in Glasgow, which meant an early start for him. Christie had taken advantage and headed for a bath and and early bed.

This morning she chose to cycle from her flat in Stockbridge. Compared to the lengths of her triathlon cycles, it was a short distance but every opportunity to get her legs moving was taken. She knew that Lyle would be driving to their interviews today, so she could get showered and changed at the station and be set up for the day, and very probably evening, ahead.

Christie took the time to admire the national rugby stadium at Murrayfield as she passed. It was as important a landmark to the Edinburgh residents as the castle, with 67,000 fans piling in for the big international rugby matches. Christie had never experienced the atmosphere herself firsthand, but Tom attended most of the matches by way of hospitality from his business connections.

As she pedalled on along the cycle route she reached Carrick Knowe Golf Course, and took a brief moment to pause and watch a couple of older golfer chip onto the green and putt out. It reminded her of her father, an avid golfer living out in East Lothian and still playing most days. It was a far cry from his days of alcohol abuse that he endured following the death of Christie's mother to cancer. The moments reflection reminded her that she must pay him a visit soon.

The time was now approaching 10:30 and she wanted to be at her desk by 11:00, so she decided to up the speed for the final stretch. She was a highly competent cyclist and knew to look out for the dangers of runners, walkers and dogs off their leashes. She decided to head onto the main road at Corstorphine Road which led onto Saint John's Road. She soon passed the guitar shop on her left hand side and thought of Lyle. After the case involving Miles' partner, they had all met up at the Classic Crock Cafe and

Lyle surprised her by getting up to play the guitar. To her untrained ears, he was very good, however, he was accompanied by the beautiful singing voice of Fiona, 'Songbird' herself.

Turning left at the roundabout, Christie peddled quickly down the hill before turning right into the station's car park. Lyle's immaculate GTI was in his usual spot. The whole staff at the station knew better than to park in his spot, but Lyle was not immune to the occasional prank such as a banana peel under his windscreen wiper or a condom on his aerial. He always identified the guilty party, but took it in good humour often getting his own back at a later time.

'Revenge is a dish best served cold,' he said each time he removed an offending item.

Having chained up her bike, she went into the station and had a quick shower. Not one to sweat profusely, it was just a case of freshening up for the day ahead. Her hair would remain dry under the shower cap to speed up proceedings.

Chowdhury walked over towards her desk as she was approaching, a piece of printer paper being waived in front of him. He called Lyle over as he reached the desk, considering that he would also like to hear what he had to say.

'I've been looking at Stafford's social media profile and he was quite active. It seems that his preferred platform was Twitter and he got into many a debate, some of them were quite heated. No topics appeared off limits, but he had a particular interest in relationships with large age gaps. In age gaps, I'm talking decades rather than years. He often cited older actors or rock stars fathering children with much younger partners.'

Christie and Lyle were captivated by what they were hearing, getting an insight into the murdered man.

'There is plenty more which I will look into further, but there was one thing that caught my eye and that was some abuse that he was receiving from one specific Twitter user. Assuming she is female, she went by the name of 'Mother of Gonetoosoon'. Her replies were very specific and at times downright nasty. There were also threats of what she would do to him if they were ever to meet.'

He placed the paper on Christie's desk for her and Lyle to read some of the comments for themselves. Christie was once more impressed by his attention to detail, in a short time he had already found an interesting thread to the case.

'Good work Chowdhury, can you follow that up and see if you can get the users details?'

For a moment, Chowdhury looked somewhat bashful.

'Actually, ma'am, I already have. You see, I have a contact in the Met who has access to a lot of online data. She can get information very quickly given the contacts she has built up over the years. I know, perhaps, I should have went through the proper channels, but she owed me a favour and I think you will be interested in the result.'

'Go on,' confirmed Lyle. Christie wasn't going to overrule.

'The user is Margaret Kerr, the mother of the missing girl he was accused of kidnapping.'

Day 3 - 12:45 - A71 heading towards Kirknewton, West Lothian

Lyle, in a moment of weakness, had let Christie choose the music for the journey out to Kirknewton. He was impressed when she chose Iron Maiden's 'Seventh Son of a Seventh Son' album. The second track of the album was playing and Lyle was enjoying the harmonious guitar introduction of 'Infinite Dreams'.

'Nice choice, ma'am,' he confirmed.

'I used to listen to that song 'Teenage Dirtbag' all the time. I just liked the idea of a teenage odd couple hanging out listening to Iron Maiden. I felt like I should maybe listen to some of the inspiration.'

'I wouldn't class Wheatus as classic rock quite yet, but I admit it's a great song. You can put it on next.'

Lyle had told Christie about the phone call he had received from Margaret Kerr earlier that morning and explained that he took calls from her from time to time. It was part of her healing progress and Lyle was the perfect police officer in such instances. Christie understood the reason why he kept taking the calls and would not question it. Many lesser officers in the force would make excuses not to continue with the calls so long after the event, but he would never be like them.

Lyle turned the GTI left off the A71 onto the approach road for the village of Kirknewton. The village and surrounding area has a population of over two thousand and is in easy reach of Edinburgh by road and rail. The railway is known for its level crossing that has had its fair share of accidents and work had been completed to upgrade the system to try and address this. Lyle was approaching the village from a different direction so was not having to overcome that particular hurdle today. Although it had been a long time since he had been at the house, he still knew the route, he did not have to use the car's onboard satellite navigation system for this particular journey.

The car rolled gently into the village and Lyle kept the speed of the powerful car low. Not one to always adhere to the reduced speed limit himself, he cruised along at 20 miles per hour keeping an eye out for the correct turn off. Finding it without incident, he pulled up in front of Margaret Kerr's property. He turned off the engine and let out a deep breath.

'You okay, Lyle?' Christie asked him.

He nodded confirmation, but his voice lacked the usual confidence.

'It's just been a long time since I was last here, but I can remember it like it was yesterday. Every time I knocked on the door I was met by eyes begging for positive news and pleading that I wasn't there to confirm the worst. After time, they just wanted news, some form of closure. Eventually it got too much for Patrick Kerr and he moved out. Divorce proceedings were not long after.'

He shook his head, feeling a sense of disappointment that the couple that had been through so much were now living their lives in separate pain. Without saying anything further, Lyle opened the car door and got out. Christie followed suit, deciding that given their history it would better for Lyle to take the lead in questioning. She would not, however, hesitate to jump in should the conversation fail to be heading down the right path.

Margaret Kerr's house was a traditional 3 bed end terrace property. The garden was well tended, but what you would describe as being 'low maintenance'. A rusty swing was still erected at the side lawn, a memory of times long since gone. Lyle approached the door tentatively and rang the bell.

The door was answered by a man who appeared to be in his early thirties. He was tall with dark hair, dressed smartly in a casual shirt and chinos. It took Lyle a moment before realisation occurred.

'Nicholas, isn't it?'

'You must be Sergeant Lyle, my mother said you would be coming. Please come in.' He stepped back to allow the detectives through and indicated the way to the living room. Entering the room, Christie noticed how cluttered it was. Family photographs and cheap ornaments filled every space. The outdated wallpaper was barely visible behind various printed artworks and larger framed photographs. A large number of these were of Samantha and a very young Nicholas. The room was in complete contrast to that of Bad Boy's flat they had visited recently.

Margaret Kerr was sat on a Queen Anne chair which seemed out of place compared the other furniture within the room. She acknowledged her guests with a gentle nod of her head and directed them towards the sofa. Christie sat at the end closest to Margaret, leaning on the edge of the seat. Lyle, as usual, remained standing. Margaret looked up at Nicholas.

'Go stick the kettle on, Nico, and bring through the good biscuits,' she commanded, Nicholas headed for the kitchen obligingly.

'He seems to have turned into a fine gentleman,' Lyle commented.'I think he was only about five or so the last time I saw him.'

'That's a good description, Sergeant. I have always been a stickler for good manners and I brought him up well. You ken how some of the bairns speak nowadays, I was no having that with my boy. He's a good lad and he takes care of me.'

'It must have been tough on him,' Christie added. 'Being so young when his sister was reported missing.'

'Aye, Inspector. They got on so well, those two. Despite the big age difference, they loved each other's company. It was so unusual for siblings, but they never fought or argued. Maybe when Nico grew older…'

She left the sentence hanging, the thought obviously too painful to consider. There would never be the chance for Nicholas to grow up with his big sister looking out for him. Those days were gone and even, if by some miracle, she was to come back to them it would be a difficult integration for the family.

They continued with some small talk until Nico returned with the tea and biscuit selection. Christie recognised them from Marks and Spencer and appreciated the gesture, even though it was unlikely she would eat any.

'Thanks Nico,' said Margaret. 'You can head over to your dad's hoose now.'

'Are you sure you'll be okay here on your own?' Nico asked with genuine concern.

'Aye, son. I'll be fine, I'll see you later.'

'Nice to meet you both,' Nico said to the detectives as he left the room, gently closing the front door on his way out. Margaret gave the detective a serious look once she knew her son was safely gone.

'I'm not keen on talking about the past in front of the boy,' she explained. 'He had nightmares about it for years after and couldn't come to terms with the fact his sister wouldn't be coming home. One positive thing that came out of it was that he worked hard at school because that was one of the things he remembered Samantha saying to him. She told him not to make the mistakes she did at school and work hard. He was the first in our family to go to university, studying law at Edinburgh and now works for a small law firm in Livingstone.'

She picked up a large framed photograph from the unit next to her and passed it to Christie. It was Nicholas' graduation photograph. There was pride in Margaret's voice as she spoke about him. Lyle took the frame, studied it closely to show interest and passed it back. He knew that the difficult questions would need to start now. Lyle had his notebook out, ready to be note taker as well as lead interviewer.

'When we spoke this morning,' Lyle started tentatively. 'You had already heard that Stafford was dead and wanted my confirmation. It may seem an obvious question, but we have to ask it. Why did you want to know if was him that was dead?'

'I know Sergeant, it's for the record,' she nodded at his notebook. 'Mr Stafford was arrested and charge under suspicion of kidnapping my daughter. The case failed and the truth did not come out. Since that day in 1992, I have fought to get him to tell me what he knew, but the bastard remained quiet all these years.'

There was a hint of anger in her voice, but she remained calm and was handling the situation well given the circumstances.

'Do you believe that Mr Stafford was guilty of taking Samantha?' Lyle's use of the daughter's name was deliberate. He wanted to show compassion, to show that she was a person, not a statistic.

'I'll be honest with you both, I couldn't say that I ken he did it. I couldn't say I ken he didn't do it. I couldn't even say my woman's intuition told me he did it. I will tell you one thing though.' She moved forward on her chair, balancing on the very edge with her hands gripping on the armrests so tightly the whites of her knuckles were clearly showing. 'That man knew something.'

She leaned back in her chair, glad to get the accusation out of her system. Lyle knew he had to change the line of questioning slightly to get to the reason behind their visit.

'Do you use social media much, Mrs Kerr?'

She considered the question for a moment with a surprised and somewhat confused expression on her face.

'Aye, I use social media. No much, I'm no on it everyday. I use that Facebook to keep in touch with the family, I've cousins in Canada and Australia so it good for that. I go on Twitter as well, its good for a gossip and a wee rant for time to time.'

If she knew what was coming, her body language didn't show it.

'Have you heard of a user called 'Mother of Gonetoosoon' on Twitter?'

Her face now gave her away and she could feel her own cheeks beginning to flush. She knew that there would be no point in denying it.

'Aye, I'll come clean Sergeant. That was me. That was me who said some nasty things to him. I just wanted to get some of my frustrations out and I was not happy with some of the stuff he was saying.'

'Like what, for example?' Christie had asked the question, just a gentle reminder that she was in the room. It was asked softly, in a non-accusing manner. It was important that Margaret was able to trust her as well as Lyle, so that she would open up in front of them both.

'All that stuff about older men and younger lasses. It made me sick to the pits of my stomach. It made him sound like a dirty old man and I didn't like it.'

'What I am really interested in, is some of the more personal replies.' He pulled out the printed sheet that he had been given from Chowdhury and handed it over. Margaret fumbled to put on her glasses before having a look at it and surprisingly smiling at the content.

'I think I must of had a few too many glasses of wine when I wrote these replies, Sergeant. At times I would just start to vent my anger and probably didn't do it in the right manner. That's the thing with this social media, once it's out there, it's out there. All the bairns get taught how to be careful online nowadays, but they should teach some of the old ones too.'

Lyle wondered if they had wasted their time coming out here. Perhaps like some of the questions he was asking it was just a matter of routine, for the record as Margaret had put it. Did he think that she would be capable of murdering Stafford, or even arranging the murder? She would be into her sixties by now and the events of the past had taken its toll on her, she could easily be mistaken as being in her mid to late seventies.

With the break in the questioning, Margaret took the time to clear the tea cups and biscuits away. Neither Lyle nor Christie has touched much of theirs so they took it as a hint that the time for questioning was coming to a close. When she returned from the kitchen, Margaret remained standing, subtly waiting for the officers to begin to make their exit. As she reached to open the front door, she paused and looked Lyle square in the eyes.

'As I said to you on the phone, Inspector, I didn't kill him. I ken that you know that, but you may not have realised why. I think he knew something and now that he's dead, it's going to make finding out the truth so much harder…'

She opened the door and let them pass.

'…but I won't stop trying,' she concluded before shutting the door behind them.

CHAPTER SIX

Day 3 - 14:08 - Whitebank Village, West Lothian

Miles was starting to get frustrated at the lack of progress whilst coordinating the house to house enquiries in the village. The time spend the previous day has yielded nothing of significant interest and the day so far had producing a similar result. To make matters worse, the PC that was accompanying her had an annoying habit of constantly whistling and Miles could feel the start of a migraine coming on.

After another fruitless interview, they decided to go and get something to eat. Miles realised that she hadn't eaten since an early breakfast and some food may help settle her stomach, head and irritability. The PC had been snacking of various chocolate bars between interviews, which brought only temporary relieve from the whistling. The only issue was there was a severe lack of dining options in the village, and Miles had neither the desire nor the will to make the drive into Livingston for a better choice. The local newsagent/grocer advertised the selling of 'filled rolls', so that would have to do for now.

The 'Whitebank Village Store' was as unoriginal as its name. Two aisles of generic groceries, a wall rack of newspapers and magazines and a cooler counter beside the till. The man behind the counter looked to be in his mid to late forties and beyond bored. What he lacked in enthusiasm he didn't make up in customer service. An upwards flick of the head confirmed he was ready for their order. Miles chose what was the only vegetarian option on display, a cheese salad roll. She doubted that a vegan option was likely to be on the menu any time soon. Her partner for the day ordered as many different meat options the assistant could fit onto one buttered roll.

They paid for their food and for some unknown reason, Miles decided to open up a conversation.

'Are you the owner here, sir?'

The assistant for the first time since they had arrived looked at them with an element of interest.

'Are you the police?' His accent was local and the question was neither threatening nor welcoming. The officers produced their identification, which seem to satisfy him.

'Not yet, the place was opened by my parents in the 1980's, although it's just mum left now. It will be passed over to me when she has had enough of the world, but I don't see that happening anytime soon. She comes in most days and works a few hours, well I say work, I do all the work and she chats to the regulars.'

He had suddenly come out of his shell, realisation hitting him that the prospect of talking to police officers would be the highlight of his year.

'Do you enjoy working here?' Miles for the first time since she started the door to door enquiries thought that she may have stumbled across something interesting here. She didn't want to spook him, so she decided to take it slowly.

'It was great as a kid, you know. Growing up in the eighties I got free sweets, football stickers, I could read all the comics on the day they came out as long as I left them in saleable condition. Of course, you grow out of that very quickly, but it's an honest life.'

'Can't be easy nowadays, big supermarkets, online news, etc.' Miles was making a statement rather than a question, but wanted to keep him talking. He ran a hand through his ample dark hair. It was a fine showing for a man of his age, full of colour with only a hint of grey at his temples, albeit the middle parting style probably hadn't been changed since the nineties.

'Very true. The village still has a number of older residents who still like a paper they can flick through. They don't always manage to the supermarkets and a trip here is often the highlight of their day. It keeps them active and it's good for mum too. I guess we have another five good years, maybe ten at a stretch. I think when it's time for me to take it over I may have to convert the shop to property. It would break mum's heart, so I just hope she doesn't witness it.'

'Do you live in the village, sorry I didn't catch your name?' Miles was using one of the oldest tricks in the book, but it got the desired result.

'It's Freddie, Freddie Taylor. My dad was a big fan of Queen, I'm surprised that he didn't call me Roger.' He laughed at his own joke, doubtless told many times, but it was lost on Miles. She would have to check with Lyle later for an explanation. 'Mum still lives in the village, but I have my own place not far from here.'

Miles knew it was time to move the conversation along, her partner was now eating his roll and leaving the questioning to her. That was fine, but she gave him a look, indicating to him to put the roll away rather than stuff his face in front the person answering her questions. He duly obliged.

'I assume you have heard about the murder?' Miles continued.

'Of course, most of the village knew before the ambulance had arrived. It's that kind of place.' He smiled once more at his own joke. 'Winnie the Watcher will have seen and shared it all. She's like a human, geriatric Facebook for the village.'

'Sorry, Winnie?'

'Winifred Taylor, by dear mother. If you want information you should have a chat with her. She'll be back in the shop tomorrow morning.'

'Thank you, I will call back,' Miles lifted her roll up in thanks and turned towards the exit. She had no intention of leaving and was setting up her Columbo moment, which her own mother would been impressed by, having been a big fan of the TV show. At the doorway, she turned and asked casually. 'Sorry, one more thing. Did you know the victim?' Taylor showed little reaction as if he was expecting the question.

'David Stafford? He came in from time to time for milk, bread and the odd bar of chocolate. Not one for chatting, no interest in football or music so I found it difficult to strike up a conversation with him. Didn't know too much about him, to be honest.'

Satisfied, Miles thanked him a left. Satisfied that she got answers to her questions and satisfied that he was definitely hiding something…

Day 3 - 17:12 - A71 heading towards Kirknewton, West Lothian

Following a trip back to the station to check in with Chowdhury and give a quick and unsubstantial update to DCS Hepburn, Christie and Lyle were back in the GTI heading towards Kirknewton once more.

Patrick Kerr lived in a small flat, not far from the original family home that they had visited earlier in the day. He was a man of medium height with receding grey hair. Smartly dressed in jeans and shirt, he welcomed them both with handshakes and took them through to the living room. He offered coffee and went through to the kitchen to prepare it.

The room was in direct contrast to that of his ex-wife's, a few family photographs tastefully framed in plain sterling silver. No pictures or artwork on the brilliant white emulsion walls. The furniture was modern, the sofa and matching easy chair in a simple grey colour and without pattern. The coffee was served in a smart matching set, however, Patrick continued to drink out of a large mug emblazoned with the crest of Glasgow Celtic Football Club.

'Are you interested in the fitba' yourselves?' Patrick asked as he took a gulp from the mug. The question was aimed at both of them, a typical icebreaker amongst Scottish men. Christie shook her head, leaving Lyle to answer.

'Music's more my thing, but my grandfather played as a goalkeeper for Hibernian, so I keep a wee eye on their results from time to time.'

'Ah well, any green and white team is fine by me. As long as it wasn't that other mob.' He let out a large laugh at his reference to his team's great rivals Glasgow Rangers. Christie allowed the small talk to continue as they drank appreciatively from the cups. Patrick certainly made a good coffee, fresh rather than instant. It was Patrick himself that turned the conversation round to matters relating to the visit. His jovial demeanour turned to one of reflection.

'It's good to see you again, Mr Lyle. It was a difficult time back in the day and you were the most patient and understanding officer. Some of those I spoke to treated Margaret and I like an irritation, but you always welcomed our calls and our visits. You always made time for us and for that I will always be grateful.'

Lyle nodded his appreciation of the sentiment,

'There was one bloke I remember, his name was Montgomery which I remember because he walked about with the same facial expression as his namesake golfer whenever he missed a putt. Excuse my language, but that guy was a complete fucking cock.'

It took all their resolve to retain a neutral expression and fortunately Patrick continued with the conversation.

'I think he done it.'

The statement was unwavering. The pain was there, but he had learned to mask it over time from showing on his face. There was a touch of anger and regret in the statement also.

'Are you happy he's dead?' Christie asked, Lyle glanced over thinking the question was too direct and too early. It was a risky tactic, but it seemed to pay off.

'If my Sammy's body had been found, then I would have happily done it myself. I'm not unhappy he's dead, but it's another obstacle in the course of finding her.'

Lyle took up the questioning, taking a slightly softer approach.

'You said, if Samatha's body had been found, do you believe that she is dead?'   Patrick considered this for a moment.

'Unfortunately, I do. I'm a realist Mr Lyle and I don't believe in miracles, God forgive me. If Sammy was alive she would have been found by now and there is no way she ran away from home. She wasn't an angel as a teenager, but not many are. The one thing she valued, because our mother and I installed it into her from a young age, was the importance of family. She had a great relationship with us both, let us know what she was doing and who she was with and she also spoke to her mum about any boy issues. She always made time for her family and completed doted on Nico, her baby brother. There was nothing whatsoever to indicate that she wanted to leave the family home.'

'We spoke with Margaret,' Lyle stated, treading carefully. 'She said that she will never stop looking for Samantha. I'm sorry to ask such a personal question, but is that what caused the break up?' Patrick nodded.

'I think it's what keeps her going, it's what gets her out of bed in the morning. I just couldn't take it any longer. As much as it pains me to say it, I felt we had to try and move on. We have another child and I felt that Nico was being neglected and that was the basis of every argument we had. In the end, it got too much for both of us and we decided to call it a day. I had started drinking more than I should have at that time, a mixture of guilt over what happened to Sammy and not being able to deal with how Margaret was handling it. I stopped four years ago and haven't had a drop since.'

'Did you or Margaret ever make direct contact with Mr Stafford, you don't live too far away from him?' Christie was keen to discover this and the timing for the question seemed right.

'No. We both went to the trial of course, but I didn't know where he lived or what he was doing. I would have liked to have confronted him, got the truth out of him but that will never happen now.'

Christie and Lyle finished up the questioning and thanked him for his time. Back in the car, Lyle let our a deep breath.

'I don't think either of them were involved in this, ma'am. I just think there might be something we're missing.'

Day 3 - 20:59 - The Classic Crock Cafe, Edinburgh

The cafe was closing and Frank was escorting the last customer out the door so he could clear up. Lyle, Christie, Miles and Chowdhury were sat round the Queen table, as requested by Miles, waiting for the cafe to empty so they could discuss the case in privacy. Frank would be heading off soon to leave them to it. Miles was filling them in on her conversation.

'Freddie Taylor! I'm surprised his parents didn't name him Roger,' Lyle reacted. He then explained to Miles that Roger Taylor was the name of Queen's drummer, Freddie Mercury being the charismatic lead singer. 'Hey Frank, what's your favourite Queen song?'

'Seaside Rendezvous.' Frank replied laughing.

'Stop taking the piss,' Lyle got to his feet and headed over to the counter. 'I'll make it easier, best Queen song from the 1980's?'

'Hammer to Fall,' Frank stated proudly. Lyle was shaking his head, adjusting the music system.

'Good shout, but wrong again my dear friend. Now, I'm taking the guitar playing bias here but listen to the guitar on this one.' He pushed the play button and Brian May's guitar kicked in with the powerful opening of 'Gimme the Prize'. Lyle played air guitar along with the whole introduction, gaining some laughs from his colleagues and a shake of the head in disbelief from Frank.

After a brief pause to admire the bagpipe sounding start of the guitar solo, conversation returned to the case. Miles continued with her update.

'This Freddie Taylor could be an interesting witness, he grew up in Whitebank and knows the place well. I didn't buy the chat around not really knowing Stafford, I'm sure that he was hiding something so I think it's worthwhile speaking with him again.'

'I think that would be the right thing to do, but take Lyle with you. If he's hiding something, Lyle will get it out him.'

'By extraction with rusty medical equipment if required,' Lyle confirmed, causing the others to laugh.

'We also need to speak with his mother,' Miles went on. 'She knows everyone in the village and is apparently very observant. She will be in the shop tomorrow.'

'Fine,' confirmed Christie. 'You and Lyle head back to Whitebank tomorrow and see if you can speak with them both. I'm going to stay at the station tomorrow and see what else I can find out, I want to have a look at any tip offs that have come in over the last couple of days. Chowdhury, you can continue to go over the files and give me a shout if anything come up.

Also, see what CCTV footage you can get your hands on. There won't be much on the street, but try local public transport. There's bound to be a few buses that pass through the village.'

'Yes, ma'am. Also, I would like to go through Stafford's paperwork if that's ok. It may be fruitless, but you never know what I will find out.'

'Good idea Chowdhury. Can you also see what you can find out about his finances when you are there. If anything unusual turns up we can get an access request to his bank accounts.'

Frank popped over to say his goodbyes and Lyle walked him to the door, taking a final opportunity for some musical banter. He then headed back to the table as Christie brought the work talk to a close. They were now off the clock and it was time for some socialising conversation and team gossip.

Miles confirmed that things with her and Fiona were going well and there was talk about getting a flat together. They had been together now for over 2 years and they wanted to commit to the relationship together. Fiona had previously turned down the offer of a solo record deal due to her commitment to the band and the company had recently came back to her and agreed to sign the band on a three record deal.

Christie said that she was concerned about the upcoming triathlon race as she spent more time in Lyle's cafe drinking his coffee and eating his sandwiches than training. She was worried that Tom would finish hours in front of her and she would fail to live it down.

Chowdhury told them that he had just had an offer accepted on a flat in Gorgie. He was loving life in Edinburgh and was so happy that he made the move up from London. He had also been on a couple of dates and said that the 'Edinburgh Lassies' were so much prettier than the ones down south. No one at the table was going to disagree.

Lyle managed to avoid questions of his own love life, mysteriously saying that when there was something to tell them, he would let them know. His big news, however, was that his two sons had agreed to come and visit him. Lyle's ex-wife had emigrated to Canada and taken his sons with her. It had been a difficult time for him, but over the years he got used to his own company and the mixture of Police Scotland and the Classic Crock Cafe had kept his mind off it. He was on amicable speaking terms with his ex-wife, who had recently remarried, which had made contact with the boys easier. They were now in their early twenties and would be flying over together in a few months.

Lyle just hoped that one of the toughest cases he had been part of was concluded before they arrived.

PART FOUR - GLORIFIED G

CHAPTER SEVEN

Day 4 - 09:52 - Main road towards Whitebank Village, West Lothian

Miles was scrolling through the music available on Lyle's in car music system. Having heard enough of Queen the previous night at the Classic Crock Cafe, as Lyle took the group through his own Queen's Greatest Hits collection, she wanted to choose something else. Her choice of Jimi Hendrix's 'Little Wing' surprised the driver.

'My dad is a huge Hendrix fan and I was raised on him. I love all his songs, but this one is special to me.'

'It's a beautiful song,' Lyle agreed. 'Most people have this vision of Hendrix being a big rock star that plays heavy metal and sets his guitars on fire. As well as being technically brilliant, he also wrote some gorgeous songs.'

They drove in silence, listening to the song in full and with it being so short in length Miles skipped it back to the start. Once the song concluded for a second time, Lyle decided to share some more of his encyclopaedic knowledge of classic rock trivia.

'There is an interesting connection with your Freddie and Roger from Queen and Jimi Hendrix. Freddie was a massive Hendrix fan growing up and wanted to play guitar like his idol. He used to run a market stall in Kensington Market with Roger Taylor and on the day Hendrix died, they closed the stall to commiserate.'

They were just arriving at Kirknewton when the song finished for a third time. Lyle found the store and parked right outside.

'Easier than trying to find a space in the city centre at this time of day.'

Behind the counter stood a young girl, looking equally as bored as Freddie had the day before. They initially thought that they were out of luck in catching Winnie Taylor, until the girl pointed out that she was standing at the bottom of one of the aisles, in deep conversation with a fellow elderly lady. Lyle and Miles approached, picking up a bit of the conversation.

'I'm telling you Betty,' an animated Winnie was saying. 'There was something about him, I always said so. He was hiding something and I think that's what got him killed.'

Lyle was about to interrupt the conversation when Winnie spoke.

'This will be the police, Betty, I better let you get on.'

Betty made her retreat and Winnie invited the officers into the back of the shop. It felt a bit like the Tardis from Doctor Who as when they went through a narrow door, it opened out to a substantial office and stock room. There were two chairs in front of the office table and Lyle wondered who else would be invited into the back of this shop requiring such a set up. It was as if Winnie was reading his mind.

'The table and chairs were my husband's idea. He always invited our stockists in for a chat and often drove a hard bargain from this very desk.' She gave the desk a playful thump with the palm of her hand. 'He also like to invite the bank manager in regularly, his way of maintaining what he called the most important of business relationships.'

She smiled at the memory and took a seat in her late husband's chair. Lyle formally introduced himself and Miles before starting with the questioning.

'Forgive us for our intrusion into your conversation, however, I assume you were talking about Mr Stafford with your customer just now. Can you tell me what you knew of him and what you thought of him?'

'Well he came across as a quiet gentleman, but that's not surprising given his past,' she acknowledged Lyle's reaction with a simple nod of the head. 'I remember the trial well, not much like that goes on around these parts, a wee girl going missing. I remember joining the search party and putting up posters in the shop and around the village and surrounding towns.' She paused for a moment, the recollection causing a glint in her eyes.

'We were shocked when Mr Stafford was arrested of course, you don't expect a kidnapper to be living on your doorstep, do you? I knew his parents well too, they both died young, cancer of the lungs, the pair of them smoked like a chimney. Came down here everyday for their newspaper, morning rolls and cigarettes. They were nice people and raised David as best they could. He was always a bit odd, a bit of a loner, nothing they could have done. He still lives, or lived, in the family home.'

'You mentioned earlier that you thought he was hiding something,' Lyle probed. It took Winnie a moment to recall what she had been saying to Betty and it was that which Lyle had overheard.

'If you want my opinion, I think he was involved but I don't think he was a murderer. The thing is, Sergeant, I knew his type.'

'His type?' Lyle was intrigued.

'He had a fancy for younger girls. You see, we have always employed school boys and girls in the shop to do a couple of hours before or after school. Obviously, it makes economic sense but it was good to have them cover the counter to allow us to set up the shop for the day and tidy things up at night. David always came in when one of the girls were on and he would flirt a bit. At the time I thought it was harmless and the girls didn't seem to mind or, in some cases, even notice. Of course I regret not saying anything at the time, but it was the late eighties or early nineties and it was different. Doesn't feel like much of an excuse now, but I never witnessed any inappropriate behaviour, just some unwanted attention perhaps.'

'Did you know the girl who went missing, Samatha Kerr?' Lyle asked.

'Not well, however, she came into the shop from time to time. I assumed that she had a friend or relative that lived in Whitebank. Perhaps Freddie knew her better as he was on the counter more than me, I was always floating around chatting to the older customers about their troubles.'

Lyle shot Miles a glance, who shook her head in return. She had asked about Stafford but not Samantha.

'When will Freddie be here next?' Lyle was getting a feeling in his stomach that wouldn't settle until he had had the chance to speak to Freddie directly. Winnie looked at her watch.

'He's due in any minute, in fact he should have been here by now.'

Lyle asked if they could be excused for a minute and he headed out to the car with Miles. She confirmed to him that she had not mentioned Samantha, only Stafford.

'How did he come across when you spoke with him, you said you thought he was hiding something?' Miles thought for a moment.

'He was comfortable talking to us, but he knew about Stafford and I just didn't buy the notion that he hardly knew him. Especially now that the mother says he was a regular. He said Stafford only came in from time to time.'

Lyle called through to Christie who was at her desk.

'I wasn't expecting to hear from you so soon,' she commented, intrigued.

'We've just been speaking with the mother, but I want to bring Freddie into the station. I think he needs to be in an uncomfortable environment for us to get the best out of him.'

'I'll book a room, you bring the coffee.'

Lyle and Miles returned to the shop and headed straight through the back where Winnie was still sitting in the office chair.

'The girl out front,' Lyle began. 'Would she be able to stay on a bit so that we can talk to Freddie?'

'I'm sure that wouldn't be a problem. She is saving up for a holiday so will take all the overtime I can give her.'

'That would be great, Mrs Taylor. I would prefer to speak with him at the station with my superior officer, it's just a matter of routine and the more details we can get officially, the better the chances of catching the killer.'

Winnie just nodded solemnly, her lack of objection was interesting to Lyle. They heard the welcoming chat of Freddie coming into the shop. He walked through to the back room and was surprised by the two visitors. He eventually recognised Miles and Winnie excused herself to ensure the girl would stay on for a few hours longer.

'We have some questions that we would like to ask you back at the station if that's okay? Miles asked him.

'Am I a suspect?' The question was asked with a confident grin, but there was a shadow of doubt in his eyes. Lyle answered the question.

'It's just routine at this point, Mr Taylor. We are trying to gain as much information as we can on the victim and your assistance would be greatly appreciated.'

This tact seemed to satisfy Freddie and he agreed. They headed for Lyle's car with Miles choosing to sit in the back, seated behind Lyle so that she could keep an eye on Freddie should there be any interesting conversation undertaken in the journey back to Edinburgh. In an unusual move, Lyle put on the radio rather that another helping of classic rock music.

It was important that he concentrate on the interview ahead…

Day 4 - 11:45 - Interview Room 3, Corstorphine Police Station, Edinburgh

Lyle had made a quick stop at the Classic Crock Cafe to get four coffees to go, Freddie had been happy to accept the slight delay with the promise of a decent coffee rather than the weak effort that was dispensed at the station. Christie was a willing recipient of her gift when Lyle arrived at the station.

Freddie sat in the interview room, sipping away appreciatively, as Christie and Lyle stood outside discussing tactics. They had agreed on the gentle approach, mainly information gathering but Lyle was given permission to dig deeper if he felt that there was gold buried in any of Freddie's statements. Christie entered the room first, shook Freddie's hand and introduced herself, saying how appreciated it was that he had taken the time to speak with them. Lyle, as usual, took a standing position ready to pounce if required. He did, however, lean against the wall behind Christie casually so as not to intimidate.

'As I am sure my colleague here has already told you, Mr Taylor, this interview is purely routine and is to help us establish some information on Mr Stafford.'

'I understand, Inspector. It's local knowledge you're after.' Freddie's reply was jovial and he smiled confidently.

'Tell me more about Mr Stafford, your mother said he was a regular in the shop.' Christie's opening question was a statement, but delivered gently.

'He was quiet, as I told your other officer. We didn't have much to talk about and whenever I served him, he paid for his things and left. I think the most I spoke with him was when his parents died and I was offering my condolences.'

'Did he speak more with any of the other shop workers?' It was a subtle tact from Christie, and it got the desired result.

'Just the young lassies,' he said confidently. 'He was always happy to speak with them, but me, mum and the young lads he never took an interest it.

'Any inappropriate behaviour?' Lyle asked casually, keen to see if he agreed with his mother's option.

'To be fair to him, I never witnessed anything like that. Unwanted attention at times, but nothing inappropriate. The girls knew how to handle him. Although some enjoyed the complement, no one would take them any further.'

Lyle was interested in his reply, 'unwanted attention' was the same phrase that Winnie had used. The conversation continued for a while in relation to Stafford, but nothing of interest came out. Freddie confirmed again that he liked to keep himself to himself and didn't have a partner that he was aware of. He had a few friends, some from the village that may be able to tell more. Christie decided to turn the conversation to the main reason Freddie had been brought to the station.

'What can you tell me about Samantha Kerr?' Lyle's question was deliberately direct.

'The girl who went missing in '92?' His answer was both too quick and too specific, Lyle knew there was something about to be dug out. 'Aye, I remember her and I remember Stafford being accused and taken to court over it. I wasn't convinced he did it himself, but it wouldn't surprise me if he was involved.'

Christie probed the response.

'What do you mean he was involved, if he didn't do it?' Freddie was starting to lose some of his cool.

'Look, all I'm saying to you is that he hung around with a crowd of men who I always thought were a bit dodgy. I've no proof of it, but I think they were somehow responsible. Stafford wasn't the ring leader, but he had a particular interest in Sammy.'

Lyle, who had been standing with his hands behind his back resting on the wall, pushed himself forward and approached Freddie. It wasn't a threatening movement, but it certainly startled Freddie. He was ready to play a joker, unsure if it would work but the use of Samantha's nickname was the green light he was waiting on.

'How long were you seeing Samantha for then?'

Stafford immediately went red and he could feel the blood rushing to his cheeks. He was never a good liar and there would be no point in trying to deny his relationship, especially not in these surroundings. He raised his hands, involuntary, in surrender.

'Yes, Sammy and I were a couple but we met in secret. I was 18 at the time and she had only just turned 16. Doesn't seem like much of a difference, but Sammy wanted to keep it secret. We had only been going out, not even a month when she disappeared.'

Lyle was slowing moving to angry, but in a controlled manner as this was still an unofficial interview and he didn't want Freddie to retract any of the information he had just shared.

'You never spoke to the police at the time, I was on the case. It could have been important Freddie.' He paced back to the wall, handing the interview back to Christie. It was both tactical and theatrical, for impact. Christie let the last couple of statements sink in before speaking again.

'What we need to do now, Mr Kerr, is to take a formal statement documenting everything that you have just told us. We will want to speak to you again, in a more formal setting, but once you have given your statement we will arrange for someone to drop you off at the shop. For now, thank you for coming in and being honest. I know that these things can be difficult.'

With that Christie stood up and Lyle held the door open for her, before following behind her with no further comment to Freddie. Christie and Lyle headed to her desk where Christie sat down and looked up at her partner.

'How the fuck did you know that?'

'I had an idea, ma'am. Miles is a sharp one and when she thought he was hiding something I fully believed her. I knew he was roughly ages with Samantha and he answered the questions too quickly. I could also see some hatred in his eyes when we spoke about Stafford, but the winning move was when he called her Sammy.'

'You're too good for your own good at times, Lyle. Go fill in Miles and get her to take the statement. Tell Chowdhury to go in with her, it's a team effort here and I want all four of us sharing everything all times.'

'Yes, ma'am.'

Lyle headed off just as DCI Montgomery made an unwelcome appearance. He was not looking in the best of moods and Christie felt his wrath was coming.

'Hepburn wants to see you to discuss The Chain case, apparently he's not too happy at the lack of progress. I personally think it's down to the fuck up that you left me with, but he seems to think differently. I will tell you one thing though, Christie. Don't for a minute think that because you are his special girl, his 'Glorified G' as my daughter would say, that you can get one over me.'

He turned on his heels and marched off, barking out a couple of orders to his team. Christie was taken aback, about Hepburn's invite more than Montgomery's outburst. It was something that she had grown used to over time. She knew that Montgomery, as her superior officer, had a level of authority over her but she would never let him control her.

With that thought in her head, she headed off to see the real boss.

Day 4 - 12:50 - Office of DCS Hepburn, Corstorphine Police Station, Edinburgh

His door was open when Christie approached and Hepburn was inside flicking through a pile of paperwork on his desk. Christie gently knocked on the door as Hepburn looked up to enquire on the visitor.

'Ah, Christie, come in. Shut the door behind you.'

He got up from his seat and moved some paper files off a chair and instructed Christie to sit down.

'How's the Stafford case proceeding, I appreciate that it's still early days?'

'Nothing concrete yet, sir, but we've had someone in for questioning this morning. We managed to discover that he was the secret boyfriend of Samantha Kerr, the girl who went missing.'

'I've read up on the case, it was before my time but I know that DS Lyle was involved in it. I assume that you are keeping an eye on him, make sure he's not blindsided by the previous case.'

'Yes, sir. I think it's better having him at the centre sharing his knowledge and recollection. I will keep an eye on him, but there's no one I would rather have at my side in a case such as this.'

'Okay, I trust your judgement, but don't be afraid to make the difficult call if it becomes an issue. Any other leads?' Christie knew there wasn't much to share, but she had picked up an interesting thread that had been mentioned by Freddie in the interview and also in one of the tip offs she had been reviewing early this morning.

'There was mention of a group of friends back in the day when the girl went missing. I'm interested in this as there is not much in the files from the kidnapping case about this group and everyone now is saying that he was a bit of a loner, kept himself to himself. I need to track down these friends, I have Chowdhury going through his background at the moment.'

Hepburn nodded, quietly impressed that she had something concrete that she was working on in contrast to Montgomery's lack of progress in The Chain case.

'The main reason that I asked you in, Christie, is that I've been getting pressure from above over The Chain case. We still have a serial killer wandering about the place and I need him back behind bars as soon as possible. I'm keen to get you and your team back on the case as quickly as we can, so I'm keeping an eye to ensure this case is moving at a pace. It's only been a few days, I know, but I want you to ramp things up and I want suspects found. It's a small village, so someone must have seen something. Go speak again to the lady that found her and go back round the neighbours.'

Christie had planned to go back out and speak with Barbara Stewart with Lyle. She was interested that Hepburn was aware that she hadn't done this, so he was obviously closer to the case than she thought. She was not concerned about this, she knew Hepburn would be happy to throw in a suggestion or two that could help.

'Montgomery is a good officer, but he lets his ego get in the way at times. I know the pair of you don't see eye to eye, but that hasn't had an impact on your results to date so I'm not too concerned about that at the moment. I would, however, like you back on the case as you caught him before and I have faith you will catch him again.' Christie was interested in the phase he used, your results, as if he had concerns about Montgomery's results. It was true that he had not solved a big case in a while and Christie had concluded a number recently.

'Yes, sir. I'll throw everything at this case.'

With that Christie was excused, relatively happy how the meeting had gone. She knew, however, that she had better ramp up progress to keep it that way.

CHAPTER EIGHT

Christie had only just managed to get hold of Barbara Stewart and had agreed to go out to speak with her tomorrow. She still sounded a bit shook up and had a niece staying with her for a few days. The niece had taken her to Livingston for the day to try and take her mind off things. Barbara didn't have a mobile phone, so the only contact they had was her landline.

It gave Christie the time to go through the tip offs once more and there was not much that she could use at present. She had spoken with Chowdhury for an update and he confirmed that he was still working through the background. Going back to 1992 was not as easy, as there was no social media or internet blogging that he could refer to. He had been reading through the newspaper articles of the time but nothing was showing up. He was still waiting for the bus company to supply him with the CCTV footage, but he was expecting that by tomorrow at the latest. She reiterated the importance of finding this group of friends that was being referred to.

Christie was starting to feel the effects of the long days, and decided to finish up and get off to an early start tomorrow. She had a busy day planned at Whitebank and she needed to take her mind off the case for a few hours and go into tomorrow fresh. She pulled out her mobile phone and scrolled through the contacts and dialled. Her call was picked up straight away.

'Hi Tom, I need food and company tonight, can you come over?'

Tom was just getting off the train at Waverley after his two day conference and agreed to pick something up on his way to her flat.

Day 4 - 23:07 - Undisclosed Location, West Lothian

The killer once more found himself standing in his spare room, admiring his handiwork. The meticulous detail that he had added, each victim thoroughly researched and everything planned to the last detail. He wondered if he was too hasty in his first kill, he had been watching some documentaries about assassins and recalled that they rarely shot once, that was something for Hollywood. He knew Stafford was dead by the mess the shot had made, but he should be careful with the next one.

The next one would be more challenging, being a family man, but again his research had allowed him to pick the perfect time. Tonight was pint night and he always walked home alone just before midnight. He walked through to his bedroom to check his attire in the full length mirror. Happy with the image, he fetched his car keys and headed out the door with his ruck sack on his back.

He drove in silence and pulled into a deserted spot on the outskirts of Whitebank. This was one of the trickiest parts of the plan, where he would have to exit the car and cross over fields to a small wooded area at the end of the village. His research, though, has led him to the perfect parking spot. There were no cars around and his car was out of sight from passing traffic. Keeping low, he paced slowly through the field for around one hundred metres before he reached the wooded area. His gloved hand grasped the wooden stake as he climbed over the barbed wired fence careful that he didn't leave a trace.

He reached the spot that he had visited a few times already, when he had been doing his planning. It was the perfect place, as he could clearly see both up and down the secluded path that his victim walked home alone each week. When he had been here before, the path had been unused by any other person so he knew that this was the best place to complete the task. Again,

80

he would not take any unnecessary risk and if it was not going to plan, he would abort the mission.

He looked down at his watch, the time having reached 23:45. The victim would be here in the next five to fifteen minutes. It was just a matter of being prepared and patient. He had taken out the gun from the ruck sack and held it lightly in his hand ready to take a second person's life. He crouched down and waited, a predator awaiting his prey. Hours in the gym had made him physically strong, but not imposing. He despised those who went to the gym to become some sort of muscle freak. His bulk was subtle, easily hidden in his day to day life, but his strength was awe-inspiring. He had been working hard on the strength of his knees for this very moment and could remain in this position for a good half hour without it affecting him.

As it transpired, he was only waiting for ten minutes when he spotted him staggering along the path. His next victim was dressed mainly in black, but his jacket had a distinctive pattern. The killer waiting for him to pass then left his position and fell in close behind him. A quick look back to ensure they were alone before he raised the gun and called out his name. He turned round at the sound of his name and the killer had the confirmation he required that it was definitely the right person. The shock in his eyes only lasted a fraction of a second before the first bullet entered between those eyes. As he lay motionless on the path, the killer pulled the trigger three more times, once more into the head and twice in the chest.

He didn't have to wait any longer, knowing the bullets were fatal, and disappeared once more into the woods, pausing only slightly to ensure the path remained empty. He climbed back over the fence and crouched low through the field once more. Reaching his car, he threw the back pack onto the back seat and drove off.

As he reached his home, he allowed himself a few deep breaths and headed into the house to update his wall chart in the spare room.

Two down, three to go…

Day 5 - 06:54 - Christie's Flat, Stockbridge, Edinburgh

Christie looked at her watch in the early morning light seeping through a gap in her bedroom curtains. She knew her alarm would be going off in 21 minutes, so she snuggled in tighter to Tom, allowing a wandering finger to stroke the hairs on his chest. He hadn't planned to stay over after feeling the effects of the two day conference, 'long, monotonous and extremely boring' was how he had described it. After the post meal love making, he couldn't pull himself away and Christie didn't realise how much she needed his company.

She was starting to feel the pressure of getting a quick result on the Stafford case so she could get back onto finding The Chain. She was keeping a close eye on Montgomery's progress, one of his team had going through CID training at the same time as her and they continued to get on well, despite the conflict that Montgomery would try and impose. He would give her updates at the coffee machine when they were out of Montgomery's earshot. She felt that Lyle's motorbike may be the best angle to take and she was keeping that up her sleeve. The Chain was too intelligent and resourceful to make a mistake himself, the best chance was to get to his accomplice.

Christie closed her eyes and held tighter, Tom was starting to awaken and was returning her hold. She thought of how she needed more of this, more time to just be herself, be with Tom and leave work behind. She never thought of marriage, Tom already having a failed one behind him and she didn't want to be responsible for a second. Marrying a Detective

82

Inspector was not the wisest of moves if you were looking for a long and happy marriage. For now, both parties were happy with the arrangement. They were serious about each other, loved each other and wanted to spend the rest of their lives together. They also had their own lives to lead, Tom was successful if his career and Christie was still at the early stages of hers. Neither wanted to jeopardise that by rushing towards marriage or cohabiting. They had their own flats and could comfortably spend time apart, which had brought them closer together.

Christie slid her body on top of Tom's and rested her head between his head and shoulder, enjoying the warmth and comfort that it entailed. Tom's eyes opened and he gave her a warm smile, his hand gently caressing her back. Their pending moment of passion was interrupted when Christie's phone started to ring. She initially thought it was her alarm and she was ready to turn it off so she could return to Tom, but it was an incoming call.

'Shit,' she said loudly as she scrambled for the phone. Tom would never argue against her answering or plead with her to ignore it. He knew that she would not know how important the call was until it was answered. With Lyle's name showing on the display, she knew it may be a vital call, especially this time in the morning.

'Better get up, boss,' he said wearily. 'There's another body in Whitebank.'

Day 5 - 07:49 - Main Road Approaching Whitebank Village, West Lothian

Christie had changed quickly and left Tom in the flat, running down the stairs to meet Lyle outside. The GTI was parked right outside her door and he sat waiting for her, fresh coffee in his hand for her. Lyle had arrived early at the station when the call had come in. Christie was cursing the lack of progress in the first murder, a second death was the last thing she needed right now.

'What's that band with the guy with the voice that sounds likes he's swallowed a load of razor blades?' Christie asked, needed to have her mind wandering so she could approach the scene with a clear head. For once, Lyle was stumped.

'Could be anyone in the classic rock genre, you need to give me more.'

'You played one of their songs before, something about a gypsy. The singer could have been the fourth Bee Gee.' Lyle was not any the wiser.

'So the singer has a voice that is gravelly and sings in falsetto?'

'They're named after a cartoon or something.'

'Cinderella.' Lyle exclaimed excitedly. 'Stick on the Long Cold Winter album, the opening track is a belter.' Christie scrolled through the album selection and started the album. After the bluesy analog introduction of 'Bad Seamstress Blues' the song kicked into 'Fallin' Apart At The Seams' at which point Lyle increased the volume and head-banged his way through the rest of the song. Christie was grateful that he was one of the best drivers on the force or they could be heading for the nearest hedge.

The music was turned off at the end of the song as Lyle pulled into the turn off for Whitebank. The body had been discovered by an early dog walker in a secluded path that ran on the outskirts of the village. As Lyle pulled over in a street close to the path, they could see that the forensic team were already in place and they could also see Dr James's black BMW 4x4 parked ahead. They changed into their forensic suits and approached the scene. A local PC was standing at the police cordon and allowed Christie and Lyle through after a thorough inspection of their ID's. Lyle smiled at Christie during this, but they both knew he was young and doing an important job. It was possibly his first murder scene and he was looking a little white round the edges.

Dr James spotted their arrival and stood up from inspecting the body.

'We're not long here, but his ID confirms that he is a Dennis Robinson, aged 59 and lives in the village. You're the first CID on scene, so you may have to visit the house and inform the family. The dog walker recognised him, he's lived in the village for a while and is married with a grown up son.'

Robinson's ID was in an evidence bag and Lyle inspected it, taking down the personal information. Christie viewed the body for the first time. The man was laying on his back, almost as if sunbathing. She could see bullet wounds in both the head and chest area.

'Same killer.' Christie's question came out as a statement.

'Too early to say, ballistics will need to confirm. What I will say, is the entry wound is consistent and this time they fired four shots rather than one. It may be a different killer, however, two murders in a village with a population in its hundreds? I think it is unlikely.' He gave her a smile, 'Strictly off the record, of course.'

'Of course,' Christie agreed. 'We'll leave you to it, best get the unpleasantries out of the way. We'll see you for coffee later this afternoon?' It was a cheeky request that Dr James would have dismissed had it been anyone else.

'I've taken delivery of a new blend, your timing is good.' With that he returned to the job in hand and Lyle handed the ID back to the forensic officer as they headed back to the car. Lyle brought up a map of the village on his phone to find out which street they were heading to.

'Fuck,' he said aloud. 'His house is at the top of this path. He was about thirty seconds from his front door.' They stripped off of their forensic suits, and made their way around the cordon towards the house.

The property was a smart and modern detached house with a tidy garden. Some dog toys were lying on the grass.

'Please let it be friendly,' Lyle commented as they walked up the path. Their knocking was greeted by deep barking within. The door was opened by a young man in his twenties, he was holding the golden retriever who looked more excitable than threatening.

'Bouncer, calm down,' he shouted at the dog who seemed to comply. Christie and Lyle introduced themselves, showing their ID, and requested to come into the house to speak with the homeowner. They were led through to the main sitting room, where a bored looking lady of late fifties to early sixties sat motionless watching a quiz show on the television.

'Who is it, Adam?' She asked the question without taking her eyes from the screen, oblivious to the two detectives standing in the room.

'Mum, it's the police,' Adam replied in a worried tone, a tone that immediately gained his mother's attention. Lyle suggested that Adam go and sit with his mother.

'Has something happened to Dennis?' Her question was asked in contempt, rather than in concern. 'That useless drunk bastard is always getting himself into bother, he didn't even make it back last night from the pub.' Christie, being the senior officer was the one to break the news.

'I'm afraid your husband is dead.' It was never easy to deliver news like this and it never got easier. Christie knew that if the day came where she could break such news to someone without her stomach churning, it would be time to quit the police force. The scream of Linda Robinson was piercing, Adam moved quickly to hold her. Christie and Lyle remained standing in silence, giving them time to let the news sink in. After a couple of minutes, which often felt like a lifetime in these circumstances, Lyle left in search of the kitchen and tea making facilities leaving Christie to take a seat on the sofa.

'I know that this will be a really difficult time for you both, but it's important that I ask a few questions once my sergeant is back. Before that, is there anyone you want me to call? Anyone you want to be with you?' Linda looked up towards Christie, her inflamed, bloodshot eyes seeking comprehension which would not be coming at any time soon.

'Adam is all I need just now. I'll call for Betty my next door neighbour later, it would be good to have her around.' Lyle came back with cups of tea and laid them down on a coffee table in front of the family. The enormity of what was happening was starting to sink in. 'What happened?' Linda asked softly, at almost a whisper. Christie knew she had to balance what she could say and what she needed to say.

'He was found this morning, not far from the house, and we believe that your husband was murdered. Unfortunately I am limited to what I can say at the moment, but I promise I will tell you everything I can as soon as this is possible.' There was no objections from Linda as she accepted a mug from Lyle of the strong, sweet tea.

'Jesus, that's disgusting,' she complained taking a sip. 'Dennis took four sugars when I met him, I managed to get him down to one.' There were more tears at the recollection. Christie decided to start gentle with the questioning.

'What can you tell us about Dennis.' She took a moment to find the words.

'He was a useless big shite, but he was *my* useless big shite. He liked a drink, you will have gathered that already, but he was generous and gentle.

87

He was never violent when drunk, the opposite in fact. He would come in with declarations of love, I just wish he could have said it more when he was sober.' She squeezed Adam's hand. 'He was not a bad dad, was he?' Adam smiled and nodded his head.

'Aye, he was not a bad dad.' His answer lacked some conviction, but Christie let it pass, it being neither the time nor the place to challenge the young man's answer. Linda didn't seem to notice the lack of sentiment behind his answer, her mind obviously on other things. She answered Christie's next question before she had had a chance to ask it.

'Why would anyone wish to hurt Dennis? He was no angel, but he was not a confrontational person and he was definitely not someone to make enemies.'

Christie considered her answer, it was something that they would have to check when they looked into his background and spoke with his friends and associates. The big difference between him and Stafford, was Robinson appeared to be a very social person. He was a regular at the local pub, he was married with a son. Stafford was an isolated individual, keeping himself to himself. No family or friends of note, the ultimate loner. Christie wondered if that was why they had failed to make any progress. Christie decided to have a go at one last question, then would leave the family for now.

'Just one last question, Mrs Robinson, then we will leave you for now. We will probably have to come back and speak to you both some more, but we will give you some privacy for now.' Linda nodded her head in understanding and agreement. 'Did your husband know a David Stafford?'

'The man that was killed the other day? Do you think they were linked?' Christie didn't show the frustration she felt at being answered with a question, especially a question that she had been asking herself from the moment Lyle called her that morning.

'We can't rule anything out at this stage, Mrs Robinson.' She left the sentence handing, hoping the silence would prevent her having to ask the question again. Linda clicked.

'No, not that I am aware of. Of course, he may have known him down the pub. Most of his pals were regulars in the pub. Perhaps he was in the darts team?'

Christie thanked her for her time and left her business card should she need to be contacted. They agreed to see themselves out and as they crossed the threshold the were faced with a small, angry looking lady.

'Who are you? Are you the polis, whit's going on here?' Lyle approached her, speaking firmly but calmly.

'Yes, we are the police and we are the ones who tend to ask the questions. Who might you be?'

'I'm Betty, I live next door.'

'Well Betty, I suggest that you go on through and comfort Mrs Robinson. I'm afraid Dennis Robinson has died.' He chose the word carefully. Died, not killed, not murdered. It would be down to Linda and Adam to tell who they wished and in what way they wanted. Betty barged passed the officers into the house and they continued down the path heading back towards Lyle's car.

'So what do we do now?' Lyle asked.

'Breakfast,' Christie replied. Lyle checked his watch, started the engine and drove out of the village.

Day 5 - 09:24 - Corstorphine Police Station, Edinburgh

Chowdhury has now amassed a large paper file in relation to David Stafford. He had been informed of the second murder and wanted to get a strong lead in the Stafford case so that he could start working on the background of Dennis Robinson. He knew that Robinson would be an easier case to do the research on and he would have the opportunity to speak with family and friends, something that had been lacking in the Stafford case. The CCTV he had been trawling through had yielded nothing of interest, his chances of finding anything now rested on the paperwork.

He had been given access to Stafford's property and allowed to take away his personal paperwork that he had kept filed neatly in the spare bedroom of his house, which had been converted into a study and home office. Chowdhury had also managed to have a long conversation with Stafford's boss and she confirmed that he came into the office daily but also did a lot of work from home. He was a hard worker, who excelled in his field although he was very quiet and did not have much of a relationship with his co-workers or clients. There was no indication of any issues at work and the manager did not believe that his tragic death could be linked to his work. It was an angle that Christie would have to explore as part of the investigation, but Chowdhury did not expect there to be a link.

Stafford's paperwork was kept in immaculate order and was easy to review. Chowdhury flicked through the bank statements that went back five years. He was a wealthy man, but the statements confirmed that his wealth came from a lack of spending his wages rather than a personal windfall. He had invested his savings wisely; low risk, fixed returns seemed to be his preferred option, which would have seen him through any financial downturns. He kept two current accounts, one for his wages and bills and the other one for his day to day spending. Aside from supermarkets and petrol, he did not seem to spend much money on himself. Chowdhury recalled from visiting the house that it was tastefully decorated but there was not a lot of personal possessions. A TV and DVD player were in the main living room and a bookcase full of old books, but no games console or modern gadgets were seen.

Putting down the bank statements, he looked through Staffords bill receipts. Again, there was nothing of note within that file. He changed his utilities supplier often, obviously keen to get the best deals at all times. He scribbled notes on the bills, ensuring that they were accurate and up to date. Meter readings were also recorded, with dates and times taken and submitted. Again all the bills went back for five years.

There was a file of receipts, instruction booklets and guarantees for his electrical appliances and again there was nothing of interest in this file. He flicked through a file marked 'Tax' and similar to his bills there were scribbled notes and calculations. Tax receipts from dividend payments were also carefully filed for the last five years.

It was in the last file that Chowdhury spotted something that made his heart beat a little faster. The file was marked 'Home Improvements' and it was obvious that Stafford was not one to undertake any DIY himself. It reminded him of his own grandfather, who would say 'Every man to his job', which was an expression that suggested each trade should be done by a trades person in their own field. His grandfather was a joiner to trade and would have various friends round Chowdhury's parent's house fixing electrics or plumbing whilst the grandfather would do all joinery work. The file had all the receipts for painting, some plumbing and electrical work all carried out in the last five years. It was obvious that Stafford was not one for 'cash in hand' as all jobs came with a proper VAT receipt.

There was one receipt that seemed out of place, not only in this file but in all of Stafford's paperwork. The receipt was from a landscape

91

gardener and was for the construction of a patio. Chowdhury remembered the patio from his visit, it was in the rear garden, running along the back of the house from the back door that the killer had entered. The killer must have stood on this very patio that may be a clue in this case. The patio had seen better days and most households would have replaced the dated patio with modern decking. So why had Stafford not done this, as the rest of the house was decorated to a modern taste?

And when all other paperwork went back exactly five years, why would Stafford hold on to a receipt for a patio that had been laid more than twenty five years previously?

PART FIVE - DISSIDENT

CHAPTER NINE

Day 5 - 11:01 - Whitebank Village, West Lothian

Christie and Lyle had enjoyed breakfast at the Classic Crock Cafe before heading back to the station to plan the rest of the day. They would return to Whitebank to interview Barbara Stewart first, now that she had had some time to recover from her ordeal. They also wanted to speak to the shop owner Winifred and perhaps Freddie briefly. They also planned to visit the pub at some point once it had opened. Now with Chowdhury's revelation, they would be having a close look at that patio before deciding if they needed to see if anything was hidden beneath it.

'It can't be coincidence, ma'am,' Lyle was saying as he pulled the car over in front of Stafford's house.

Christie had been silent, mentally facing the endless task of trying to tie up all the threads of the investigation, before all the threads had even been discovered. She had been thinking constantly about the patio since Chowdhury had told them of the misplaced receipt. Perhaps that's what is was, just a misplaced receipt, a random piece of paper that got lost amongst the other receipts. Chowdhury had been adamant, the filing system was immaculate bordering on obsessive compulsion. They got out the car and walked to the rear of the property to see for themselves.

The cordon tape whistled in the wind, as Christie pulled the collar of her overcoat up against her neck. Lyle never seemed to be affected by the cold, he always wore his suit and rarely an overcoat over it. They stood staring at the patio, the slabs now fraying at the edges, the colour long drained out of them. Weeds were growing in places, unlike the rest of the garden which was kept to Chelsea Flower Show standards. Chowdhury had mentioned some landscape maintenance receipts in the paperwork files. Lyle was racking his brain for recollection of the house at the time of the disappearance case.

'There use to be a gravel path here,' he recalled. 'I remember when we came to arrest him I was sent round to this back door, should he try and do a runner. I remember treading carefully so that the stones would make as little noise as possible.'

'I'm worried about pulling the whole thing up on a whim, Lyle. I'm not doubting Chowdhury's hunch, but in a village this small word will get out straight away. I can't have the family being traumatised thinking we know that there is something buried under there. What's your gut saying?' Lyle didn't have to consider his response.

'My gut is telling me that I won't be able to sleep again until a thorough search has been carried out. There may be clues hidden under there, preserved and with luck containing DNA traces. Yes, it may be a false lead. Yes, it may upset people if nothing is found...' he trailed off in his own thoughts.

'To be honest, I won't be able to sleep either, Lyle. I'll make the call and see what we can do.'

Christie headed back to Lyle's car to get out of the wind and have a clearer line to DCS Hepburn. He answered straight away and listening intently. He approved her request immediately, but told her to tread carefully and speak with the neighbours discreetly. He would pull as many strings as possible and try and get a team out that day. He was being backed by his superiors to get a result in the two cases, that were quickly becoming the focus of the whole of the Edinburgh region of Police Scotland. There were a lot of eyes on them and it would not be long until the station would be getting swamped with 'outside influence', so he was keen to get moving on the case. If that meant spending a bit of the budget, then so be it.

Christie exited the car with a thumbs up to Lyle confirming her success. They decided to walk to Barbara Stewart's house, letting the wind blow out the current thoughts allowing them to arrive with a clear mind ready for fresh questioning. They would be spending a great amount of time in this village, so they may as well get to know the streets. It was like being back on the beat once more.

Barbara Stewart lived in a tidy bungalow and, to the surprise of Christie and Lyle, she was standing in her front garden, hoe in hand, de-weeding her borders. Her niece was observing from the doorway, coffee cup in hand, chatting away to her aunt.

'Morning officers,' Barbara exclaimed cheerfully. 'Please come in, I'm due my next cup of tea anyway.' Her niece re-entered the house and headed for the kitchen, taking the hint of her aunt. Barbara ushered them through to the living room. The room was spotless, albeit very dated looking. The room had a three bar electric fire, a television set that was larger behind the screen than it was across it and a video cassette player. A wireless radio was playing Radio 4 quietly in the background. Lyle recognised that it was playing on the long wave frequency, not many radios would have that option nowadays. Invited to sit on the sofa, Christie asked the first question.

'How are you feeling now, Ms Stewart?'

'Much better than the last time we met,' she replied with a smile. 'It was an awful shock and I don't think I will ever get the vision out of my head, but you have to move on. I don't know how many more years I've got left so I'm going to enjoy them. I'm already passed my three score and ten, so I will focus on the good things that have happened in my life and leave these thoughts and memories behind me.'

She was certainly a spritely lady for her age. The niece came through with tea for everyone, served in an antique bone china tea set. She introduced herself as Eva, the great niece of Barbara. She informed them that she lived in Livingston on her own and had agreed to stay with her aunt for a week just to make sure she was ok.

'As you can see, my great aunt is more than capable of looking after herself,' she said with a genuine grin. 'I have some time off work, so I thought I would keep her company anyway.' Christie turned back to Barbara.

'We need to ask you about Mr Stafford. You have lived here a long time, you know him and his history. What can you tell us about him?' Barbara took a sip from her teacup, considering her answer.

'I assume you will have already heard that he was a loner, kept himself to himself, didn't socialise, etc. I knew him to say hello to, and he was alway polite if we bumped into each other in the street. Not the best conversationalist in the village and after a while I kept any chats with him to a bare minimum. I could tell he was uncomfortable in those situations and there was no point in making it any worse for him.'

'Did he have any family, friends or associates that came to visit him?'

'No, I never seen anyone go into the house, with the exception of tradesmen when he needed something repaired or sorted. I believe what family he had stopped speaking to him after the trial. The only person he had any conversation with was Old Edward.'

'Old Edward?' Christie asked, her interest perked instantly,

'His gardener, Edward McMillan. He has lived in the village as long as I have and keeps many a garden beautiful around these parts. He's in his seventies now and should be long retired, but he keeps riding his old bike around doing odd jobs around the village.' Suddenly she moved forward in her chair and beckoned Christie forward, her next statement almost at a whisper. 'If anyone knows anything about Mr Stafford, it will be Old Edward.'

'Where can we find Mr McMillan?' Lyle was sensing that at last they may have found someone that could tell them something about the elusive Mr Stafford.

'He lives in Holly Cottage, it's the beautiful little house on the right hand side just as you enter the village from the Edinburgh side. You can't miss it, lovely array of rose plants in the front garden and a climbing holly bush covering the left hand side of the house.'

Lyle nodded, he had noticed the property when they had arrived. The cottage must be well over 100 years old and, although not much of a gardener himself, he had remembered the stunning front garden as he passed it earlier that morning.

'Thank you, we will pay him a visit when we are done here,' Christie commented gratefully. 'I just have one further question for now. You said that you thought he was innocent when he was charged in 1992, why are you so certain?' Barbara had drained the last of her tea, Lyle moved forward to refill her cup.

'Nothing exciting has ever happened in this village in all the years I have lived here, so when a resident was accused of such a crime, the whole village could talk of nothing else. I remember your sergeant here going round asking questions,' she looked up towards Lyle with a smile. 'I always remember a face, even one that has aged slightly. It's your eyes, if you don't mind me saying, they are very kind.' Lyle felt himself starting to blush slightly. 'Some of your colleagues were very arrogant and rude, trying to trip people up to help the case. Your sergeant was different and I respected him for that.'

'I always try and treat people fairly, Ms Stewart.' Lyle confirmed. Barbara gave him a grateful smile.

'I had known David for quite a while before he was arrested. As a teenager, he was not always as quiet as he became when he was older. The trial changed him forever and I was amazed that he chose to remain the village. Most of the village agreed with my assumption, but I know there were some who suspected that there was no smoke without fire. He would get up to the usual mischief that boys of that age would do, stealing apples and strawberries from peoples gardens, chapping doors then running away, then having a fly smoke and drink in the woods behind the village.'

She actually laughed at the memory, a recollection of youth. Perhaps she herself had undertaken some of these past times in her own younger days. It was a thought of the innocence of being young, reminiscing of days long gone. She continued.

'I seem to recall that he hung around with a group of friends, mostly from the village. They were inseparable, the five of them.'

'Five of them?' Christie asked.

'Yes, there were five in the group always. I remember because I used to think of Enid Blyton's Famous Five. David always appeared to me as one to hang on to the rest of the group. He always walked slightly behind them, I think he may have been slightly younger than them.' She was giving good background and Christie has taking a copious amount of notes, some of which she knew would help the investigation. Barbara was now coming to the answer of Christie's question.

'Despite this little rebellious phase, David was a kind person. He often helped the older people around the village by carrying their heavy shopping home, or helping with odd jobs. That, of course proves nothing, but there was one incident that I witnessed that makes me sure that he could not have done anything to harm that young girl.' She was pausing for effect, the officers knew, once more reaching for the bone china cup to finish the last of her drink. She even shuffled forward in her chair, looking for maximum impact. The two officers were gripped at this point.

'He was standing outside of the village shop, with the rest of the famous five, and a young girl came out of the shop. I had been heading in to get some biscuits and witnessed the whole thing. It was a hot day and the young girl was wearing a mini skirt. Some of the group started to wolf whistle, disgusting practice of course but it happens. Anyway, one of the boys crept up behind her and lifted her skirt up, showing off the girl's underwear. The rest of the group laughed, all except David. He ran over and punched the guilty party straight on the nose, causing it to bleed profusely. Without stopping, he checked the girl was ok and offered to see her home. The girls was crying, thanked him but said she was okay. I went over to confront the injured thug, but they all ran off. David walked off in a different direction.'

It was an incredible story and Lyle and Christie let it sink in. Lyle was the first to respond.

'Was this ever discussed at the original case?'

'I did recall the story to one officer, but he didn't seem to pay much attention and it was never mentioned again.' Christie and Lyle both knew what was coming. 'An Inspector Montgomery, I remember comparing him to Field Marshal Montgomery.' She paused once more, laughing at her own pending punchline. 'He didn't compare well.'   Lyle could feel his mood change, this could have been a vital piece of evidence had it been investigated and confirmed. Despite all the years of hurt and frustration, he was now starting to question his own conclusion about Stafford. Christie decided to ask one final question.

'The other four boys in this gang, can you remember who they were?' Barbara thought for a moment then shook her head in resignation.

'Most of the boys have long since left the village. The only one who still lives here is a man called Dennis Robinson. I don't speak to him as he is usually with that dog of his, and I don't like dogs. I was bitten as a child and never stopped being scared of them, although Bouncer appears more friendly than most.'

It was the connection that they were looking for and it fell onto their lap. The first piece of positive news, the cases could now be officially connected. They would have to try and find out about the other three, because if Christie's gut feeling was correct, they may have another serial killer on the loose.

Day 5 - 12:42 - Holly Cottage, Whitebank Village, West Lothian

Christie felt it only right that she tell Barbara about the death of Dennis Robinson, she would have heard before the day was out anyway. She took the news relatively calmly, but Christie was glad her niece was there with her as support.

They drove out of Barbara's street and back towards the Edinburgh side exit to the village. Holly Cottage came into view and there are a small area in front of the cottage that Lyle could pull onto to park. The cottage was exactly how Barbara had described it. It was simply stunning and the front garden was as you would expect of a gardener of such reputation. The view was like what you would find on the box of a jigsaw puzzle. There was a bicycle lending against the garden wall, an old black cycle that Lyle recognised.

'It's a Norman if I'm not mistaken. I think this is from the 1950's, my father had one just like it.' Lyle approached it, his eyes wide and grinning like a school boy. 'This one is a beauty, what condition for its age.'

'1955, to be precise and I've had her since then.' Old Edward made an appearance from the rear garden. He was small in stature with a slight hump on his back. We wore old brown corduroy trousers, a woollen crew neck jumper with a shirt and tie underneath. He wore a flat cap on his head, strands of brilliant white hair protruding from beneath it. He had a weather beaten, friendly face. 'I have looked after it the same way since then, cleaning and drying it after every cycle, oiling the chain every week and replacing any parts that are starting to get worn. It's amazing the things you can order on the internet nowadays. The parts ain't cheap, but they last a hell of a lot longer than the rubbish they put on bicycles nowadays.'

Christie and Lyle formally introduced themselves, although Edward knew straight away who they were. It was unlikely Barbara had phoned to warn him, he was a person with the ability to spot a police officer from a mile away.

'Please come in, I was expecting you to come for a chat about young David.' He led the officers through to his kitchen, which was large in comparison to the rest of the house. An old wooden bench table took up much of the middle of the room and the back door was open looking out to the even more impressive rear garden. Had it been a nicer day, they would have no doubt have ended up out there. Edward laid down three glasses without offering and retrieved a large glass jug from his fridge. 'Homemade apple juice.' He nodded his head towards a large apple tree in the back garden. 'I've been making this since I was a kid.' He poured the cloudy liquid into the three glasses. 'The boys in the club have been trying to get me to make cider for years, but I don't touch alcohol myself. I have a sweet tooth and I would rather drink pints of this than anything else.'

'Slainte Mhath,' he raised his glass in toast. Christie and Lyle repeated the toast and both took a sip. A beautiful mixture of sweetness with a hint of tartness, the juice was the best that either of them had ever experienced.

'You should sell this, you'd make a fortune,' Lyle complemented.

'Not for me, young man. I make enough of this juice for myself and a few selected friends only. Production would ruin the magic.' Lyle liked that thought, producing something for pleasure rather than profit. The world could learn a lot from Old Edward. 'I make enough money from my pension and my real passion, which is gardens. I would do most of them for free, the joy I get out of transforming dull boring spaces to a palace of plants, a fortress of flowers.' His face lit up once more, expressions that he had no doubt used hundreds of times, but it visualised his passion to perfection. They continued with some small talk, comfortable in each other's company. Edward lived alone, his late wife had passed ten years previously. He made a comfortable living for his modest needs and the gardening and cycling kept him fit and healthy. The 'club' he referred to was the local dominos club which operated out of the village pub, which he attended every Tuesday and Thursday evening. Pleasantries concluded, Christie turned the conversation around to Stafford.

'We understand that you were one of the few people that spoke to Mr Stafford on a regular basis,' Christie asked him. His facial expression started to turn to one of remorse. 'Can you tell me about him?' He took a deep breath and shook his head.

'I wish I had taken more notice to him. I did spend a lot of time speaking with him and I have been doing his garden and other little odd jobs for him for over 20 years. I always found that he was a genuinely nice lad, of course there was all that business that he got himself mixed up in.'

'What do you mean, got mixed up in?' Lyle question was asked in somewhat frustration, although he was just on the right side of the line of asking it appropriately. Christie threw him a warning glance nonetheless.

'He hung around with a bad lot in those days. At the start, they were just kids larking around. I chased them away many a time from my fruit trees, but would let them have an apple or two from time to time. It was good natured then. Of course, young lads become young men and cigarettes and drink made them feel tougher and then they start to act in more inappropriate ways. David was one of the the gang, but his part was unconvincing, especially to the likes of me who knew him so well. One or two of the others were particularly cruel.'

'Do you remember the names of any of the others in the gang?' Christie asked him. He thought about this for a while before shaking his head.

'At my age, names start to lose themselves in the history of time. I can remember the faces, I'm good with faces, but names are another thing. Just the lad that stayed in the village, Dennis Robinson. I've done his garden from time to time but his own lad does it now.'

Once again, Christie was forced to reveal the discovery from early that day. Old Edward looked genuinely shocked and said out loud what Christie had been thinking about.

'Then there's a link between the two murders,' he said with respectful excitement. 'They didn't speak to each other, I believe that they fell out after the trial over something or other. I hate to speak ill of the dead, but I never liked Dennis and he didn't improve with age. I would see him occasionally in the pub but I found him loud and obnoxious. I kept my distance from him as much as possible.'

'Any idea who would want to harm him or Mr Stafford?' Lyle asked with more composure than his last question.

'I can't think of anyone who would want to harm David, unless it was someone with a grudge linked to the original case. That doesn't make sense though, because why wait this long?' Christie and Lyle had thought the same thing. 'More people would be likely to hold a grudge against Dennis. He wasn't always popular at the local pub and got chucked out a few times. Never barred from the pub, in a village this size the owner needs all the customers she can get.'

Christie was now keen to speak with the landlady of the infamous pub and would be heading over there to speak with her before the pub started to get too busy.

'Tell us more about the kind of work you did for Mr Stafford.' Christie asked.

'Mostly the usual stuff, lawn mowing, weeding, planting of flowers, tidying the border, et cetera. Nothing of the heavy stuff anymore, in my younger days I could build walls, smaller houses, paving, patios and sheds. Many of these I did are still standing, I did not take shortcuts, my work was built to last.' Christie knew the time had approached to ask the one question that they had really came here for.

'Did you lay the patio at Mr Stafford's house?'

'I certainly did, must be what early to mid 1990's. Not one of my best efforts though.' Christie and Lyle were surprised by this, encouraging Edward to elaborate. 'Well, the materials were fine, but when I do a patio I like to do it all myself from preparation to finalising it. David insisted that he do the preparation work and he and some friends laid the groundwork. I could see straight away it was not perfect, but I carried on against my better judgement. Anyway, after a few years the slabs still hadn't settled right and I suggested to David that I lift and relay the slabs but he said that he was happy the way they were. Most people now go for decking and I did discuss this with David, but again he said that he liked the garden as it was. In the end, I just accepted it. David inherited the house just before his trial, his parents died not knowing that their son had been mixed up in the case. Anyway, he once told me that the patio was the first thing he paid for with his inheritance money, so I suspected there was some sentimental value to it.'

Christie had all the information she needed and now felt more than ever that the patio hid something. She may even find out later that day should Hepburn's string-pulling be successful. Of all the sentimental possessions that a person would own, she thought it unlikely a patio would be high on the list. She had one more question to ask.

'We won't take up any more of your time, however, I have one final question for you. You said at the start of the interview that you wished you had taken more notice of him, what did you mean by that exactly?' Old Edward's remorseful expression returned.

'He told me, in some confidence, that there was something worrying him. When I pressed him, he admitted that someone had been asking him questions about the young girl that went missing.' Lyle pounced on this, realising the importance of this information.

'Did he say who it was?' Edwards shook his head.

'I think he knew the person, or knew of them. The only thing he said was the person was too young at the time of disappearance and wanted to find out the truth.

106

CHAPTER TEN

Day 5 - 14:14 - The Mole Catchers Arms, Whitebank Village, West Lothian

Christie and Lyle approached the local pub on foot, having left the car outside Edward's house. The old man had promised to keep an eye on it until they had returned. He had insisted that the pair take away a bottle each of his prized apple juice, which they had locked safely in the boot of the GTI.

The pub stood on its own, detached from the surrounding properties. There was an outside smoking shelter and a picnic bench that had seen better days. An old style pub sign swung gently in the breeze, depicting a man all dressed in black with a small sack over his back. He looked like some sort of evil Father Christmas. A blackboard sign outside the main door advertised live sport, Monday quiz nights and Sunday evening karaoke. The small windows were illuminated in yellow and the place felt that it belonged in a Charles Dickens novel.

Entering the pub, it had a tasteful blend of old and new. The building dated from the early 19th century and many of the original features remained. The yellow glow came from a huge roaring, open fire in the centre of the room. The wood burning smell filled the air giving a sense of the history of the place. A large screen television and fruit machine brought the atmosphere up to modern times. On the other side of the fire where tables that could handle 20-30 covers, although modest it would have been a vital addition to ensure the pub's survival in the recent difficult times for the industry.

The bar was well stocked with a geography of single malts from all over the country and local craft beers sitting alongside the more popular brands. It was hard to identify the demographic that the pub was aiming at, perhaps it was looking to please all. Three customers were nursing their drinks, two older gentlemen were sipping at their malts as they were debating over the horses listed in the their Racing Post newspaper. A postman, still in uniform, was enjoying a post shift pint by the fire looking up at the Sport News channel playing on the television. Behind the bar stood a smart lady, polishing glasses and wiping down the already spotless surfaces.

'What can I get you?' She asked kindly having spotted the two enter the premises for the first time. Lyle ordered fresh orange and lemonade for himself and Christie accepted his offer of a soda water and lime. After paying for the drinks, Christie and Lyle formally introduced themselves, the landlady smiling having already spotted their profession.

Andrea Wood was a striking lady in her early fifties, with long straggly greying blond hair. She wore tortoise shell spectacles over sharp, pale blue eyes. She was comfortable in her surroundings and managed to dismiss the curious glances from her punters both subtlety and professionally. She poured herself a diet coke and moved to the top end of the bar away from the ears of the Racing Post drinkers.

'Nice place you have here,' commented Christie.

'Thank you. Not the most trend setting of places, but I do enough to get by.' Christie noticed the absence on a wedding ring and wondered if she ran the place alone. Background on her was not important at this point. Andrea went on. 'I took over the place about twenty years ago and gave it a bit of a makeover. Before then it was a typical 'Old Man's Pub', the type I grew up loving. Traditionally comfortable, commercially disastrous is how I would have described it. When the smoking ban came in during 2006, I had to rebrand again and created the restaurant wing. Fortunately, I managed to get a superb chef at the time who helped me design a menu that would bring people in. He became my business partner and has been with me since, effectively saving the business. I must admit, although I miss the smokey atmosphere of the pub, I love the clean air and fresh aroma that the pub has now. Only the comforting smell of wood burning fills the pub now and I think it's better for it.'

'It's an unusual name for a pub, if you don't mind me saying,' commented Lyle. 'Has it always been called that?'

'Oh no, it was called 'The Whitebank Arms' when I took over, everyone just called it 'The Arms'. When I rebranded I wanted to give it a name that was personal to me. I was always going to retain the Arms element of the name, but Mole Catcher is all me. My grandfather was a mole catcher in West Lothian and had a reputation of being the best at dealing with the problem. He had a secret that he told me when I was a little girl and after he retired. He said that he used to catch all the moles that was upsetting his customers' lawns and farmland. Then, once he was finished, he would let two go back into the wild. It was important that he guaranteed his future business.'

It was an interesting story and Christie knew that this personal information being shared was allowing a build up of trust between the parties, just as a shared drink had at the start. Andrea could turn out to be a valuable asset to the investigation, both in background and being the eyes and ears to the locals. They would need to be careful that they did not push the trust too much.

'You will have heard of the death of David Stafford,' Andrea nodded at Christie to confirm such. 'Did he ever come into the pub?'

'I knew of him and had seen him around the village a few times, but he never came into the pub.' She thought for a minute before revising her answer. 'Actually, he came in once with a group of lads. Must have been about six months ago.' This was an amazing revelation to Christie and Lyle. The loner, the man who mixed with no one, was seen in the most social of places - the local pub - with a group of men.

'What happened, did you know the other parties?'

'He came in and had one drink with the group, there was a mild altercation and he stormed off. It blew over before I had to get involved. I didn't know most of the group, however, one of my regulars was there. Dennis Robinson.' For the third time that day, Christie had to break the news that Dennis had been killed. The news visibly shocked Andrea, who shook her head in disbelief.

'What was he like, Andrea?' Lyle had asked the question, compassionately using her first name.

'Well he was one of my regulars, came in a lot and was well known both in the pub and in the village. I appreciate the seriousness of the situation, so I won't beat about the bush. Dennis was a lovely guy for his first two pints, then he turned into an arsehole. He had a good sense of humour for his first two pints, then he became loud, obnoxious and just kept in the right side of being inappropriately rude. He was a regular drinker, but not by any means an alcoholic. The thing about Dennis was I never had to tell him to stop drinking. He would often say, 'Right Andie, I've had enough now I'll head up the road soon'. He would then spend half an hour or so chatting to the punters, slowly turning back into the nice Dennis, and would head home.'

'Did he have any enemies that you were aware of?' Christie was starting to build a picture of the second victim in the case.

'Not that I was aware of. He had his fall outs with some of the other locals, but they were all pals again the next day. This is a decent pub, with a good mixture of punters, drinkers and diners. In the twenty odd years I've been here, I've thrown one guy out my pub and he was a German tourist who had just returned from a whisky tasting experience and passing through on the way back to Edinburgh. I think Mrs Robinson may have wanted to strangle Dennis sometimes, but she saw the good in him more than anyone else in the world.' Andrea dabbed a bar towel against the side of her eyes, starting to feel some emotion of the regular who wouldn't be returning. 'He was the only person to call me Andie,' she said softly. 'and I quite liked it.'

'I know it was a long time ago, but can you remember anything about these other people in the group that day?' Lyle was pushing to get the information, feeling it could be vital. They had to track these people down.

'I couldn't describe them as I didn't pay much attention to them. All I recall was that they obviously knew each other. When I was clearing glasses away from the tables I heard them saying something about 'forgetting the past'. Anyway, it was not long until David stormed out, Dennis returned to his group of regulars and the other three left.'

'Other three?' Lyle asked, trying to retain control of his voice. 'Are you sure it was definitely three of them?'

'No doubt about it,' Andrea replied confidently. 'One of the punters asked who the Famous Five were, then went on a story about some Hibernian Football Club players from the 1950's.' Lyle smiled both at the recollection and the confirmation. It was very likely that the Famous Five from the early 1990's had met, in this very pub, just six months ago.

And now two of them were dead…

Day 5 - 16:04 - The Whitebank Village Store, Whitebank Village, West Lothian

Christie and Lyle had one final interview to conduct in Whitebank. It was a short ride from Old Edward's house to the store, but Lyle was desperate to fit in a song before they arrived. Christie had been complaining that Lyle wanted to drive round, she wanted to walk, but music helped to clear his head and it had been a busy day with a lot of information to take in. His choice of music may have been his get back at Christie's gripes.

'Now, you will probably recognise this one,' Christie raised her eyebrows in mock surprise. 'But, I won't be playing the hip hop 1986 version. Oh no, you will be hearing the classic and original 1975 version.'

With that, a drum introduction led into Joe Perry's famous guitar introduction as Aerosmith's 'Walk This Way' started to play. Lyle tapped along to the song on his steering wheel as they drove back into Whitebank toward the village store.

As they pulled over in front of the store, Lyle's phone started to ring. His puzzled look was picked up by Christie who lent over to see that it was Bad Boy that was calling. He did not often call Lyle directly, so they knew it was important.

'My little dissident has something to say,' he commented as he pushed the answer key on the phone.

Bad Boy was animated on the phone, losing some of his usual composure.

'I won't fucking risk my new life, my family for you Mr Lyle and you have to promise me that you can give me some discreet protection.' For once, Lyle became very serious with his informant.

'Look William,' it was the first time he had ever called him by his first name. 'I appreciate all the information that you give me and I will do everything in my power that the source of your information is not leaked. If, for whatever reason, I need to make anything you say official I will ensure you and your family are protected. I hope that it does not come to that, but I have your back.'

'Thank you Mr Lyle. I only do this because you cut me a break when I most needed it. I wouldn't have the family back had you not got me to see sense.' Lyle smiled at the complement.'

'Kind of you to say, but you got your family back by changing yourself, don't forget that.' There was a slight awkward silence on the line before Bad Boy remembered the reason for his call.

'I have put out some feelers and I have a warm lead on the motorbike. I don't have all the information yet, but I think I can get you a name. I'll need a bit of time, so please don't come to the flat, let me phone you when I have it.'

'Deal,' confirmed Lyle before ending the call. He filled Christie in as they entered the store. Winnie was once more floating around the shop floor, although as there were no customers in to talk to, she busied herself straightening the items on the shelf. She came rushing over at the sight of Christie and Lyle, ushering them once more into the back of the shop. The same bored looking girl was behind the counter, wrapping chewing gum round her finger before popping it back in her mouth.

'Terrible business,' an animated Winnie was commenting. 'First David, now Dennis.' Christie was glad that she did not have to break the news for a fourth time. 'I just can't believe what is going on in this village. People are getting worried, this was a safe place to live. Not so much as a stolen bicycle around these parts and now two men have been bumped off by some psycho killer.' Lyle mind started singing the Talking Heads song.

'What can you tell us about Dennis Robinson?' Lyle asked her, keen to get the song out his head and focused on the job.

'Well, he always was nice enough when he came in here. I understand from some of my customers that he could be a bit funny at the pub, but he was always pleasant when he came in here. Bought his newspaper every morning, and would get the main essentials, bread, milk, eggs, etc.'

'Do you know how well Dennis and David knew each other? Lyle continued with the questioning.

'Well they would hang around together when they were younger, but they stopped talking after the trial. I think David resented the fact that no one stood up for him, I think some of the locals started to believe he was guilty. David took that really badly, stopped socialising and went into his shell.'

'Did you ever see them together, recently?' Winnie though for moment.

'Not personally, but Betty that comes in here said that she spotted David with a group of men a while back. I'm sure she said that Dennis was there but didn't recognise the others.' Winnie was unable to provide much more information, so Christie thanked her and they headed back to the car. Lyle fiddled with the controls to the music system.

'Well, ma'am. Where to next?' Christie's phoned beeped and she checked the message.

'That was Hepburn, the team have arrived at Stafford's house. Shall we go and see if there'e anything hidden under the patio?' Lyle nodded I agreement.

114

'There was one thing that Winnie said that may be useful.' Christie looked somewhat confused, feeling that she gave very little useful information. 'She gave a good description of who we are looking for.'

With that, Lyle drove off smiling, with The Talking Heads' 'Psycho Killer' coming from the stereo.

Day 5 - 17:02 - Undisclosed Location, Lanarkshire

The Chain hated being stuck in this godawful flat, in this godawful place and longed for the comfort of his affluent property back in Edinburgh. He knew that he had to keep low and both the flat in was in currently and its location could not be traced by looking through his financial records. He had made that mistake before which had led to him being tracked down and his ego had led to him being caught. He had a final trick up his sleeve, however, which led to his escape.

He smiled at the recollection, the plan had gone smoothly, much better than he ever could have anticipated. His accomplice had been handsomely paid in advance, he knew the plan should he get caught during the lifetime of his father. The Chain knew his father didn't have long to live, so the funeral would be the best chance of escape. He had other plans in place should he be caught after his father's death, but the original plan had worked.

The Chain looked around the flat, it was is a state of disrepair but it had the basic amenities that were required for his time underground. The flat had been bought for renovation by his accomplice and The Chain had being paying him a small rent to hide in it. He had left money in various locations and still had plenty left from his initial recovery. He also had foreign currency and his accomplice was in the process of getting him a fake passport should he need to flee the country. He was deliberately allowing time to pass before making that particular move.

The mirrored wardrobe doors in his bedroom gave off a sorry sight. He was wearing an old tracksuit and trainers. His hair had been shaved off and he had grown a beard. He was completely unrecognisable in his current attire which is what he wanted. He had ventured out to the local shops a few times and had mastered the local accent, a far cry from his time at private school in Edinburgh.

He felt that it was soon time to get back to work once more. The last three months since the escape plus the time spent in prison had been unbearable and his desire to kill was beyond any pain he had ever encountered. He knew, however, that he had to be patient once more or face the consequence of being ill prepared. The journey back to Edinburgh would be tricky, but he had it all planned out. Rather than go with stealth, he planned to travel by train during rush hour when everyone would be too busy to notice him. He had chosen the location and the time, it was the victim that would be random.

The Chain put his hand under his bed and pulled out a sports bag. He lifted it onto the bed and opened the zip. He lifted up a large towel and sports wear to reveal a separate plastic bag. Inside he reached for his weapon of choice, the bicycle chain that had already killed three people. He gently wiped it with a cloth, then took out a small bottle of oil which he rubbed vigorously into the links of the chain with a piece of rag. Putting the materials back in their own separate bag, he lifted up the chain to admire his handy work. It sparkled in the evening light coming in through the window, a chain that looked brand new, unused, ready to go on a new bicycle. It has cost a small fortune to get the weapon back, but a break-in at the evidence room has recovered it. It was so perfectly executed that the break-in and theft of the chain has still not been noticed.

'Don't fear my pretty weapon,' he said out loud. 'Once more we shall dance in the moonlight.'

PART SIX - W.M.A

CHAPTER ELEVEN

Having been told that it would take at least a couple of hours for the patio to be removed and the ground prepared for the forensic officers, Lyle decided to nip back to the Classic Crock for coffee and a bite to eat with Christie. Returning to the scene, the building contractors had left, the patio slaps were stacked up at the rear of the garden and the forensic officers were hard at work with a newly erected police cordon.

Two uniformed officers were posted at the front of the house, moving on any curious onlookers. The news would be all round Whitebank by now, Christie just hoped that it didn't reach as far as Kirknewton and the Kerr family. Christie had called them to say she wanted to speak to the family this evening and had agreed to go there later. Her main reason for the visit was to establish if there was any link between Samantha and Dennis Robinson. Other news would depend on what was or was not found here.

Lyle was pacing up and down just outside the cordon. He had already been warned off by a senior forensic officer, but he remained with his eyes fixed on their work. Christie sent him to the car on a needless errand so she could speak with the senior forensic officer in private.

'I know you are in charge here,' Christie said to her firmly, 'and I fully respect your work and regulations. I just ask you to extend DS Lyle a little courtesy for this specific case. He was involved in the original child abduction case from 1992 and this is the only one the got to him personally. He needs to know if there is anything there, he needs closure as much as the family do.' The officer nodded her head solemnly.

119

'As long as he keeps to that side of the cordon, and let us do our work I don't have a problem. I know what it's like to have a case like that, so I will extend him the courtesy you ask.' With that she returned to her work.

A few moments later, Lyle returned and went back to pacing round the cordon. It was not long until he stopped, frozen to the spot.

'THERE,' he shouted pointing over next to where one of the team members were working. Christie rushed over to join him, unconsciously taking his arm. She could feel him shaking slightly and, becoming aware of her action, decided to hold on to him anyway.

She could see what he was pointing at. Just penetrating the top of the soil was the back heel of a trainer.

'Diadora,' Lyle whispered softly. Christie knew at this point that the whole case would take a turn and they would be looking at a third, historic murder. Lyle's eyes remained as all three forensic officers gathered around the shoe and carefully dug around it. After what felt like days, the shoe was fully exposed and the horror of the skeletal remains attached to it confirmed that they had indeed found a body.

They waited around until the full skeleton had been exposed and Lyle could tell from the shoes, the remains of the clothes and the estimated height that it fitted everything he had been hunting for. Formal testing would have to take place, but Lyle had no doubt he had finally found Samantha Kerr.

Day 5 - 20:02 - Margaret Kerr's House, Kirknewton, West Lothian
Christie and Lyle drove in silence. No music played out of the stereo, Lyle kept his eyes on the road ahead, Christie kept hers staring out of the passenger side window and the passing landscape. There was nothing to say

at this stage, she wanted to let the news sink in, let him process the information. This was his case, his past, his obsession and he needed time to process it all. She wondered if it was a mistake going to the Kerr's house so early or a mistake taking Lyle. She had called Hepburn and he had given the go ahead, so she at least had the comfort that she was following direction from above.

They pulled up once more in front of Margaret Kerr's house just behind a new BWM. The private plate had the initials NIC and Christie wondered if their son, Nico, was doing very well for himself in his law career. Lyle turned off the ignition and turned to Christie.

'Please ma.am. Will you let me be the one to tell them.' His voice lacked its usual confidence, but she knew how important this moment was to him and agreed. He gave a small smile in way of appreciation. They exited the car and walked once more to the front door. Lyle took an audible deep breath then rang the doorbell, following it up with a couple of bangs with the ball of his fist. The door was opened by Nico, who welcomed them in and took them through to the sitting room.

To their surprise and relief Patrick Kerr was sitting on the sofa talking to Margaret. He rose to shake hands with the officers, before returning to the sofa where Nico joined them. The Kerr family could sense an atmosphere and looked towards Lyle for answers. He had seen that face before, he had always told them he had no further news. Now, all these years later he was finally going to break the news they least wanted to hear. Lyle cleared his throat.

'I must warn you that formal identification has still to take place, however, earlier today we found what I believe to be the remains of Samantha.' There was a sharp intake of breath and Margaret Kerr burst into tears, her throat refusing to let out the scream her body was attempting.

Patrick and Nico raised in one from the sofa and rushed over to each side of her. Patrick's eyes filled with tears, Nico's face drained of all colour. Lyle let the news sink in and remained quiet. Christie noted the words he used, especially 'I believe' confirming that he was taking responsibility for the news and 'remains' to let them know that Samantha was deceased. In a move most unlike him, Lyle took a seat on the sofa. Christie expected that his legs were struggling with the enormity of the situation and she chose to sit next to him in support.

It felt like an eternity before anyone spoke, it was Margaret that broke the silence.

'I knew in my heart of hearts that ma wee lassie wasn't coming hame, but when there is no news you keep a wee glimmer of hope. I knew this day was coming, Mr Lyle, and it will take time for it all tae sink in. Thank you for telling me yourself.' Lyle was visibly moved by the sentiment and spoke quickly to maintain his composure.

'I promise you one thing Mrs Kerr. I won't give up on Samantha. I can't promise I will catch who did this, I can't promise you that I will find out the truth, but I promise I will try every single day of my life to do just that.' Christie was moved herself by Lyle reply and decided it be best to take over.

'We have someone from Family Liaison coming over to see you and they will stay with you for a while. I don't mean to pry in business that has nothing to do with me, but I would suggest that you all stay here together for now. Is that possible?' Nico nodded his approval, Patrick looked at Margaret pleadingly who said she would like that very much. Patrick took her hand and gave it a squeeze, a moment of solidarity in grief.

'Thank you,' Christie said softly. 'We will wait until the officer comes, but we shall not bother you with questions at this time. We will, of course, have to come back as the investigation will be fully re-opened. Do you have any questions?' Patrick looked directly at Lyle.

'Will you be working the case again?'

'It's not for me to say, Patrick, but I will do everything that I can to be involved.'

'We would like it if you were, Mr Lyle. Like it very much.' The doorbell rang and Lyle left to answer it. The Family Liaison officer came in and introductions were made allowing Christie and Lyle to leave. Christie's phone rang and she spoke briefly to the caller before getting in the car.

'Back to the station,' she told Lyle. 'Hepburn has called an urgent meeting.

Day 5 - 21:32 - Corstorphine Police Station, Edinburgh

Hepburn was very animated as the staff collated in Meeting Room 1. The room was packed and Christie noticed a few faces that she hadn't seen for a while. Montgomery was floating around Hepburn, who seemed to be ignoring him for the time being. The room looked tired, many colleagues had been putting in long hours. The overtime budget was going to be busted before they got half way through the financial year. Christie herself was feeling the effects, but she was more driven and focused than ever before. Her desire to solve these new murders, to help The Chain be caught and returned to his prison cell and now the body of Samantha Kerr was being added to the mix.

'Listen up people,' Hepburn bellowed. 'I'm going to make this meeting short and to the point. We now have three major investigations to deal with and the Chief Constable is keeping an eye on proceedings. I am expecting a visit from the Assistant Chief Constable in the coming days, so everyone needs to up their game. We need to pull as much of our resource onto this as possible and every available officer across Edinburgh and the Lothians will be used. The CC may wish to go further, so let's make some fucking progress before then.' Montgomery had sheepishly taken a seat near the front rather than act the usual right hand man to his boss. He knew that The Chain case had not moved much and he was now starting to feel the pressure.

'So this is what is happening, Montgomery will continue to lead The Chain case, but I want you to liaise with Christie to ensure you are both pulling the same direction. Christie, you will continue to lead the Whitebank case but you liaise with me on this. As for this cold case, Samantha Kerr, I want Lyle leading this. I would not normally ask a DS to lead such an important case, but Lyle is not an ordinary DS and he knows the case inside out. He will also liaise directly and frequently with me. Are you up for that Lyle?'

'Of course, sir. Thank you, sir.'

'Now does anyone have an issue with what I have instructed?' For a moment it looked like Montgomery may protest, but he thought better of it. He would have been devastated that one of his team didn't get the chance to lead the Kerr case.

'Right, I don't need to explain to anyone how vital it is that I see progress in the coming days. I want regular reports from all leads, and it better be decent.'

With that, he stormed off into his room. There was little murmuring in the room as the crowd filed out to get on with the task in hand. Lyle and Christie walked back to her desk to agree the next stage.

'They may be linked, ma'am.' Lyle said once she was seated. 'I'm happy to take the lead, but I need us to still be working together.'

'I full agree, Lyle, but this is a good opportunity for you. Nail this case and it opens your career up. I will help as much as I can but this is all about you and you are more than capable.'

'Thank you, ma'am. I do appreciate the sentiment. There is only one thing though.'

'What's that?'

'I like being your DS and I have absolutely no desire to become anything higher.' Christie gave a slightly bewildered look, Lyle leaned down to whisper in her ear.

'I wouldn't want to turn into fucking Montgomery.'

Day 5 - 22:58 - Undisclosed Location, West Lothian

The killer was particularly happy how the second killing had materialised. He knew that the risk was higher as it was taking place in a public place, compared to the private dwelling house of David Stafford. He had wanted to look into the eyes of Dennis Robinson slightly longer, just like he had done with Stafford, but it was a risk he was not willing to take. He wanted the men he was killing to see him, to know who it was that was taking their life. They would already know why he was doing it, they knew who he was and he had deliberately entered their lives recently, albeit indirectly. It had been vital for his research that he got the right people.

Once more he stared admiringly at his wall chart, the steaming cup of Ethiopian coffee in his hands. Victim number three would be raising the stakes further, adding more risk to what he was looking to achieve. Once more, he had everything planned to the finest detail and it would not be long before he would bring out his grandfather's fountain pen and mark the photograph on the wall chart with a large cross in the red ink from the cartridge he had recently installed.

With that glimmer of excitement, he place his coffee cup down carefully on a coaster on the antique table he worked at and unlocked the drawer. He sat on the chair and lifted the pen case out and stared at it, an act he had done countless times since his grandfather had passed on the gift to the eleven year old boy. Opening the case he pulled out the beautiful pen, black hard rubber casing with gold clip and nib. The Swan fountain pen was made in the 1930's by Mabie Todd and Company and the killer's grandfather had been given it on his birth. The killer remembered as a small child being fascinated by the pen and would often sit on his grandfather's knee and ask him to write out a story with the 'magic pen' as he called it. His grandfather had beautiful writing, having worked for the Registers of Scotland, and was required to write up land registers in neat fountain pen writing or be made to write it over again. He often wrote 4 lined stories, rhyming like a poem and always making them both descend into fits of giggles. He remembered one in particular.

> *There once was a landowner, with a large mansion house,*
> *You would say he was a spoiled old Toff,*
> *He used to wave his arms, when I crossed on his land,*
> *Until one day, both the limbs, they fell off…*

The killer found himself smiling at the recollection as he carefully returned the fountain pen back to its case and locked it in the drawer. He wondered what his late grandfather would think of his pen being used to mark off the killings of the five evil people in front of him. He knew that his grandfather was born during the Second World War and grew up in post-war Scotland so perhaps he understood the devastation that evil can bring to a person's life.

He would perhaps also understand the need of revenge…

CHAPTER TWELVE

Day 6 - 07:17 - Christie's Flat, Stockbridge, Edinburgh

Christie had been poor company for Tom the previous night, barely eating much of the meal he had prepared for her getting home at eleven o'clock and falling asleep on the sofa before midnight. He had carried her through to her bedroom and wished her good night as she stirred, leaving her to get a good rest and heading off to his own flat. Christie, for the first time in months, had a completely undisturbed sleep and was woken by her alarm feeling refreshed.

She smiled at herself noting that she had not made it to her pyjamas, sleeping in her t-shirt and underwear. Her lounge wear trousers, that she had briefly put on after coming home from work were neatly folded by the chest of drawers, Tom's work no doubt as she had no recollection of taking them off before bed. Waddling through to the kitchen, Tom had left fresh coffee and pastries on the work surface. How and when did this happen, she wondered. He knew what was happening as she had relayed the update to the cases. She would tell him enough so that he knew what was going on but not any of the details she had to keep confidential. It was the recollection of the remains of Samantha Kerr that had finished off what little appetite she had. Tom has asked lots of questions, he had remembered the case at the time being a little older than Christie and was interested to hear that Lyle had worked the case. Christie refrained from disclosing too much, both about the case and the impact on Lyle, but Tom could read between the lines.

She decided that she would take the Mini Cooper into work today. It was likely that Lyle would be working independently from her, so her usual taxi ride was out of the question. She put the Italian coffee pot on the hob and headed for a quick shower. Once washed, she came back through to turn the heat off and get dried and changed. She sipped at the strong coffee and nibbled at the pastries as he dried her hair.

The traffic was not too bad for the time of morning and as Christie was heading out west of the city toward Corstorphine, she was travelling against the run of the rush hour traffic. She was listening to the local radio and a young kid was telling a joke. She had heard this a few times and knew that the parents often pushed to see how close to the bone a joke could be told on the radio. Today's was about a constipated Maths teacher who had 'worked it out with a pencil.' Christie smiled at the joke, failing to join the hysterics of the the male presenter whom, like most of the male population of the country, was obsessed with toilet humour.

When she entered the station Lyle was already at his desk going through his paperwork. A man of action, the avalanche of paperwork was always what he hated most about the job, although he was very competent in the requirements of his role.

'It's on your desk,' he said without looking up. Christie was amazed that he knew what time she arrived at the office and that there was often a coffee waiting for her. She picked up the cup, still warm, and walked over to his desk. She stood leaning against his desk, absently looking at the notes he had been writing down.

'I need to keep Miles on my case, but you can take Chowdhury,' she said firmly but kindly. 'If there is anyone in this station that can go through the files and find something it will be him. In fact, had it not been for his attention to detail we may never have found Samantha is the first place.' Lyle was nodding his head in agreement.

'I was hoping to take him on board for the same reasons. I was speaking with him yesterday after Hepburn's meeting and I think that this case is hitting home for him too. No one likes working a case that involves the death of a child, but we all want a result more than other cases.' Christie knew what he meant and couldn't agree more. Certain cases, given the nature or the individuals involved, get under the skin.

'What's your plans?' Christie asked.

'Well, I want to speak with Freddie again. He was in a relationship with Samantha at the time of her murder.' Lyle took a moment, it was the first time he had mentioned the term murder rather that disappearance. 'He knew Stafford, he knew he hung around with a bad lot and he would have know Robinson too. We need to get all the facts from him, it could be vital to getting something significant in the case. What about you?'

'Truth be told Lyle, I'm not sure where to start. Miles and I will head back to the Robinson's house and interview the family again. I want to see more of Robinson's house, go through his possessions, his paperwork see if it turns up anything. I'll get one of the DC's to do some background checking, they might not be as good as Chowdhury but they can lay the groundwork.' Lyle smiled in agreement of Chowdhury's skills.

'I want to get Chowdhury out with me. He's turning into a great detective, his work ethic is tremendous and he has really stepped up recently. I thought he was a bit quiet when he first joined from the London Met, but he seems more settled now. I don't know what happened to make him move, but I guess he will tell us if he feels the time is right.' Christie thought the same thing, and also wondered if they would ever find out the secret that Chowdhury was keeping so close to his chest.

Day 6 - 09:42 - Main road towards Whitebank Village, West Lothian

130

Following their conversation at the station, Lyle revealed that he had left a present on Christie's desk and told her not to open it until she got to her car. It was wrapped in a small gift bag, with ribbon and a tag that said 'Don't miss me too much on your drives'. Miles and Christie debated what it could be and after they both had their seatbelts on, she untied the ribbon and lifted out a ring box.

'He's not proposing to you is he, ma'am?' Miles quipped. Christie slowly lifted the lid if the box and burst out laughing. Miles leaned over to peek inside and laughed herself at the USB stick.

'No prizes for guessing what is on this,' Christie said, inserting the stick into the Cooper's music system.

'Brace yourself, ma'am,' laughed Miles as Christie headed out of the car park and on their way to West Lothian. They were surprised and quietly impressed by the gentle guitar picking of the opening track. It was not long before the rock guitars came to the fore of Boston's 'More Than A Feeling'. Despite themselves, the two found themselves singing along with the chorus, making up some of the lyrics as they went. Lyle had chosen a few songs in the 'soft rock' category for them to listen to and as they were approaching Whitebank Christie realised how much she had enjoyed the songs. With the village in sight, however, she turned off the music and switched her focus back on what was happening next. The music had indeed cleared her head, another one of Lyle's lessons that she was picking up in her career.

Christie pulled over in front of the house. She had filled in Miles on the initial interview she had conducted with Lyle and set out her plans for this visit. Christie would lead the questions but she was happy for Miles to jump in with any relevant questions that she thought appropriate. This was Christie showing the faith that she had in Miles, however, they also had a subtle signal should Christie feel she needed to take over and relegate Miles to an observer. Christie did not imagine that should have to use the signal.

By the time Christie was locking the car, Adam was standing at the door restraining a very excitable Bouncer. Miles being a dog lover herself, took over and introduced herself to the dog rather that the owner. She allowed Bouncer to jump up softly and let him rest his paws on one arm whilst using the free hand to rub behind his ears. In a matter of seconds, the dog had calmed down and Miles had a friend for life.

'We never get him to settle that quickly,' commented Adam. 'You certainly have the talent.'

'My parents bred golden retrievers when I was growing up, so I was surrounded by them.' Adam invited them in and once more Christie found herself in the sitting room.

'My mum is just getting dressed, she won't be long. She hasn't slept since the news, I guess it's understandable.' Christie nodded sympathetically, but also saw the chance to ask some questions of Adam on his own.

'How did you get on with your father?' The question was asked quickly, Miles fumbling for her note book to record the reply. Adam's facial expression was one of regret.

'Growing up as a kid, it was great. He was a fun dad, taught me how to play football and just about every other sport you could imagine. Straight after work, he changed and took me to the park to play. We would go to the woods and play games, he would climb a tree to make me a swing and we would play Star Wars or Power Rangers or Action Man, whatever I was into at that particular time.' Christie sensed that the tone of the answer was going to change.

'What happened?' she asked softly.

'I grew up and discovered that he was not the fun dad I thought he was. I started to notice the drinking in my early teens. He never got violent, but I sensed a rage in him, especially when he was drinking.' Christie felt he was holding something back, perhaps the source of that rage, but the conversation was curtailed at the entrance of Linda Robinson. Christie rose to shake her hand and introduce Miles, who passed on her condolences for her loss.

'We won't take up too much of your time,' confirmed Christie. 'I just have a few questions and I would also like to see Mr Robinson's personal belongings. I know this is difficult but we need to build up a picture of his life and see if there is anything that may help the investigation.' Linda was surprisingly compliant, most newly widowed individuals would resent the police going through their deceased loved ones belongings.

'I fully understand, Inspector. I can show you where he kept his things.'

'Thank you, Mrs Robinson. I wanted to ask if Mr Robinson was acting any differently in the days leading up to his death?'

'Not that I can recall. He was his usual self, pottering about waiting until he could sneak off to the pub. We live a very simple here and not much happens. I can't think of anything that happened out of the ordinary.'

'What about his friends from the pub. Can you tell me anything about them?'

'I know them to look at, but I never went to the pub that often and couldn't tell you much about them. David and Paddy must have been his best mates, as they are the only ones I can remember him talking about often. I think they were both on the darts team, you could check with the landlady.' Christie paused letting Miles ask the next question. To her pleasant surprise, it was the same question that she was thinking about.'

'When Mr Robinson was growing up, do you know who his friends were and if he kept in contact with them.' This question seemed to throw Mrs Robinson, but she quickly regained her composure.

'What a strange question. I know that he hung around with a few lads and got into the usual trouble and mischief that boys of that age do, stealing apples and knocking at doors and running away. I have no idea who they were, he told me they all moved away from the village and he lost contact with them.' Christie recalled her conversation with Old Edward who has said the same thing about David Stafford and his friends, which he said included Dennis Robinson.

'You said before that Mr Robinson didn't know David Stafford,' Christie asked carefully. 'Could David have been one of the boys he hung around with?' Linda thought for a moment and shook her head. Adam, who had been until this point a silent observer, spoke softly.

'He could have been, dad was known to tell a few fibs about growing up.' Linda shot him a glance, but knowing what her son had said was true she never objected. 'When I was growing up,' Adam continued, 'my dad said that he signed for Celtic when he was 19 and played for two seasons until he had to retire with a knee injury. I believed this and told all my friends how proud I was that my dad played for Celtic. Of course, not long after the internet could tell you every football team's starting line up going back decades and there was no record of him playing. I was teased and bullied because of it and he finally admitted that he made it all up.'

Adam excused himself, saying that he had to go out and reassured his mum that Betty was popping in shortly. Christie decided to end the questioning there and asked to be shown to where Dennis Robinson kept his things. They went upstairs to the main bedroom, his clothes were still hanging up in the wardrobe. 'Betty will help me take it all to the charity shop, I wanted to wait until after the funeral though.' Christie and Miles put on gloves and flicked through the clothes, checking the pockets and the going through his chest of drawers. There was nothing found of note and they were then taken into the spare room which was a gym come study. There was a desk and chair in the corner and a filing cabinet was used to neatly file all the family paperwork, Linda's role she confirmed to them.

After twenty minutes of reviewing the paperwork, which did not appear to show anything significant, they found something that was of interest. Tucked in at the back of one of the drawers in the desk was a leather bound journal. Christie asked about it.

'He's had that since he was a kid,' Linda confirmed. 'I've never read it, but he told me that he had written little notes in it from time to time. He said that he didn't have the discipline the keep a proper diary and there are some years he wrote nothing. I guess it would be interesting to read it now. I had completely forgotten about it, I can't remember the last time I seen it.' She paused in realisation. 'I assume that you need to take it though.'

'It may be important,' was all Christie said. Linda nodding in agreement. Linda was less impressed when Christie informed her that they needed to take the family computer, but promised to have it back as soon as possible. She confirmed that Dennis didn't use it much but finally understood and agreed for them to take it.

Back in the car, they drove away from the house but Christie pulled over in front of the pub. It was still closed, so she decided that she would have a look at the journal to see if there was anything interesting. The entries were both sparse and erratic, some notes about childhood birthdays and Christmases, some football notes. She flicked further on and read some interesting entries about girls, typical of adolescent boys she considered. Suddenly there was something that did grab her attention.

On one of the pages there was a business card printed and stuck on with yellowing sellotape. The card was cheaply printed, basic font on a standard cream card. The card was dominated by three large letters - 'W.M.A.'. In smaller writing underneath the initials was confirmation of what it stood for, 'Whitebank Male Association'. In italics at the very bottom was a quotation, *'Five Against One'*.

Day 6 - 11:37 - Main road towards Whitebank Village, West Lothian

Lyle and Chowdhury had been going through paperwork for most of the morning as well as discussing and agreeing how the investigation was going to take place. Chowdhury was obviously delighted to have been allocated such an important role, however, Lyle had warned him about complacency and to follow his lead at all times. In return, he would share his thoughts and plans throughout the investigation. Getting an end result, getting to the truth and getting closure for the family of Samantha Kerr was what was important.

Heading out of the city, Lyle turned to ask Chowdhury the most important question of the day.

'Right, young man. What is your musical taste of choice. Be very careful how you answer.' Chowdhury had worked long enough in the team to have expected this integration.

'Well, I like a bit of everything but I know that answer won't wash with you. A bit of R'n'B, a bit of soul, a bit of Motown. I'm not into the modern day stuff, only the classics from the Sixties and Seventies. I do, however, have a particular liking of band that you may or may not approve of.' Lyle's interest was raised like his eyebrows. 'I always got teased as a

136

kid, but my dad played them all the time in the car, of course they were always better live.'

'Out with it then, we will be there soon.' Chowdhury looked a little sheepish.

'Status Quo.'

'Yes, that's the ticket. The most classic of classic rock artists, and you are right about them live. Seen them so many times over the years, so sad that Rick passed away.' He scrolled through the music system, turned up the volume and blasted out 'Down Down'. The pair started singing along, badly, together.

'There are two people in this world, Chowdhury,' Lyle shouted over the music. 'Those who like Status Quo and liars.' Chowdhury laughed in agreement.

As the song was finishing, they were entering Whitebank and Lyle headed towards the village store. He had not announced his visit and was hoping to catch Freddie Taylor unprepared. He planned to propose it as a follow up informal conversation, having already had him at the station once. Now that the investigation had moved on he would need to gather some further information before deciding if he wanted to get him back to the station. He expected the next time he did that, Freddie would see the sense in getting a solicitor along with him, so he had to make the most of today. He also told Chowdhury that the discovery of Samantha Kerr's body would not be discussed. They did not believe that the gossip had started yet and the body had been removed in the early hours and the police had ensured that the area was cleared.

They entered the empty store and Freddie was behind the counter scrolling through his phone. After a moment he looked up and spotted the detectives, putting his phone away swiftly in his pocket and coming around the counter to shake Lyle's hand. Lyle introduced Chowdhury, and once more Freddie offered his hand in friendship.

'Terrible news about Dennis,' Freddie began. 'I can't believe that we had one murder in Whitebank, but now we have two. It's really unbelievable. When word gets out, I think the place will be swamped like Edinburgh in August.' Despite himself, Lyle smiled at the reference. Edinburgh swells annually during the festival period of August and the word given by the locals is that it doubles in size, although no one is really sure exactly. He did think that, indeed, when word got out there would be people swarming to Whitebank.

'What can you tell me about Dennis?' Lyle opened the questioning.

'In short, I thought he was a good guy. Always polite when he came in here, which was most days. Liked to get his newspaper early, rolls or bread and the usual essentials. We would often have a chat about the football, big Celtic fan. I support Livingston for my sins, but always enjoyed having a chat with him.'

'Did you mix with him in the pub?'

'Not my scene sergeant, never been much of a drinker. It's the early rises that kills me, I could never face this place with a hangover. I did hear the locals talk about him being a bit of a drinker and that he could be a bit of an arse in the pub, but I never experienced it firsthand.'

'Was there anyone who you knew had a grudge or a particular dislike towards him?' Lyle was impressed with Chowdhury's question, well delivered and presented at the right time.

'None that I was aware of, a few who would bad mouth him in here after he had been an arse the night before. I think it was often to do with his darts playing rather than his personality. Apparently he was an exceptional darts player, but tended to start drinking too early which affected his performance. Sober he played like Jocky Wilson, drunk he played like Jackie Wilson.' Chowdhury laughed at the joke, being a big fan of the late American soul singer. He glanced at Lyle nervously, but Lyle was smiling confirming that it was fine. He wanted the conversation kept light, so was happy with the progress thus far.

'Do you know if Dennis Robinson was aquatinted with David Stafford.' Lyle asked.

'Not anymore, as far as I was aware. I think they knew each other when they were younger, but I don't think they talked recently. I don't think David spoke to anyone from his past after the trial.' Lyle had one final question, a question he wanted to ask when Freddie was off guard. He seemed relaxed enough answering the questions so far. He decided to have a reconfirming question prior to the final one.

'So, no one else you can think of that had a dislike? No one, perhaps closer to home?' It was a leading question, but it got the confirmation that he was looking for.

'I don't think his son got on with him particularly well. I would often ask after his dad when he came into the shop and he would ask me not to speak about that arsehole or prick. To be honest, I just thought he was showing off in front of his mates. There was a real hatred there though, I could see it in his eyes. Saying that, a son doesn't go round killing his dad just because he thought he was a prick. If that was the case, there wouldn't be many dads about in the world.' Lyle smiled at his reply, thinking that Freddie would be surprised at the truth. He thanked him for his time and apologised for disturbing him again. Freddie confirmed it was not a problem. As he reached the door, Lyle asked the killer question.

'Dennis Robinson,' he said turning over his shoulder from the doorway. 'Did he know Samantha back in the day?'

139

'Not that I am aware of,' Freddie replied. Lyle thanked him again and left the shop.

He was not overly convinced that the final answer was the truth…

PART SEVEN - BLOOD

CHAPTER THIRTEEN

Day 6 - 12:14 - The Mole Catchers Arms Whitebank Village, West Lothian

The pub was open and serving lunch, so Christie decided to kill two birds with the one stone. The landlady was out on an errand but was expected back soon. Miles was impressed with the range of vegetarian options and they both decided to risk the halloumi burger and large chunky chips. The waiter was very friendly, without being creepy and gave them enough space to enjoy their meal and have a non-work catch up chat.

As the waiter was taking away the cleared plates, Andrea Wood entered the pub and immediately spotted Christie. She walked over to the table and was introduced to Miles.

'I hope you enjoyed your meal, very kind of you to stop in during this awful time.'

'We did, very much,' confirmed Christie. 'Although we also came in to have a chat with you if you don't mind.'

'Not at all, just give me a minute or two.' Andrea went to speak with the waiter and the girl behind the bar before returning with a chair and sat at their table. There were a few other tables occupied with diners, however, they were secluded enough to have the conversation in private.

'We wanted to ask some more about the people that Dennis mixed with in the pub, it's important that we build up a complete picture of his life and often it's his friends that help that the most.' Andrea thought for a moment.

'It's difficult because he was never with the same people when he came in. He often sat at the bar and would just chat to whoever would listen to him. I don't think he had close friends, but he chatted to most people who came in. Often, he was good company and gave intelligent conversation, which is more than I get from most.' She smiled at her own little joke.

'What about the darts team? Was there anyone in the team that he was close to?'

'Ach, they were always arguing in that team. Dennis was a great darts player, but if he started drinking too early or too much, it could send the others into fierce competitive banter. Although it was mostly good natured, underneath they knew that Dennis was turning victories into defeats and they were not happy about that.'

'Who in particular in the team?' Miles asked.

'Paddy and David are the team co-captains, so if you wanted to speak to any of them they are the ones to see. In fact, if you come back before seven this evening you will catch them. A home tie against one of the Livingston pubs. They are holding a minutes silence for Dennis before the match I believe.'

Christie thanked her for her time and promised to pop back later to see Paddy and Davie. Christie had a final question, but Andrea had one for her first.

'Nice to see you again and to meet you DC Miles, but where is the other man that came the last time? DS Lyle was it?'

'He's working a different case, but he may be back to speak to you.' Andrea had a smile and a twinkle in her eye.

'You can tell him I will look forward to that, he is more than welcome in here anytime he likes.' Christie filed the knowledge for future teasing. She asked her final question.

'Davie and Paddy, what are their surnames?'

'Davie Gibson, he's a local. Retired lawyer I believe, always telling stories about his old cases in the High Court. Paddy Kerr, he's a bit quiet but a very good darts player. He's been coming here for a few years, previously played with another pub but asked to join the Good Guys.'

Christie thought for a moment. Paddy Kerr, Patrick Kerr? It was too much of a coincidence.

'Is Paddy not a local then, does he travel in from elsewhere?'

'Aye,' confirmed Andrea. 'He comes in from Kirknewton, I think.'

Day 6 - 15:14 - Undisclosed location, West Lothian

The killer was getting impatient and tried to focus on his plan. He had spent years planning this fortnight and the first two had gone exactly as expected. He was debating if he should strike tonight or wait until tomorrow. Both days would be fine for his plan, but Livingston was a busy place and not as easy to slip away unnoticed from. There would be CCTV cameras around and he would have to use a mixture of driving and public transport to arrive and leave carefully and well planned from the murder site.

He had the gun laid out in front of him, broken down into separate pieces to allow for proper cleaning. He travelled to America and visited some of the Southern States and booked lessons at various gun clubs. He struck up a friendship with a gun obsessed Texan, who taught him how to fire various hand held pistols. The killer had asked to be shown how to look after the weapon to ensure safety and accurate shooting. The Texan had been only too happy to show him and after his three week 'vacation' he knew how to operate, shoot and clean a number of different handguns. When he returned to Scotland, he had been surprised how easy and how cheaply he had managed to get one. He had travelled to Glasgow, using a false name and a subtle disguise and managed to strike lucky in an East End pub. He had bought and received his weapon, with bullets and silencer within an hour. He had rented a remote cottage in the Highlands of Scotland and took his weapon and an archery target with him, perfecting his shooting when there was no one around to witness it, testing the silencer to ensure any unlikely passing hikers would not hear him.

Number three out of five, he would be over half way there. He would also be classed as a serial killer, three murders was what was required for that particular tag. He was not interested in notorious reputations, he was only interested in justice. Justice and revenge. Revenge, a dish that would certainly be served cold as the saying goes. He would be getting both, as long as he could finish the job he had started. The police presence would be increasing with each kill and he knew he was taking a risk acting so quickly, the murders coming so close together. If he was to be caught, so be it. He just wanted to rid the world of these five individuals that had caused so much pain.

He put the gun back together, wrapped it up carefully and put it back in its place. He wandered through to the kitchen, feeling the need of more coffee. He knew he was getting worked up and needed calmness once more. Unlike most people, coffee actually calmed him down. The effect of the caffeine no longer had the same impact on him, he found the process of making the coffee more satisfying and focused his mind. He opened his cupboard and looked at the selection of beans available. The Columbian Rosabaya was a particular favourite and he decided to treat himself. He was nearly half way through his task and deserved to be rewarded. He decided to use the Italian coffee pot that he had purchased on a trip to Naples, the Italians certainly knew how to make and enjoy coffee.

Suitably relaxed, he sat down in the living room and started once more to contemplate killing number three. Livingstone was going to be a tough location, but he had a perfect window in which to do it. It would be difficult, the window was small, but the chances of success were high enough. He had had another thought about his escape plan and it was simple, less complicated than he thought and it would work perfectly. He would need to set things up, but that could be done quickly and easily.

And there was no time like the present…

Day 6 - 17:54 - Corstorphine Police Station, Edinburgh

The update meeting with Hepburn was brief, and he was not pleased. There had also been little movement in The Chain case, so Hepburn's wrath was aimed around the room rather than any individuals. The pressure of the cases were starting to show, he was losing some of his cool, some of his reason. He needed results and to get results he needed solid leads and to get solid leads there was a requirement to wade through an ocean of time wasters and dead ends.

Christie, Lyle, Miles and Chowdhury convened afterwards to discuss their own cases. Christie spoke first.

'Miles and I are back at the pub this evening, we need to speak with Davie and Paddy, the captains of the darts team. The main bit of news is that Paddy is likely to be Patrick Kerr, Samantha's father. If this is the case, he had a link to Dennis Robinson and possibly David Stafford. It may be too soon to call him a suspect, but he is certainly a person of interest.' Lyle was obviously taken aback by this statement.

'I think you're wrong, with all due respect, ma'am. I've known Patrick for over 25 years and I just don't see it in him. He wanted justice, yes, but I couldn't imagine for a moment that he could be capable of this.'

146

'We will keep him as a person of interest for the moment,' Christie replied firmly. 'We can't afford to rule anything out at this stage.' Lyle lifted his hands in mock surrender. 'What have you got, Lyle?'

'Well, Freddie gave a couple of interesting pieces of information. Firstly he said that Dennis' son,' he checked his notebook. 'Adam. He said that Adam was no fan of his father and was quite vocal about it. Now, as Freddie himself stated, it's a big step to go from hating your dad to killing him, but it may be worth keeping an eye on him in case be becomes a person of interest.' He gave a cheeky glance at Christie who let him away with it, for now. 'The second thing is I think that Dennis may have known Samantha. I can't remember him being spoken to back during the original trial, but if he knew David back then it's not unlikely he was around at that time and he may even have been involved. If that is the case, then David and Dennis may have been involved in Samantha's murder. Chowdhury and I are going through the case files once more, but they're both useless suspects to me dead.' Christie reached for something on her desk and handed it to Lyle.

'We picked this up from Robinson's house. It's a journal that he kept for many years, going back to the time of the original case. I've only flicked through it, but it may be more relevant to your case than mine.' She pointed out the business card that she found, Lyle carefully picked it up. 'I think that you need to discover who was in WMA and if there is a link to either of the cases.

'I'll make that a priority, ma'am. This is very interesting, going by where in the journal it is, and the yellowing of the card with age, I would suggest that it fits our timeline.'

'What's next for you, guys?' Miles asked them.

'I'm going to visit my first autopsy,' replied Chowdhury somewhat sheepishly. 'I've been reading up to make sure I'm prepared, but I'm a little nervous truth be told.' Chowdhury always liked to be honest with his colleagues and had built up enough respect to be able to share his fears within the group of four.

'Very good Chowdhury, but I hope you included coffee variations in your reading list.' Lyle had managed to lighten the mood once more and stood up to start the journey to see Dr James.

'Oh Lyle,' said Christie playfully, bringing an immediate smile to the lips of Miles who knew what was coming. 'A certain landlady was asking after you.'

'Andrea?' Lyles answer was too quick and he knew he had been caught.

'Yes indeed. Ms Wood said you were welcome to pop in any time you liked.' Lyle waived off the banter and called on Chowdhury to come, who himself was enjoying the moment.

'I just hope she isn't a suspect,' he said joining in.

Day 6 - 19:01 - The Office of Dr Arthur James, Edinburgh

Dr James was typing up a report when Lyle and Chowdhury entered the room. He immediately stood up and greeted them with warm handshakes.

'DS Chowdhury, what a pleasure to welcome you to The Office. Let me furnish you both with a special coffee and then we can discuss the details.' As was the usual procedure with visit to Dr James' office, he fussed over his coffee machine and looked through his collection of capsules to choose the latest offering to share.

'Now, as it's Mr Chowdhury's first visit here, I would like to offer a limited edition blend for enjoyment. Now, this is a bit different to my usual

148

tastes, I tend to go for the more traditional, rather than flavoured blends but I must confess to having a liking to this. Have a taste and see if you can guess what the flavour is.' He handed over two small coffee glasses and Lyle mimicked a wine taster, swirling the coffee around the cup and sticking his nose into the glass so he came out with froth on his nose. 'Don't even think about spitting that out Lyle,' James warned.

'I'm getting the taste of rhubarb and custard, with a hint of Irn Bru and old socks.' Lyle was obviously not taking this seriously, leading to a disapproving stare from his host.

'I'm getting vanilla definitely,' confirmed Chowdhury taking a second sip. 'and possibly almonds?'

'Top of the class, Mr Chowdhury. It's Vanilla Amaretti to be precise and I think Mr Lyle can learn a lot from you.' Chowdhury looked pleased at the complement and took a final appreciative sip of the coffee.

Coffees finished, it was time for attention to turn to the purpose of the visit. Dr James, picked up a file and flicked through the pages to find the part he wished to discuss. He then looked at his computer monitor, clicking the mouse until he found what he was looking for.

'So, I know this case is important to you Lyle, so I managed to pull some strings and got some tests rushed through. The most important one was confirmation through DNA testing. We had the foresight to retain some of Samantha's personal belongings and from that managed to get a profile. Despite the passage of time, we managed to get sufficient samples from the body to confirm that it is indeed Samantha. The results arrived just before you did, so I will be informing the family shortly.

'Thank you,' Lyle replied in gratitude. It was the outcome that he was expecting, the outcome that he had prepared for and yet hearing the formality of it still stirred up the feeling of helplessness he had been carrying for so long now. His drive to get a result was hitting maximum speed and he knew that he would have to focus like never before to ensure that he did not let the Kerr family down.

'Cause of death is still to be fully established, but if I may speak off the record?' Lyle quickly confirmed that the news would go no further than the four walls and Christie. 'I would guess strangulation, going by the damage of the hyoid bone. My initial examination found no other major signs of injury. I will conduct further examination and write up my final report in the coming days, but if I was a betting man - and I am not - I would not expect to see much variation to my initial findings.

Lyle stood up and shook Dr James' hand, with more warmth and appreciation than normal. The moments eye contact between the two experienced professionals said everything that they did not need to say verbally. Lyle was starting to find closure in a case that had haunted him for so many years.

Closure that wouldn't be complete, he knew, until he found out what happened and who was responsible.

Day 6 - 19:44 - The Mole Catchers Arms Whitebank Village, West Lothian

The pub was much busier than Christie had imagined as she entered and they waited a full ten minutes to be served. There was a large crowd around the dartboard, and the latest match was in full swing. Miles insisted on buying the drinks having been treated to lunch by her boss. She had to shout out her order above the noise of cheering and booing after each round of darts thrown. An excited punter shouted out a 'one hundred and eighty' that the legendary commentator Sid Waddell would have been proud of. Christie had a glance over at the crowd, but could not see if Patrick Kerr was amongst them.

They found a table away from the action and sat down, toasting each other's soft drinks. They had missed the start of the match, so were unsure if there had been a minutes silence or not. They spent ten minutes catching up, although colleagues there was a bond of friendship there also. They both knew, however, that there was a professional hierarchy between them and they both respected that. Miles spoke fondly about her blossoming relationship with Fiona and Christie shared her own relationship situation with Tom.

In many ways he was the perfect partner, not pushy or demanding of her time. He fully understood the pressures of her job and that at times she could be tired, distant and cranky. They loved each other's company, but knew that time apart worked well for them both. Christie had concerns of being too committed with Tom, but also worried about losing him. He always said he was happy with the relationship and the experience of one failed marriage had put him off somewhat of making that commitment again at present.

Andrea suddenly appeared at the table and took a seat beside them. She had tied her hair up, added some make up and was not wearing her glasses. She certainly was an attractive lady and Christie wondered if the change was a usual evening transformation or if there was other reasons. Her opening statement seemed to suggest the latter.

'No Mr Lyle again, I think he might be hiding from me.' She had said it laughing, but Christie knew there was feeling behind the sentiment.

'I passed on your message. He may be wishing to visit you soon, however, I suspect that it will be in a professional capacity.'

'Any excuse suits me.' She seemed pleased with the news, before she returned to the reason for coming over to their table. 'They shouldn't be too much longer with the first half. You can have a chat with the guys during the interval, I told them that you would be passing by.'

'How did they seem when you told them this?' Miles asked.

'Davie was fine, Paddy seemed a little sheepish but I think his mind was on the match. It's a big game, if we win we will go above them and into second place in the league table. I guess that I'd better go and give them some moral support.'

With that she left the table and went off towards the game, chatting to and hugging customers on the way. Christie reflected on how suited Andrea Wood was to this lifestyle. She fitted in with the surroundings perfectly and you could not imagine her doing anything else. Except perhaps a rock music themed cafe, she thought mischievously.

Ten minutes had passed when the match came to a halt. Davie was the first to appear, confirming that Paddy was having the team talk and he would fetch him once they were done asking him questions. Christie was happy with this set up, as it meant that they could get separate opinions on Dennis Robinson, without the fear of speaking ill of the dead in front of each other. Davie sat down in front of the two officers and laid his fresh pint glass on the table. He formally introduced himself and waited for the detectives to do the same.

'Terrible business about Dennis,' he began. 'Terrible business indeed. Fine darts player when he put his mind to it, he'll be a big loss. We're two games behind tonight and I'm not sure we will pull it back. Dennis always won his early games to put us in a good position.' He took a long drink from his pint, shaking his head as he did so.

'I believe that he didn't always put his mind to it, as you would say.'

'Very true, DI Christie. His mind was often on the drink rather than the game. We always put him in first, that way he was more likely to win. By the second half he was mostly useless, although on occasion he still pulled out a win regardless of the state he was in. He was unpredictable with a drink in him.'

'What was he like, away from the darts?' Davie considered his answer.

'To be honest, I didn't mix with him much away from the oche. Paddy spoke to him more than I did. I didn't really like him if I am being truthful with you, but we needed him in the team so I tolerated him.'

'Do you know anyone that held a grudge or would want to harm him?'

'He wasn't popular, but I never witnessed anything like that. At times I wanted to strangle him for his darts playing, but if I gave in to these emotions, I would have killed everyone on the team at some point.' It was obvious to Christie that they wouldn't get much more out of Davie, his focus was on darts rather than people. It was as she was bringing the interview to a close that Christie spotted Patrick Kerr for the first time, confirming her suspicions that it was indeed Samantha's father. He pointed to his mobile phone and the exit to indicate he was taking a call then would be back. Christie thought for a moment about going after him, but she knew where to get him if he decided to run. She didn't expect that he would be so stupid.

A few minutes later he appeared, looking somewhat forlorn. He sat down holding up the phone.

'It was Margaret, seven texts she had sent me during the first half so I knew it was serious. Of course, you know what the call was about...'

'I'm so sorry for your loss, Mr Kerr,' Christie condoled, Lyle having updated her on the confirmation that the body was indeed Samantha Kerr. 'I know this is a terrible time, but it is important we speak to you.'

'Can I see her?' The question came as a surprise, even to Patrick. 'Sorry, that was a stupid question.'

'Not a stupid question, Mr Kerr, but I think you know what the sensible answer would be.'

'You're right,' he agreed. 'Remember her for who she was, not what she became.' Christie nodded. 'I guess I owe you both an explanation for all this.' He waved a hand around the room.

'I would be interested in that certainly. The man who was arrested for the kidnapping of you daughter lives five minutes away from the pub you chose as the place you wanted to play darts. Now, there is a second man murdered in this same village and shortly afterwards we find you are the co-captain of the darts team.'

'I know, it doesn't look great. The truth is, I wanted to get close to David Stafford without anyone being suspicious. I thought he knew something, or was even involved in it. What I didn't know was that he became a recluse and never stepped foot inside the local pub. By the time I discovered that, I was enjoying the darts too much and was made co-captain of the team.'

'Did you know that Dennis Robinson knew David?'

'Dennis never mentioned David, no one in the team did. No one in the team knew I was Sammy's dad and after a while I stopped subtly bringing up the subject. As hard as coming here was with the connection to Sammy's case, and now learning that she was buried five minutes from here, I found this place a comfort. This pub is like a family and Andrea is the nicest landlady you could meet. After a while, I just liked to come here

154

to forget the pain of the past and enjoy the company of the future.' Paddy excused himself as the match was about to restart. Christie and Miles finished their drinks, bid farewell to Andrea and headed back out to the Mini Cooper.

'Well, ma'am. What are your thoughts?' Christie took a while to compose all the thoughts that were running round her head.

'Patrick Kerr is someone we need to keep an eye on. He came here to find out information. We just don't know what information he found out.'

CHAPTER FOURTEEN

Day 6 - 22:54 - Livingston, West Lothian

The killer had set everything up over the course of the afternoon. He had driven to the key locations and left everything he required to complete the task as planned. The anticipation was building as he set to work and now he was finally in place awaiting the attack.

Livingston was not too far from his home, his safe location and he knew that if he managed to complete the first part, the following stages would click into place perfectly. He had only one concern and that was ensuring that the victim was alone when he struck. During his research and stakeout sessions, he had occasionally walked home from his back shift with a colleague but mostly he walked alone. His shift finished at eleven o'clock and the night shift workers were always punctual ensuring a sharp exit after each shift.

The pathway was dimly lit, older yellow lighting would assist his plan. Some of the pathways had had the bulbs changed for white lights or modern LED, but this stretch was still awaiting the upgrade. The killer was crouched behind some trees that lined the pathway, enough to provide temporary cover but not enough that he could spent too long in the position. He deliberately arrived just before eleven so that he would not be here for long. Once more, he may not have the opportunity to face his victim, it was too risky and the location did not suit this indulgence.

His watch showed it had now passed eleven o'clock and any minute now he would strike. He held the gun gently in his right hand, steadying himself with his gloved left hand on the tree. From his vantage point, he could see down the lane towards the direction his victim would be approaching. Seconds later, he came into view.

A quick risky glance in the opposite direction confirmed no one else was on the pathway and he waited until the victim has passed him. He had earphones in, he wouldn't hear his killer approach. That was fine also. The killer waited a few more seconds, before appearing behind his victim raising the gun to fire. That was when he made his first mistake…

A shout appeared to come out of nowhere, as a colleague of the victim had been running to catch up with him. By the time he heard the shout, the killer had already squeezed the trigger. A splattering of blood sprayed towards the night sky and the man went down heavily. The killer had no time for a second shot and ran through the woodlands, over a wall towards a connecting path which had a bicycle leaning against a tree that the killer had left. Jumping on the bike, gun already returned to the backpack with the safety catch on, the killer could not hear anyone following. The colleague had obviously gone to the aid of the victim and this should give him enough time to escape.

The killer cycled hard until he reached his second checkpoint. There was a small river, just deep enough to cover the disposed bicycle to ensure that it would not be discovered for many years. With little effort, he tossed the bike into the water, waiting momentarily to ensure that it sunk as planned. Following confirmation, he jumped on the motorbike which would be his final transport home. He had cleverly put a food delivery box on the back so that any witnesses would only spot a delivery driver rather than someone suspicious. He kept his speed low, ensuring that he did not catch the eye of any passing motorists. He kept to the main streets were there was still plenty of traffic at this time of night, blending into the crowd.

He reached his property and parked up the motorbike, to be dealt with at a later time. His neighbours didn't really know him that well, he hadn't lived here long and he did not planning staying much longer. He deliberately avoided conversation with the exception of a passing hello. He knew that this was a safe place and he had done well.

As long as the one shot fired had been fatal…

Day 7 - 07:03 - M8 Motorway towards Livingston

Lyle and Christie were speeding along the M8 motorway in the GTI, heading towards the St John's Hospital. News had come in that a patient had been taken there with a gunshot wound to the head in the early hours. His condition was confirmed as critical and no one would answer Christie's enquiry if the patient would live or die. The proximity to Whitebank and the fact that a gun was used were two coincidences that were too strong to ignore. Although this was more likely to be part of Christie's case, it may have an indirect bearing on Lyle's, so he insisted in coming.

Lyle had music on, trying to keep his mind off the speed that he was traveling at. Meat Loaf's 'Bat Out of Hell' seemed most appropriate given the speedometer was touching three figures. The near ten minute song had barely finished as they pulled into the car park. They headed straight to the Intensive Care Unit, in search of the doctor in charge. Once more they were kept waiting, before being approached by Dr Elizabeth Davis who was in charge of looking after the shooting victim. Dr Davis was in her fifties, the ultimate professional and reputedly took no nonsense. That said, she had also dealt with scores of detectives in her distinguished career and knew the importance of her flexibility to the investigation. Her priority, however, was always to the patient. Following introductions, she took them into a private consulting room so they could talk freely.

'He's still in a critical condition, however, he was lucky where the bullet struck. It penetrated through the left hand side of the head, had it passed through the centre, he would already be dead. We performed emergency surgery on him last night, but with head injuries it is touch and go if they make it. If he does survives, and early indications are positive, he may not be able to communicate. The next 48 hours will be crucial.'

'Has he spoken at all?' Christie asked the doctor.

'No, he has been slipping in and out of consciousness since it happened. He won't be in a position to see anyone for a while yet, but I will keep you posted.'

'Is the person who found him still here?'

'No, she left in the early hours not long after his wife arrived. She was a brave girl, certainly if he survives this a lot of it will be down to her. She called the ambulance straight away and administered first aid until the paramedics got there.'

'Thank you, doctor,' Christie shook her hand warmly, in preparation for her next question that sounded more like a statement. 'Can you tell us where the wife is?' They were given this information without resistance and were directed to the family room.

Tracy Mearns sat alone, her eyes swollen red from hours of crying. The introduction of the detectives caused the tears to flow once more. Lyle went off in search of drinkable coffee for her as Christie sat next to her and gave her time. Tracy reached for Christie's hand and she let her take it. The questions would not be easy for Mrs Mearns to hear, but it was important that they were asked quickly. Lyle returned with a latte and handed it over with some sugar sachets. Tracy nodded to him in thanks as the tears stopped once more.

'I'm so sorry about what has happened to your husband,' Christie began. 'I promise I will do everything in my power to catch whoever did this. I know that you will still be coming to terms with what happened last night, but it is really important that we ask you some questions.'

'I understand,' Tracy replied, showing strength that Christie feared was not there, an underestimation that would be proven.

'Tell me about you and your husband.' Tracy smiled, readying herself to discuss the happy memories.

'Luca celebrated his sixtieth birthday last week, and I have known him since his teens. We were childhood sweethearts, but we drifted apart when I went off to university in Ireland. I came back to Scotland in my late twenties and we bumped into each other and rekindled the romances of the past. Within a year we were married and living together and have been happy ever since.' She took a moment fighting the tears, a struggle she was currently winning,

'So you knew him from his Whitebank days?' Lyle asked, pitching it perfectly as he normally did. Christie knew the questions would be balanced between the two cases. The question was an assumption that the victim was part of WMA, the answered confirmed it.

'Oh yes. My family were one of the first to move to Livingston in the sixties. Most of the Whitebank kids went to school in Livingston and I first met Luca in our first year of high school. I was attracted to him straight away, his Italian heritage, his exotic first name and he also used to flirt with me, speaking in Italian. Years later, I found out he was taking about football, the only Italian that he knew, but it all sounded mesmerising to me.'

'Do you know if anyone wanted to harm him?' Christie asked.

'God no,' she said in an offended manner. 'Luca is the nicest man you could meet, doesn't have an enemy in the world.' He obviously had

160

one, thought Christie. The question set off the tears again and Christie felt that they shouldn't push her any further yet, but would want to speak to her again no doubt. Lyle felt there was one more question in her, a question that would answer another pending question if the answer was affirmative.

'Did Luca ever mention an organisation called WMA.?'

Tracy's laugh caught them both off guard.

'Organisation is a strong word for it. The Whitebank Male Association was a club that Luca joined with four of his other Whitebank pals. It was just an excuse for the five of them to meet up and get pissed on a regular basis. I think they aspired to be successful business men that frequented the private gentlemen's clubs of Edinburgh and London. I once interrupted one of their meetings by accident and they were sitting in Luca's bedroom sipping brandy and smoking cigars. It was hilarious and I just burst out laughing in front of them and Luca didn't speak to me for days.' She started to giggle herself at the memory. Lyle knew the answer to the next question, but needed to ask it for confirmation.

'David Stafford and Dennis Robinson were in that room that day, were they not?'

'They were. I think Dennis was the ringleader of the group, Luca once confessed that it was Dennis' idea. David was always a bit quiet, I think he just went along with it to be part of the group. The other two, I always thought were the trouble makers at the time.' She wouldn't elaborate on the last statement, but she did confirm the information that could prove vital to both cases. 'Donald McIntyre and Fraser Wilson, both live in Livingston and are still friends with Luca.'

'Thank you Tracy,' Christie touched her gently on the arm 'We may need to speak to you again, but we will leave you for now. Here is my number if I can be of any help in the meantime.' Tracy took the card and looked at it closely before placing it her her handbag. Christie and Lyle headed back to the GTI.

'First job, Lyle, is to find these two men. They are linked to all three attacks and if we are to prevent any further murders we need to get to them first.'

Day 7 - 08:05 - St John's Hospital Car Park, Livingston

The killer sat in his car, watching the two police detectives heading out of the hospital and walking towards the car park. He had spent a restless night replaying the botched attack over and over. The other person came out of nowhere and shouted just as he had fired. He had a superb aim and the gun was pointed at the centre of his head, almost certain death awaited, but that shout had changed everything. He snatched at his shot but he still hit his target, sending him to the ground, blood pouring from the wound. He regretted not shooting at the witness and finishing the job off, but that was not in the plan. The plan was to kill and escape, unfortunately he had only exceeded in the latter.

In the early hours of the morning, he called the hospital from a remote payphone. He was surprised that it still worked, but he got through and played the part of a concerned relative asking about Luca. They wouldn't give him much information over the phone, but it confirmed that he was at the hospital and he was being treated in Intensive Care. Local police had come and gone, but he waited patiently until the police detectives arrived. Of course he recognised them, having already met them and he knew how talented they were. This would make finishing the job all the tougher, but it was a challenge he was ready for.

The detectives drove off and the killer exited the car. It was a risk, but a calculated one. He just wanted to get close enough to Luca to know

162

where he was. He was wearing a suit and walked with confidence so as not to attract attention. He wandered through the corridors, occasionally referring to a floor plan to get his bearings. He soon found the ICU but knew he would not get access, but that was not the purpose. The purpose was to locate, should he need to take matters into his own hands. Of course, he may have already done sufficient damage and the patient may not even make it through the next twenty four hours. He had spent part of his sleepless night researching gun shot wounds to the head, over ninety per cent were fatal. The odds were in his favour that Luca would not recover from the trauma.

Then he would be able to get his fountain pen and change the question mark on Luca's photo to a large cross like his first two victims.

Day 7 - 08:34 - Undisclosed Location, Lanarkshire

The Chain had been looking forward to this day for such a long time and now that it had arrived he had to control his emotions. He sat on the train, looking out of the window as the towns of Lanarkshire gave way to West Lothian on the approach into Edinburgh. He could not believe how much he had missed the old city.

He had acquired a new tracksuit, a black Adidas Firebird design which went well with his current persona. He had given his head a fresh shave with the hair clippers he kept in the flat, and touched up the colour on his beard which was growing well. The sports bag sat on the table in front of him and the businessman in the opposite seat was obviously annoyed that he could not spread out his broadsheet newspaper. Annoyed, but not willing to challenge the lowlife in front of him. If only he knew that this lowlife was worth a few million pounds and had killed three people. Killed three people with the weapon that was currently lying within that very offending sports bag.

The train stopped at Edinburgh Haymarket and the businessman exited the train, muttering under his breath. The Chain allowed himself a smile and picked the sports bag off the table, and moved towards the door as the train made the short journey to Waverley station. He even strained his neck to catch a glimpse of the castle as they passed, another view that he had been missing. He would spend the day reacquainting himself with his city before he made his move. It would have to be late enough that there was a cover of darkness, but not too late.

He had a train to catch back to Lanarkshire.

Day 7 - 13:24 - Livingston, West Lothian

The witness had managed to get some sleep, but was still looking groggy when Christie and Miles went to visit her. Lyle asked Christie to fill him in as soon as she was finished speaking with her as the two cases were now unmistakably linked. Lyle had remained in Corstorphine with Chowdhury and together were working on the background of Luca Mearns. They knew he had a connection to the other two victims and it appeared that they now knew about the five members of the Whitebank Male Association.

Christie pulled up outside the home of the witness and turned off the engine of the Mini Cooper. She felt as if this case was bouncing around like a ping pong ball and she was looking for the one piece of evidence that would head them towards the killer, rather than towards another victim. She doubted that she was going to find that in this visit, although this was the first person who may have actually seen the killer. Miles had called the hospital on the way over, but there was no change in Luca's condition.

164

They approached the modern, semi-detached house and were welcomed by Erik Larsson, a tall blond man with his hair tied up in a man-bun. He took them through to the living room where his wife, Kim was sitting on the sofa. Photos of the couple were all around the room and the lady in front of them looked pale and drawn compared to the smiling tanned expression beaming from the photographs.

Erik explained that his wife was a colleague of Luca and, on occasion, worked the same shifts. As their respective family homes were in close proximity, they walked each other home when finishing a shift together. The previous night, Kim had been held back by her boss to discuss a client and she had decided to run to catch up with Luca once she had finished. Kim was able to pick up the story from there.

'We always walk the same way home when we go together, and I was only detained a few minutes. I decided to catch up with Luca as he had been dealing with a difficult client earlier in the shift and I wanted to hear what had happened. I spotted him in the distance and picked up my speed. It all happened so quickly…'

'Just take your time, it's important that you tell us as much as you can remember.'

'I'm not sure I will be able to help much. As I said, I spotted him ahead and started to jog a bit quicker. The man came out of nowhere, calm as you like, and I watched him raise his hand. I saw the gun straight away it glistened in the street light and I just shouted. He turned towards me for a moment, before running off through the trees. I ran towards Luca and by the time I reached him, the man was gone.'

'What was the attacker wearing?' Christie asked.

'He was dressed in all in black. I think he was wearing dark jeans and a leather jacket. I never seen the shoes, but I assume they were trainers going by how quickly he moved.'

'Did you see a face?'

'No, he had a dark cap pulled down and I couldn't make out any facial features, the nearest street light was directly behind him.' Christie thought for a moment.

'You said that the attacker was a man, but you didn't see any facial features. I admit that it is very likely that it was a man, but how can you be sure?'

'The clothing was male, the way he walked towards Luca was masculine, but I would also say that he was over six feet tall. Luca is about five foot eleven and this guy was a good couple of inches taller in my option.'

'Thank you Kim, that has been really helpful. Was there anything else you can remember?' Kim shook her head.

'I just can't get the vision of Luca out of my head. There was blood everywhere, I held his head in my arms and the blood was flowing so fast.' Erik moved closer to her, taking her hand, giving her the strength to continue. 'I'm not usually squeamish, I am a first aid officer in the work, but my hands were covered in blood trying to stem the flow. I struggled to dial 999 as my phone kept slipping from my hand.'

'Would you be able to describe the gun?' Miles asked her. 'It could be important.'

'I don't know much about guns, but it was a hand held gun rather than a big one.' She suddenly realised something. 'The noise it made.'

'The noise?' Christie asked.

'Yes, I would have expected a loud bang, but the gin didn't make much of a noise.'

'It had a silencer attached?' Christie could feel a minor breakthrough coming.

'Like in the movies,' Kim confirmed. 'It made a swooshing sound rather than a loud bang.'

Christie thanked them both for their time and headed out the room with Miles. Kim remained on the sofa and Erik escorted them through.

'Beautiful church,' Christie commented, pointing at a wedding photograph of the couple on their happy day.

'Thank you, it is my local church in Helsingborg, where I'm from.'

'Sweden, I have always wanted to go there.'

'You should, it's beautiful although I am very biased.' They shook hands and went back to the car.

'Could you get a more Swedish looking guy?' Miles asked.

'Well a Scottish bloke couldn't get away with a man-bun like that.' Christie replied as they laughed and drove off.

PART EIGHT - REARVIEWMIRROR

CHAPTER FIFTEEN

Lyle had taken the call from an anonymous number and could hear the pips of a public payphone. He was surprised that they still existed in today's mobile telecommunications world. He recognised the caller's voice, who only gave an instruction to meet in a car park in South Queensferry at six o'clock.

He was driving towards the town with Chowdhury in the passenger seat. He thought it was time that Bad Boy and Chowdhury met each other. Lyle had been filling Chowdhury in on the history of his informant, before turning his education to classic rock music once more. He started playing 'Waterfront' by Simple Minds.

'Now Chowdhury, the lead singer of Simple Minds, Jim Kerr, was married to the even more talented singer, Chrissie Hynde, in the 1980's and they had a place in this very town.'

'The Pretenders.' Chowdhury answered before Lyle could answer the question.

'I'm impressed, we will make a rock fan out of you yet.'

'She was in an episode of Friends.' Lyle shook his head.

'Much work still to be done, I fear.'

The car park was at the west end of the high street, near the police station. Chowdhury gazed out of the window at the sight of the three bridges connecting Edinburgh to Fife to the north of the River Forth.

'I've never seen the Forth Rail bridge before,' he commented.

'And you won't again if you continue to call it that,' Lyle replied to a confused looking Chowdhury. 'The Queensferry Crossing is that nice new shiny one over there. The Forth *Road* bridge is that one that is falling down, well not quite but it needs some TLC. That magnificent piece of 19th century engineering is THE FORTH BRIDGE.' He shouted the name to make his point. 'You need to watch Billy Connolly's World Tour of Scotland, he'll teach you.'

'I will order the box set,' replied Chowdhury with hands raised in defeat. 'It is a beautiful bridge though.'

Lyle nodded in agreement and made his way along the high street, taking a right turn at the police station to enter the car park. There were plenty of spaces to choose from and Lyle chose one with a good view out to the water. The detectives exited the car and went off in search of Bad Boy. They soon spotted him, sitting on the grass looking out at the water. Lyle approached him, gaining his attention and then introduced Chowdhury.

'Nice to meet you, DS Chowdhury,' Bad Boy said warmly. 'I know that if Mr Lyle can trust you enough to meet me, then I can trust you too?'

'You have my complete discretion.' Chowdhury confirmed.

'Okay then. I have some information that may be of interest to you Mr Lyle, of great interest indeed. There is, as you may expect, a little catch to this. The people that I am about to tell you about are very dangerous and I do not exaggerate when I say that I am putting my life at risk by talking to you,' he waved his arm across the viewpoint, 'hence the reason for meeting in such a beautiful spot not frequented by such people.'

'Go on.' Lyle was keen to get to the punchline.

'Not so fast, Mr Lyle. I have my conditions first. You know how hard I have worked to turn my life around. I have Maria and Michael back in my life, my business is doing legitimately well and I have rid my life of some unsavoury characters. I will not put any of that at risk, not for you and not for anyone.'

'I've heard the speech before, William, I suspect you have an encore you wish to play.'

'You're a smart man, Mr Lyle, that's one of the things I like about you.' Bad Boy said this with a smile, but the sentiment was genuine. 'I know that my information does not carry a financial reward, I know how these things work. You have helped me in the past, but my gratitude and repayment is almost complete. I just want to ensure the safety of my family and secure their future. If this information leads to the capture of your number one most wanted, I want you to put a word in for me. If there is a budget for some compensation, I would like to be considered for it.'

'Sounds reasonable,' Lyle agreed.

'I'm not quite finished. The other promise I need you to make is of complete protection. If I want a plain clothed armed police officer parked outside my flat every night for a month, I will get that. If I feel my family are at risk, I want to be relocated and full witness protection. If I need to take someone out, I want a blind eye turned.'

Lyle was about to object to the final point, but Bad Boy put up his hand.

'I jest about the last condition, of course. In fact, I don't expect to need any of these things but I need to know they are there if I do.'

'This information better be good,' conceded Lyle. 'I can only promise you that I will pull every string I can and beg to every person that will listen to give you what you want. If I have to park outside your flat every night for a month, I will do it. Your safety and protection of your family will be my priority. You have my word.' Bad Boy took Lyle's hand in acceptance of his promise.

'Last condition is that you do not ask me where or how I obtained this information. I had to go through a few layers to both find the information and protect the source of the enquiry.' Lyle nodded. 'Your place of interest is in Lanarkshire and you are looking for two known bike thieves that have suddenly came into money and are splashing it around a bit. The word on the street is they obtained the cash windfall from helping a very rich man in Edinburgh hide from the police. Their names are John Cooper and Tommy Lambert.'

'If this information reliable?' Lyle asked.

'The guy who got it for me has not let me down in the twenty years I've known him. I'd put the mortgage on the information being good.'

'Thanks William, I didn't hear any of this from you. Did you hear anything Chowdhury?'

'Sorry, sir, I was miles away. Didn't hear a thing that was just said.'

Lyle and Chowdhury left Bad Boy staring out at the River Forth once more. Lyle started up the engine and reversed out of the parking space to exit. He looked in his rear view mirror and saw Bad Boy walking away. He wondered if this was some kind of sign. Was his information stream about to dry up? Was he putting Bad Boy at risk by relying on his information. He hoped, however, that the information would bring the criminals to justice.

And perhaps lead his one step closer to The Chain.

Day 7 - 21:44 - Secluded Cycle Path, Murrayfield, Edinburgh

The Chain had enjoyed his day back in the city and felt comfortable in the embracing arms of the old city once more. He felt in his current attire and changed personal grooming that he was an invisible presence as we walked the streets. He blended in perfectly, his look was not overly threatening but you would not choose to stop and have a chat or ask directions to the castle if you seen a person of such an appearance approaching.

172

He was always proud of his disguises, not just the disguises but the playing of the part as well as the clothes and make up. He had previously dressed as a tramp, an old man and a drag queen. The latter had led to his arrest, but that was due to his bad choice of choosing a victim in DS Lyle rather than picking at random that he had done before. He would learn from that mistake and was back to choosing a random victim once more.

Throughout the day, his excitement was rising as the anticipation of the kill was getting more intense. He had to slow down his mind and focus on other things, focus on his city and getting reacquainted with the streets. He had passed his office block where he built up his property empire. He had managed to split off some of his more profitable assets through a series of shell companies that would continue to provide an income into his private Swiss bank accounts should he need to access funds in the future. When his fake passport came through, he planned to check out his remote property in Sweden and if it was still safe he would use that as a base. He didn't know when that would happen, he wasn't sure if he was near the end of his killing spree, but the more he killed the more chance he had of getting caught. He wasn't ready to go back to prison, an escape is highly unlikely, doing it for a second time would be near impossible.

He dare not approach his main residential property at this time, as he would stick out like the proverbial sore thumb in such an affluent area. He did take a walk along various cycle paths in the city, having chosen this as his area of attack. He felt a sense of irony in the fact that the bicycle chain murder would happen on a cycle path. The idea appealed to him, so he walked various paths before he found his perfect spot.

The path was secluded, not far from the Murrayfield stadium. There were no matches planned and the place would be deserted on this day. It was also close enough to the train station that he could make his leave and head back to Lanarkshire and ideally be on the train before the body had been discovered. He walked along the path and found the spot he had seen earlier in the day. There was some thick bushes next to a bridge and he placed his sports bag behind the bush, and put on his gloves carefully before bringing out his chain.

He then stood by the bridge and waited for his next random victim.

Day 8 - 07:49 - Secluded Cycle Path, Murrayfield, Edinburgh

DCI Montgomery stood over the body, barely believing his eyes. Dr James had already examined the victim and there was no doubt about it. The Chain had killed again.

There was a change to the pattern though. Previous killings had been young single females, albeit there did not appear to be any sexual motive to the killings. The latest victim was a male, in his fifties, overweight and dressed in Lycra. His bicycle lay, slightly damaged, in the bushes next to the path. The forensic team where hard at work at the preserved scene, looking for evidence of the latest crime. There was always the chance that it was a copy cat killer, especially since the details of his crimes were exposed at the trial, but Dr James did not think so.

'It is to do with the angles of the neck wound,' he was explaining to Montgomery, explaining his reason. 'Based on the height of the victim and the height of the killer, we can tell by the direction of the wound. All his previous victims were roughly the same height, and significantly shorter than the killer. This resulted in an upward angle to the wound. This latest victim was also quite short and the wound in near identical to the other three. This poor chap may not have all the characteristics of the other three, but the method and process of the killing was identical.'

'I thought he would stay underground,' Montgomery was saying in disbelief. 'If he had managed to escape once, why risk it again? Why come back to Edinburgh where a whole city know who you are and what you have done? Why not crawl under some rock in some remote place and live out your life, knowing that you got one over Edinburgh's finest?'

'I'm no psychologist, Fergus, but I think the allure of killing again proved too much for him. He knows Edinburgh better than any other city, it's where he is comfortable and he knew that this would have been as good a spot as any. He also has proven to be a master of disguise, so he would have had the confidence to walk around the city in whatever get up he has chosen now.' Montgomery nodded at the wise words he was hearing.

'I just hope we can work out what disguise he has used this time so we can nail him before he strikes again.'

Day 8 - 08:52 - Corstorphine Police Station, Edinburgh

Christie had been sitting at her desk in silence for over an hour now, ever since she heard that The Chain had struck again. She was completely focused on her own case, but the distraction of The Chain was overpowering. She felt a sense of responsibility for his escape and was desperate to see him back behind bars. She also knew the best way to do that, was to solve her case, help Lyle solve his and then get her whole team back onto finding The Chain. Lyle had let her know of his tip off from Bad Boy, but they were keeping that up their sleeves for now. Lyle had Chowdhury doing some research this morning into to the two individuals and would be paying them a visit as soon as they got their address.

Christie, meanwhile, had called a meeting at nine to go over what they had thus far. The two cases must be linked, with the three victims all having a connection to the WMA which linked them to Stafford which in

175

turn linked them to Samantha. Miles, Chowdhury and Lyle were waiting for her in the meeting room.

'Okay, let's start with the connections. David Stafford was in a club called the Whitebank Male Association. The club included Dennis Robinson, the second victim and Luca Mearns, the third victim who is currently in a critical condition at hospital. There were two other gentlemen in this club, Miles have you managed to trace them both?'

'Yes, ma'am. I have addresses in Livingston for them both.'

'Well done, thanks. We need to speak to these men and warn them that their lives are in danger. I'm not convinced that the failure to kill Luca will stop him trying to kill again. Lyle what do you have?'

'Well, ma'am, I believe that Stafford had help in burying the body and I think that is where WMA come into this. We need to ask these other two if they knew anything about it, but it may be difficult to get a confession out of them after all these years. Stafford may have killed and buried Samantha, but if he did I do not think he acted alone. There are two things that indicate to me that Stafford did not act alone. Firstly, why did he remain at the house with the buried body? He could have sold up and moved at anytime. Was he worried that a new owner would dig up the patio and find Samantha? Secondly, why keep the receipt? It led us to Samantha, was that his intension all along? I believe that the receipt and the house were his security against another person or people, possibly one or more of the WMA. It will just be very difficult to prove it.'

'So,' said Christie, picking up on the thread. 'If WMA were involved in Samatha's murder, then the killer is seeking revenge by killing each of them.

'It's possible and may be the most likely,' continued Lyle. 'Unless the WMA did something else that we have yet to discover.'

The room went quiet for a while as the four considered this.

'There has been no other major crimes involving the village of Whitebank, confirmed Chowdhury. ' I could widen the search to the surrounding areas, but the Samantha Kerr case was the only one of note in that area that I have found so far in my background searches.'

'Right, let's keep that thought in mind but focus on the Samantha Kerr case. Chowdhury, you keep on your background checking for Lyle and go back through the Samantha Kerr case notes. I want to know if any of the WMA were interviewed as part of the case. Miles, I want to you continue on the background work of all the members of WMA, especially Luca and the final two. Also, keep your ears open for when Montgomery gets back and let me know what you can find out about The Chain's latest victim. If you give me those addresses, Lyle and I will head to Livingston.'

The meeting adjourned and Miles handed the addresses to Lyle. Christie wanted to arrive without warning and she and Lyle headed out to the GTI.

'Right, Lyle, give me an interesting fact on any classic rock song or artist or album or anything to help clear my head. There is too much noise in there at the moment, so I need something to distract me.'

'As you wish, ma'am,' he said with a wide grin. 'So many facts to share and so little time.' He scrolled through the music system, before selecting ZZ Top's 'Sharp Dressed Man and pulling the GTI out of the station car park. 'What can you tell me about ZZ Top?' Christie thought for a moment.

'Is that those guys with the massive beards?'

'The very same. Well they were formed in the very late sixties but became pretty big in the 1980's due to their music videos being played on MTV. The interesting fact is that the bad are a trio and the drummer, who

177

was famously clean shaven, is called Frank BEARD! I believe he did eventually grown one in recent years but not to the extent as the other two'

Christie found herself laughing at the image of this rock star called beard playing in a band with two highly bearded individuals. Her phone started to ring and she answered the call from Miles.

'It's Luca Mearns, ma'am. He's awake and talking.'

CHAPTER SIXTEEN

The killer slowly ground the coffee beans, letting his mind wander over the events of the last week or so. He had successfully killed two men and critically injured a third. He had considered going to the hospital again to finish the job off, but thought he would leave Luca Mearns for now. He had two other targets and perhaps he would focus on them now, let Luca suffer his injury for a while before going back to complete the task.

He put the coffee pot on the stove and walked through to the spare bedroom, looking at the board and in particular the last two in the group. He had his choice of who to pick next. He always knew he would start with Stafford, as he was the easiest target. The loaner, the one who had a routine of almost military precision. He never deviated, so the killer knew exactly where he would be each day. His house was also secluded so he knew he could slip in and out without too much trouble.

Of the last two, one would be the hardest yet and the other would be quite straight forward. He had a choice to make, easy or hard. Given the close call of the third attempt, perhaps he would go for the easier option. The buzz, however, of achieving a difficult kill, could swing the pendulum in that direction. No need to decide now, he had time before the next kill.

His coffee was ready and he poured himself a large cup, noticing the deep dark colour of the strong blend he had chosen. He took the cup with him back to the spare bedroom. He placed the mug down on the table and pulled out a large black marker pen. There was something missing on his board, under the 'Motivation' section. He had only written two words, JUSTICE and REVENGE. This was true, but there was a third reason, possibly more important that the other two reasons that were recorded on his wall chart. He took off the lid of the pen and wrote the third word down in large capital letters.

LOVE.

Day 8 - 09:29 - St John's Hospital, Livingston, West Lothian

Christie and Lyle were waiting outside a private room that had been allocated in the High Dependency Unit for Luca Mearns. Tracy was in the room currently and Christie had managed a quick peek through a small window before they were asked to take a seat. She only saw Tracy, in floods of tears, holding tightly to Luca's hand.

Dr Elizabeth Davis arrived and sat down with them. She confirmed that following further surgery, Luca had woken up and had started talking straight away. She knew that the damage caused by the bullet was not as grave as early indications and that Luca had been a very lucky man. Even so, she was amazed herself at his recovery speed, albeit, he was groggy and under a lot of medication still. He would remain in hospital for a while yet, under her supervision as they monitored his recovery. His condition was now being classed as critical but stable. She left the officers to attend to another patient, but promised she would return to let them in to see Luca, however, she would be observing and would cut the interview if she felt she had to.

Twenty minutes later, they were given entry but told that their visit would be limited to five minutes only. Dr Davis led them into the room and Tracy stood up, deciding to go and grab a coffee and let the police officers ask their questions. She had comfort that Dr Davis would be there to look after him and she cursed herself that she did not have the strength, at present, to listen to the full details of what had happened. The nightmares

180

had already begun and she had failed to get more than the odd ten minutes sleep, here and there, since the attack happened.

Luca was propped up with pillows on the bed and had various wires and tubes coming out of him. He wore a large bandage on his head and traces of blood were showing through. Dr Davis had confirmed that he had received blood as part of his treatment and Lyle, being a regular blood donor himself, wondered if his recent donation was part of it. Luca's glazed eyes watched his wife exit the room and he looked around at the new occupants, recognising only the doctor.

'Luca, these are the police officers investigating your case. I said they could come and ask you a few questions only, as long as you are still okay with this?' She had an excellent bedside manner and wanted to ensure the protection of her patient. She would happily throw the officers out if Luca was not ready to speak to them. He asked for some water before the questioning began, Christie witnessed how weak he was and was starting to question her decision to come so soon, regardless how vital the information she needed may be.

'How are you feeling?' Christie asked, immediately regretting the question.

'Like someone has shot me in the head,' Luca replied with a smile, which appeared to cause some discomfort.

'It's an obvious question, but any idea who would want to do this to you?' Luca closed his eyes and Christie was unsure if he was thinking or drifting back to sleep. The doctor started to move forward as he answered the question.

'I do not know the who, but I can guess the why.' Christie was taken aback. Luca was the first person who indicated that they knew what this was about.

'Okay, can you tell us why?' Luca kept his eyes closed as he spoke, carefully trying to keep his wounded head as still as possible.

'If you don't know about it already, when I was a kid I was in a group of friends with the now deceased pair of David Stafford and Dennis Robinson.'

'The WMA,' Lyle confirmed. Luca opened one eye and found Lyle's gaze.

'Very good, you have done your research. I only found out about Dennis shortly before I was attacked and was still getting my head around it. I was worried for my safety, as I had put two and two together, and was going to speak with Tracy about it when I got home. I had no plan, just a need to be careful. Unfortunately, I was too late in my considerations.'

'What can you tell us about Samantha Kerr?' Lyle asked, he was keen that his case was discussed, even briefly, before they were thrown out. Once more Luca opened an eye to look at Lyle, before closing it again to speak.

'You were on the original case, I thought I recognised you. I would like to talk to you about Samantha Kerr, but not now and not here. I'm sorry, but I think the drugs are kicking in again so I would like to sleep.' This time, he appeared to drift straight to sleep and the doctor quickly checked on him before escorting the detectives out of the room. Christie was first to speak when they were back in the car.

'What do you think he wants to say to you about Samantha?'

'What I think and what I want may well be polar opposites. I think he knows there is a connection between his group of friends and the Samantha Kerr case. I also think that he wants to speak to me to distance himself from the case.'

'And what do you want him to say?' Christie asked. Lyle put the car into gear and revved the engine answering simply with two words.

'The truth.'

Day 8 - 11:07 - Corstorphine Police Station, Edinburgh

Miles and Chowdhury were at their respective desks working on their respective backgrounds. Miles had found out some further information of the five members of WMA, including their individual social media profile. Unsurprisingly, David Stafford did not have much of a profile, however, the others had been pretty active. She could not find much connections with them and they did not appear to communicate via this medium.

Chowdhury had been doing the same of the two individuals that Bad Boy had disclosed to them. He had tracked down addresses for them both and had also tracked down their social media profiles. There was no obvious link to The Chain that he could find, but both had been posting photos of recently purchased items online. It made for interesting reading and he was keen to find out what Lyle thought.

Montgomery suddenly appeared in the room and started to make noise about the latest victim of The Chain. Both Miles and Chowdhury stopped what they were doing to listen in, taking notes subtly to share with Christie and Lyle later.

'RIGHT LISTEN UP PEOPLE,' he shouted to anyone who cared to listen. 'The Chain has struck again and unlike his last attempt, he succeeded.' Miles thought this comment was in bad taste, given the last attempt was of DS Lyle - one of their own. She was quickly realising that much of what came out of Montgomery's mouth was in bad taste. 'I want everyone who is even remotely available,' he continued. 'To be working day and night on catching this fucker. I will not let down the people of this city again.'

Identification of the victim was still ongoing and there was not much information to go on at this time. Montgomery confirmed that the victim was a male, estimated to be in his fifties who was cycling passed with the attack happened. This was three pieces of information that were in complete contrast to his previous modus operandi, which had been younger, females who were walking home. Miles wondered if it could be a copy-cat killer, however, Montgomery confirmed that Dr James was pretty certain that it was the same killer.

Miles knew that Dr James was rarely wrong…

Day 8 - 14:02 - Undisclosed Location, Lanarkshire

The Chain lay on the sofa of the flat, reliving the latest kill. He had been surprised how easy it was, he had been concerned that he may have lost some of his composure and skill of the act. In the end it had been so easy and he was delighted with his latest victim. The change from younger female to older male showed that he was growing in confidence, growing in skill and growing in threat. He knew that he wanted to rock the boat with the latest killing and he was confident that that is exactly what had happened.

From his vantage point in the cycle path, he had spotted the victim approaching and knew he was the one. No one was around, he had been regularly checking and the sight of the disgusting overweight man had motivated him to act quickly. He had to improvise somewhat as he had not planned in attacking someone on a bicycle, but it all linked perfectly together. He had waited until the cyclist was close and then simply walked out and pushed him as he passed. The speed and shock of what happened sent the cyclist flying from his bike, mildly injured and very confused.

The follow up was straight forward, approaching from behind and wrapping the chain around the neck, pulling upwards and crossing his hands over the enwrap the chain tightly around his neck. The resistance did not last long and the man died quickly a mixture of his age, weight and lack of fitness. The bike was new and it was obvious that the man was new to cycling.

The Chain had placed his weapon back in his sports bags and made a hasty retreat, away from the cycle path and through the neighbouring streets until he found himself back at Haymarket Station. Sitting on the train, he had allowed himself a smile as he once more placed the sports bag on the table in front of him and watched his fellow passengers, blissfully unaware of who they shared their journey home with.

The Chain rose from the sofa and went to the kitchen to make himself a coffee, the one luxury he still indulged in. When he first arrived, there had been only a cheap instant coffee of a blend he had not seen since the 1980's. He had quickly bought himself proper coffee and maker. As he waited for the drink to be ready, he looked out the kitchen window at the scene in front of him. Dirty kids, with old and wasted clothes ran round hitting each other with sticks and shouting out profanities. The Chain could not believe he was in the 21st century, the scene looked like something out of the post war slums of Glasgow.

Reflecting on where his life was now, he wondered if the lust for killing would continue, putting his freedom as risk. He had his wealth and could move abroad with the fake passport, but that too would be a risk to his freedom. His life in this flat, though, was almost as unbearable as the time spent behind bars.

Although when in prison, he couldn't kill with his chain once more…

Day 8 - 15:32 - M8 Motorway, West Bound Towards Livingston, West Lothian

Lyle kept the GTI in the fast lane of the motorway, clocking at exactly 10% above the speed limit. He knew it was cheeky of him, but he was intent in getting to Livingston soon, so much so he had forgotten to put on music. Christie, however, came to his rescue.

'Nothing too loud or heavy, Lyle, but put something nice on.'

'Nice?' Lyle questioned in jest. 'It's all nice, but let me play you a nice song that starts with an awesome guitar introduction.' Through his steering wheel controls, he selected Little Angels' 'I Ain't Gonna Cry', turning it up very loud for the introduction, before the song mellowed out at the start of the first verse. Christie shut her eyes and listened to the lyrics, letting her mind empty.

Lyle kept his eyes fixed on the road ahead thinking about Samantha Kerr. It had been so long since the original case, so much had changed in such a relatively short period of time. Assuming she died in, or close to, 1992 then the chances were that Samantha did not experience internet search engines, e-mail, text messaging, MP3 players, a barrage of Apple products, DVD's and social media. He wondered if she would have embraced these developments, or if life was simpler back then. The lack of technology may have prevented them finding her alive, or prosecuting the right person or people. He just hoped that the current leads would lead to the truth and to closure for the family. Underneath, though, he still held a feeling of failure.

They arrived in Livingston and made their way to the home of Donald McIntyre. Donald lived alone, two failed marriages behind him and no children. Although there were some similarities to David Stafford, Donald was a very sociable character going by his social media profile. Recently turned sixty one, he was the vice captain of the local golf club and had a handicap in single figures. He retired at sixty from a job in the banking sector and had recently started to volunteer in a local charity shop. Christie was armed with all this knowledge and was once more impressed with the through job Miles had done.

Donald lived in an end terrace property not far from the golf course. The garden had seen better days, however, there were fresh bags of compost and some potted flowers indicating that Donald had plans to change that in his retirement. Lyle knocked on the door and Donald answered straight away, having been informed of the pending visit. He was a short man with a completely bald head, the remaining hair he had was shaved in close. He also had evidence of a beer belly, an obvious fan of the 19th hole. He welcomed them in and took them through to the kitchen, pointing at a small breakfast bar, inviting them to sit. Offer of coffee was declined and Christie went straight into the questions.

'You will be aware of the recent deaths in Whitebank and the attempted murder of Luca Mearns here in Livingston?'

'Of course,' he said solemnly. 'I gather that you already know we were aquatinted in our younger days, but I hadn't seen much on them over the last twenty five years or such.'

'When you say you hadn't seen much of them, when was the last time you met them?' Donald was obviously forming his answer carefully in his head. Lyle stepped in before he could answer.

'It's imperative that you tell us the truth, Mr McIntyre. Your own life may depend on it.' It sounded overly dramatic to Lyle's own ears, but it had the desired effect. He let out a long sigh, knowing that he would have to be honest.

'Not that long ago I got an e-mail from David Stafford. I genuinely hadn't heard from him since before his trial. I came across the others from time to time, especially Luca who would come for a round of golf once every couple of years. Anyway, David said that he wanted to meet as he had something that he wanted to discuss. The e-mail was sent to me and three others.'

'The WMA?' Christie asked. Donald appeared shocked that they knew about the group.

'Yes. I had not thought about the gang for many, many years. I was intrigued in what he wanted to discuss and agreed. Some of the others were more reluctant, but eventually we all agreed. We met at David's house, then went to the local pub.'

'Why didn't you stay at David's house?' Lyle asked. It was a loaded question, but he wanted to know if Donald would show any signs of being aware of Samantha's presence at the property.

'Some of the group wanted a drink and David didn't keep anything at the house. I think he was tee total, or certainly rarely drank. Anyway, Dennis was a regular at the local and said that there were secluded tables where we could talk without being disturbed.'

'So what did David want to talk about?'

'He wanted to talk about the trial and how he had not been able to live a normal life since it happened. We all were compassionate to what he went through, being wrongly accused, but some of the mud sticks doesn't it?' Donald opened a cupboard a brought out a fresh packet of cigarettes. He offered the packet to the officers, neither whom smoked. He opened the back door and stood outside on the step, allowing the conversation to continue as he fed his nicotine habit.

'Do you know what happened to Samantha?' Lyle asked, maintaining a cool head whilst his stomach twisted.

'I know that David was not responsible.'

'That didn't answer the question.' Lyle stated firmly.

'Honestly, no, but I have a feeling someone close to David knew what happened. I don't want to be difficult, but I'd rather not say anymore on the matter without a solicitor. I promise you I had nothing to do with it, but I am enjoying my retirement too much to let a slip of tongue land me in any trouble.'

'Ok, we understand,' confirmed Christie. 'We would advise that you take extreme caution, you are linked to the other victims and it is possible that you are also a target. We can arrange for the local police to watch over your house.'

'That won't be necessary. My brother is coming over to stay with me and he is ex-SAS. I will be perfectly safe with him around.' Christie left her card should he change his mind and they left the house. Lyle did not waste any time and sped off on their way back to Edinburgh. Christie knew something in the interview had clicked in Lyle and berated herself that she hadn't spotted it herself. Lyle finally gave an indication of what he was thinking.

'I think he knows who killed Samantha,' he finally said. 'And what's more, I think I now know who killed her too.'

PART NINE - RATS

CHAPTER SEVENTEEN

The killer had changed his mind, he would go for the easier option tonight. He had considered that the quicker he did the killing, the more confusion would take place. He knew that the police would have started to connect the victims, so he would have to be extra cautious. He had been hiding outside the next victim's house for over an hour now and there appeared to be no police presence to deter him. He found this equality confusing and satisfying. Perhaps his next victim was being cocky, not believing that his life was in danger.

It was time to make his move, it was now dark enough to provide the required cover. Once more, he had the whole thing planned out. Previous surveillance had provided him with the perfect moment to strike, it would just be a matter of patience. That was something that he had in abundance.

The rear garden was secluded, a six foot fence enclosed the lawn and decking area. He would have to ensure that there was no disturbance from the neighbouring property, but again his research confirmed that the old couple went to bed at ten o'clock every night. He had waited until he spotted the bedroom light go out before making his move.

He scaled the fence with ease. He was fit and had checked the best location to enter, both in terms of access and cover. The property was near a golf course and traffic at this time of evening was limited. So far everything had gone to plan, but he reminded himself of the mistakes of the last attempt. The rear garden was poorly maintained, a square of grass, no trees or plants and some old decking at the door. There was an old shed in which he was able to hide behind, giving him a perfect view of the door. He removed the gun from his ruck sack, gave it a quick check and waited.

It was not long until Donald McIntyre appeared at the back door and as per his usual routine, stepped out onto the decking. He withdrew a cigarette from the packet and lifted it his mouth. The large flame of his Zippo lighter illuminated his face just long enough for the killer to aim and fire. There was a thud as the body hit the decking and the killer moved quickly, firing off three more shots to the chest. He then retreated back over the fence and headed off towards the golf course. Once he was secluded by the trees he allowed himself a glance back to the house and noticed that the neighbours bedroom light was on, but they would not be able to view the body from their window. He knew they would have to get dressed and come out to investigate before they would discover the horror of the scene the killer had left. This would give him enough time to retrieve his motorbike and escape once more.

He reached the other side of the golf course and found the motorbike where he had left it. With gun safely back in the ruck sack, he put in on his back, put on his helmet and started up the engine. His delivery disguise was once more in place and he pulled the bike out onto the main road and headed off in the direction of the back streets and his exit from Livingston.

Riding along the back roads to his house, he allowed himself a smile. That one was the easiest one yet and it had gone perfectly…

Day 9 - 01:07 - Livingston, West Lothian

Christie and Lyle were both exhausted as they wearily made their way towards Livingston. There was no music, both feeling a sense of guilt for not taking more precaution, despite the protests from Donald McIntyre. Those protests had ultimately caused his death and Christie knew that there

192

would be blame heading in her direction. The best chance she had was to find the killer, solve the case and hope that the result would deflect some of the unwanted attention.

'What the fuck are we dealing with here, Lyle?' Christie asked. Lyle struggled with an answer, he had been wondering the same thing.

'Someone who is incredibly well organised. Someone who knows when and where to strike. Someone who has gone to a lot of bother to plan and prepare for these killings. Someone who has a high success rate, unlike the Meat Loaf song, four out of three IS bad.'

It was a lame attempt at humour, and neither were in the laughing mood. They had three murders on their hands, and one attempted murder. Christie had just had a horrible thought.

'He's been more prolific than The Chain. He has been moving quicker than The Chain did and I hope to fuck that they are not now in some type of sick competition.'

'I don't think so, ma'am,' Lyle said, trying to be reassuring. 'The Chain is pure evil, killing for pleasure, getting a buzz out of each death, perhaps even choosing his victims at random. This killer is different, he is on some sort of vendetta. He is making his way through a historic gang for what purpose? Revenge. Revenge for the death of Samantha Kerr.'

'So if it's a vendetta, we need to interview every member of Samantha's family. We need to find out where they were at the time of each killing. Lyle, this is going to put us at odds with each other.' The last part of the sentence was spoken with real concern.

'It was always going to be the case ma'am. I need to find out what happened to Samantha and give the family closure.'

'But what if that closure coincides with an arrest of a family member. What if the killer is Patrick Kerr.'

193

'I've thought of that ma'am. You know we have to consider every possibility in every case.'

'So what would you do if it was Patrick Kerr?'

'I'd happily arrest him myself.'

Once more the scene was lit up with blue flashing lights and a hive of activity from the forensic team. Dr James appeared to be leaving, but stopped in his tracks when he saw them approaching.'

'My Office is not built for this amount of bodies, you better hurry up and find this madman, I need my beauty sleep.' He was being somewhat playful, but he knew how the situation would be affecting two of his favourite police officers. 'I know it's difficult and you must be under an enormous amount of pressure, but you will catch him soon, of that I have no doubt. You will be pleased to know that our good friends in the forensic department may have just found you both a little present. It appears that the killer may have made a little error in his latest killing. I won't steal their thunder and will bid you a good night.'

'Nothing to say about the body, Doctor?' Christie asked.

'Nothing that you would not have been expecting. Four shots, one to the head, three to the chest. Entry wounds looks similar, but looks like the shot to the head was from a greater distance, followed by three close range shots to the chest. Forensics will tell you the rest, good night.'

With that, he walked off towards his BMW and a return to his beauty sleep. It was an ironic thing to say, as Dr James was a strikingly handsome man for his age and obviously looked after himself. Perhaps he was not being facetious when he spoke about his sleep.

Entering the cordon, they arrived as the body of Douglas McIntyre was being taken away. They paused and lowered their heads in a showing of respect as the body passed. The senior forensic officer spotted them and came over. Christie explained what Dr James had told them so far.

'My team have been doing a through search of the garden and the surrounding area and have found a few clues that may be of interest. With the head shot coming from distance, we quickly deducted that the initial shot came from a place of hiding. The only place to hid within this garden is behind that shed. They walked over to the area in question. 'Now, I don't think this killer is daft enough to leave fingerprints, however, we did find a hair that had been caught at the edge of the shed. In the adrenaline of what he was doing, he would not have felt a hair being plucked out of his scalp in the heat of the moment. We are sending it away for analysis, however, it had a follicle attached which gives us a great change of DNA. Of course, it may not be the killer's, but it looked fresh when we collected it.'

This was a major breakthrough. If they could get a DNA profile, it would prove a person was in the garden and would help build the case. The only problem with a DNA profile, is that you need someone to match it with.

'Secondly, we have some footprints. Although the weather has been dry over the last couple of weeks, the neighbours must have been out watering their plants earlier with a hose. Some of the water has come through into this garden, enough to leave a slight imprint. We have taken some casts and will try and identify the shoes and feet size for starters.' The news was getting better and better. Christie's mind was racing, this could help narrow down the search.

'Finally, we found something else, which has a narrower possibility of being involved, but we are studying it anyway. At the golf course, one of my officers did a search in case the killer had escaped from there, it made the most sense given how secluded it is. Anyway, he found some fresh tyre marks from a small motorbike at the other side of the course. Again we have taken impressions and it may be a long shot, however, these may have come from the escape vehicle.'

Christie and Lyle could hardly believe their luck. From having little forensic evidence at the first three crime scenes, they had three solid pieces now. Perhaps the killer had been sloppy in his rush to get the third kill.

Three mistakes that could lead to him being caught.

Day 9 - 11:07 - M8 Motorway, Approaching Livingston, West Lothian

Christie and Lyle had only managed a few hours sleep between them, before attending a roasting session from Hepburn in the morning. The Assistant Chief Constable was visiting later and he was desperate to have something to tell her. Normally, Christie would keep early clues close to her chest, but she knew the importance of Hepburn having something so she shared the evidence from the latest scene with him. The relief of having something was evident on his face and they were dismissed without further wrath.

They were now on their way to Livingston to meet the final member of WMA. Fraser Wilson lived with his wife and two teenage sons and Christie had arranged for two uniformed officers to guard the outside of the property until they got there. She had already made arrangements for a safe house and it was imperative that there were no more deaths, especially now she sensed that they were getting close.

'What's your favourite guitar solo?' Christie asked to Lyle's surprise, once more looking for a distraction to clear her mind. A guitarist himself, he often spoke about the importance of a good solo in a song. He always said it should enhance the song and be part of the song rather than just be a chance for a guitarist to show off.

'Recorded or played live?'

'Both.'

'Well, it's a bit like choosing your favourite child, but I will play along this time. You can ask me again next week and get a different answer. Now, live it has to be David Gilmour of...' Christie let out a sigh.

'Pink Floyd,' she groaned.

'Well done. His solo of Comfortably Numb from the Pulse live album. The recorded version is a travesty.' He looked at her momentarily. 'They fade it out.' He looked genuinely distraught. 'Now recorded, I'm going to very controversial and choose one that not many people talk about.' He started to scroll through his music system once again. 'This solo has a beautiful blend of harmony and incredible guitar playing skill.' Europe's 'Superstitious' started and they remained silent as they listened to the song awaiting the special solo Lyle referred to.

They entered Livingston and Lyle turned off the music to concentrate in the directions to the house. Livingston, like many of the new towns in Scotland, was awash with roundabouts and Lyle had to remember which exit to take at a number of these. Finally, they arrived at their destination and noticed that the two officers were standing outside the door as instructed. Approaching them, Christie felt they had picked the two largest officers available, both men were standing well over six feet and were no stranger to the gym going by the strain on the sleeves of their uniforms.

Christie and Lyle showed them their ID and headed into the house where Fraser Wilson was sitting with a glass of whisky, next to his wife with the two sons looking nervous on the sofa. Suitcases were lined up in the hall and instructions had already been given that they were to leave. Fraser stood up on shaky legs and shook hands with the detectives, before draining his glass and sitting down once more. He admitted that it was just one glass for his nerves after finding out his life was at risk as he knew he needed a clear head for what was coming.

'We do have some questions before our colleagues arrive to take you to a place of safety.' Christie informed him. Fraser nodded and then asked the boys to go to their room for now, he didn't want them to get any further upset than they already were at the prospect of leaving their friends behind for an unknown period. He took his wife's hand and nodded for the questions to begin.

'There is no doubt that these murders are linked to WMA, can you tell me of your part in the gang when you were younger.'

'It was all such a long time ago. We started off as kids just getting up to mischief, then when we were in our mid-teens we started drinking and smoking. Someone, I can't remember who, came up with the idea that we would be like a private gentleman's club and smoke cigars and drink fancy spirits - port, sherry, brandy and the likes. We got business cards printed, to be honest I thought it was all a bit silly.'

'Not silly when David was arrested, I presume.' It was Christie's turn to ask the challenging questions.

'That took us all by surprise. Around that time the group had petered out and we all kept a low profile so not to get involved. I was always waiting for the police to come round to my parent's house to ask questions, but they never came.'

'Guilty conscious?' Lyle asked.

'Guilty by association, not guilty of any crime.'

'So you think David was involved in the disappearance of Samantha Kerr?' Christie asked.

'I know that David knew her, but I'm not sure he had anything to do with the disappearance. I just don't think it was in him to do something so evil, I guess his acquittal proved that.'

'Did you ever meet Samantha?' Christie continued.

'No, I never met her. I know that David spoke about her, he had feelings towards her, but he said that she had a boyfriend. He never mentioned who it was, I'm not even sure he knew.'

'We understand that WMA met recently though?' Fraser looked at Christie and knew there was little point telling her anything but the truth.

'That was David. To be honest, I have no idea why he wanted to see us, I thought it was just a bit of nostalgia. I think there was something that he wanted to say to us, but either changed his mind or never got round to it. By the time we got to the pub, Dennis was getting drunk and arguing with some of the locals. It was his idea we went there in the first place as he said we could get some privacy to talk. Those talks, however, never took place.'

'We believe he wanted to speak about the trial?' Lyle interjected.

'Yes, he did speak about the trial for a while, but it was more of a rant than a discussion. I think that is why Dennis hit the booze. We all felt for what he went through, but we did not necessarily want to be reminded of it.'

The doorbell rang and one of the officers confirmed that it was time for the family to move. Christie and Lyle thanked Fraser for his time and left the house.

'Do you think he is telling the truth?' Christie asked. She knew that Lyle was the expert when it came to reading witnesses.

'I believed what he was saying about the recent meeting. He looked frightened and worried for the safety of his family.'

'Did it help you with your case, you said that you think you know who was responsible for Samantha's death.' Lyle hadn't mentioned it again since they had left Donald McIntyre's house.

'I was not convinced on what he was saying about Samantha, but I was never going to find out anything from him about that,' he confessed starting up the engine. 'It's Luca Mearns that I need to speak to again to get that answer. I just need to wait until he is well enough and not so affected by drugs that I can interrogate him.'

CHAPTER EIGHTEEN

Chowdhury had got solid confirmation of the address of the bike thieves that Bad Boy had tipped them off about. John Cooper and Tommy Lambert shared a flat in Coatbridge and Christie knew they would have to bring them in for questioning. She called Montgomery and asked if he minded that Lyle and Christie head to Lanarkshire to speak with the pair at one of the local police stations. As they were in Livingston, it was quicker for them to attend. Montgomery reluctantly agreed although was pissed off at only now just finding out about this lead.

Christie had called ahead and spoken with a fellow DI who had arranged for back up. They were to meet at Coatbridge police station before heading out to the property. Lyle was in unfamiliar territory and had checked carefully where he was headed. Despite his best efforts, it was only after a few wrong turnings that they arrived at their destination.

DI Scott Higgins was a tall, well built man, in his forties. He was very welcoming to the pair and insisted that they have a coffee before heading over. He confirmed that he had two undercover detectives at the scene and the two suspects had just returned from the supermarket carrying a box of beer, so it was unlikely that they would be heading out anytime soon. He also wanted to get the lowdown on the most talked about case within Police Scotland.

Both Edinburgh detectives took an instant liking to Higgins. Well mannered, polite and ounces of the famous West Coast sense of humour had already been shared. He kept them just long enough to discover what he needed to know, then they made their way to meet the two for questioning.

Higgins confirmed that he knew of the two petty crooks and the link to the motorbike theft was bang on the money. He was happy to arrest them both under suspicion should they not speak voluntarily. Lyle confirmed he wanted to speak with them informally at the house, before they got their lawyers involved. They may chose their right of silence, but he felt that he had a card up his sleeve to play.

'It's your case, I'm just here to help,' Higgins confirmed. Lyle only had one question before they headed.

'Which of the two is the rider of the bikes?'

'Cooper. His dad used to ride professionally so he grew up around them. He knows the machines inside and out, hence why he is such a good thief. Lambert is the muscle should anything go wrong.'

Lyle and Christie followed Higgins' car, who was travelling with DS Jackie MacDonald. She was a no nonsense cop, but happy to play what might only be a minor role in the case. They travelled through a number of streets before turning into an estate of ex-council houses and pulled up in front of a block of four flats. They alighted their cars as they were joined by the two undercover officers who confirmed that they were still inside. Higgins banged on the door loudly.

One of the pair opened the door and Higgins flashed his ID and asked to come inside. The man looked unfazed and invited them in, the two plain clothed officers had already departed, but remained close by should the two try and run off. The house was on the upper floor and upon reaching the stairs the four detectives entered the living room. Empty cans, bottles and take away cartons lay all around. The newly purchased box of beer had been opened, however, it appeared that they were both on their first drink. The large TV was showing a live football match, the big Scottish derby between Celtic and Rangers. Higgins was the first to speak, addressing the man who answered the door.

'Right, Cooper, I would like you and your acquaintance Lambert here to answer a few questions to my colleagues here.' He nodded towards Christie and Lyle.

'What if we don't want to?' Cooper asked, leading to a snigger from his friend.

'Not a problem, of course, but I'd rather leave you to your unhygienic surroundings and your match rather than having you handcuffed and marched down to the station. I would like to catch some of the second half as I've a tenner riding on Celtic.' Cooper seemed to contemplate this for a moment, then with a shrug of his shoulders, he sat next to Lambert and awaited the questions. Christie had already agreed to allow Lyle to ask the questions, knowing that he would be able to read the pair and pitch them accordingly.

'We are here to ask you some questions and, depending on your answers, make you a favourable deal.' The opening gambit immediately got their attention. Lambert picked up the remote and muted the television.

'Go on,' he said.

'My colleagues here have some information in relation to a bike theft in the local area, a theft that may be very much linked to yourselves. Now personally, I'm not too interested in such matters as I, and my superior officer here, have been investigating much more serious crimes. Now, these more serious crimes may also be very much linked to yourselves and would result in an incredibly uncomfortable length of stay in prison.' He paused for a moment to gauge their reaction. He could tell he was having an impact and these petty thieves were no master criminals. 'So what I am about to offer you, is a way to both stay out of prison and for these petty thefts to bypass your door. Are you with me so far?' If they had planned on a showing of bravado, they had failed miserably. Lyle had them right where he wanted them and all they could do was silently nod their heads. If Higgins was offended by Lyle overruling a superior officer, he showed no signs. In fact, he was most impressed with the current showing.

'Good. Now I believe that you have both recently come into a large sum of money, how else would such petty thieves afford such a fine new television and to be eating take away food every night of the week. If I am not very much mistaken, you will still have plenty of that cash to enjoy and if you stick with me, that will still be the case.' Colour was starting to drain from their faces.

'My esteemed colleagues and I will shortly leave you both to have a wee chat and we will wait outside the room for a little while, allowing you to discuss the proposition. Should you decide to decline, you should expect an arrest forthwith. Should you decide to accept, it may be the best decision that you have every made.'

'Doesn't sound like you are giving us much of a choice.' Lyle remembered a political comedy show that had a similar scene in which the main character had answered that the person could chose exactly how they said yes. He decided to let the statement hang.

'This sudden influx of funds could only come from one source and it is not the sale of a few knocked off motorbikes. The source of those funds is very powerful, very manipulative and, most importantly, very dangerous. I suspect that he has already planned how to dispose of you both and I guarantee that it will not be pretty. The money is of no interest to him, he has plenty more where that came from and I suspect the amount that he paid you was pocket money for him and he would have no desire to recover it. After all, it paid to get him out of prison.' The pair knew they had been rumbled and Lyle felt the satisfaction that his educated guess had just hit the bullseye.

'I must admit, Mr Cooper, that I admired your riding skill in the escape despite the fact of who you were helping. I also imagine that Mr Lambert was waiting close by with a second vehicle, a van perhaps, as there was no sign of the bike after we lost sight of you, despite the whole of Police Scotland being alerted to the escape.'

'These accusations…' Cooper started, trying to regain some of his composure.

'Would be difficult to prove, but we have enough evidence to arrest you both and start a long investigation while you both get locked up in the meantime. My offer is this. Tell us where he is, where you have hidden him and the cases against you will be dropped. We can place you both in witness protection until he is safely behind bars. At that point, you can live your lives again. Also, one of the victim's families has put up a substantial reward for information leading to his arrest and incarceration. I will personally ensure that this substantial financial windfall goes to you both and that should prevent the need for you to restart your less savoury career.' This last statement was complete fabrication, but he knew money talked where these two were concerned.

Lyle nodded to the other officers and they left the room, shutting the door behind them. They stood at the top of the stairs, waiting for the decision.

'Do you think they will bite?' Higgins asked in a whisper. Lyle nodded.

'I hope you don't think I was stepping on any toes about the bike theft charges being dropped.' Higgins laughed.

'If these two lead to the capture of The Chain, I would give them the freedom of Coatbridge, if such a thing exists.' The door opened and Cooper indicated for them to return.

'We have one question, then we will give you our answer. What guarantees do we have that you will stick to your promise?'

'I can't give you any promise except for my word and I always stick to my word. I do, however, think you should consider the alternatives of declining as well as the rewards of accepting.' It didn't take them long to agree and soon they were all back at Coatbridge police station recording their statements.

It transpired that The Chain had known them for a couple of years as he had a small property letting company in Lanarkshire that the two had undertaken some 'off the books' maintenance work on. The Chain had got them drunk one night and learned all about Cooper's skills around a motorbike. Shortly before he was caught, he had approached them about a prison escape should he ever end up behind bars. A large payment was set up with his solicitor that would be activated in part before the escape and in full afterwards. Cooper had bought a small flat in the local area for renovation and rental and that is where The Chain had been staying, paying double the going rate.

Address in hand, Christie and Lyle headed out to the GTI with Higgins and MacDonald following behind. Armed response vehicles were just ahead.

'That was mighty impressive, Lyle. I can't believe you got them to talk.'

'I knew that they were a couple of rats as soon as I laid my eyes on them. I just needed to squeeze them gently to get them to squeal.'

The Chain lay on the threadbare and uncomfortable sofa, planning his next move. He wondered if he had overestimated his associates, as there was still no passport. The latest kill had quenched his thirst and he no longer had the urge to kill again that he had experienced before. He thought it may have been the time spent planning, preparing and approaching the latest kill. He realised that he had enjoyed this, just as much as the final act. Perhaps he didn't have to kill so often, he could be like an alcoholic that chooses to sip slowly a single malt for enjoyment rather than drink it so fast as to miss out on the taste.

Yes, he would plan his next killing and enjoy the process and the build up. He would take his time, perhaps stalk his latest victim. He could find out things about them, he had thus far chosen his victims at random, their deaths a result of a cruel hand of fate. He cared little for these victims, but perhaps he could now focus on killing people who deserved it. He could be a vigilante, killing fellow murders, rapists or abductors.

With this thought in mind, he fired up the old computer that was in the flat. It took forever to log on and the internet was mind numbingly slow. He decided to make coffee while he waited, choosing his favourite blend to enjoy. He would start to live his life in a new manner, one of slowness. One of enjoying each moment, not taking for granted the comfortable lifestyle that he had. He would enjoy his freedom and take precautions when heading out. He would consider changing his appearance again, choosing different clothes, a different set up again. He would continue to remain anonymous.

Coffee in hand, he returned to the computer which had loaded up the search engine. He decided to read some local news websites, something that he had mostly been avoiding. His attention was immediately drawn to an article on a series of murders in West Lothian. How had he missed this?

He spent the next twenty minutes reading every article he could find. Although there had been limited information leaked to the press, there was no doubt that the killings were linked. All deaths had been shootings, some news reports commented on rumours of execution style killings. The Scottish press were not always correct on their reporting, but many rumours came from solid sources and would be proven to be correct. He knew that from his own experiences.

This is perfect, he thought. He could hunt down and kill this other serial killer. How serendipitous would that be? He wanted the notoriety of being the most famous serial killer in Scotland's history and now he had a threat to that. He had resources, money talks in this country and he could bribe his way to information. He also had the intelligence to work on the case as well as the mind of a serial killer, which no police officer could comprehend. He had contacts from his business world who would facilitate him at a price. Many of them had achieved success fraudulently and The Chain could manipulate this to his advantage.

In the excitement of the moment, The Chain spilled his coffee and went through to the kitchen to get a cloth to clean it up. As ran the hot tap he heard an earsplitting crash at the front door. He knew instantly what was happening and he had no where to go. Within seconds, two armed police officers had their guns pointed at him and he raised his arms in surrender. Lyle appeared between them and moved forward to handcuff him. He read The Chain his rights and one of the armed officers led him away. The Chain remained silent throughout the process, but he had one further trick up his sleeve.

DI Higgins walked through and congratulated Christie and Lyle on their work and told them how happy he was and that he would be getting drinks bought for him for years to come, telling people how he had helped to capture The Chain. He was willing to exaggerate for the benefit of a free pint.

'That's not all the good news for today,' Lyle said, looking over Higgins' shoulder at the television. 'Celtic have just won 3-0.'

PART TEN - ELDERLY WOMAN BEHIND THE COUNTER IN A SMALL TOWN

CHAPTER NINETEEN

It was late before they got back to Edinburgh, but the adrenaline of having captured The Chain once more had kept them alert. Lyle was in ecstatic mood on the drive back, playing his music at a ridiculous volume, but Christie was happy to endure this, safe in the knowledge that their Nemesis had been caught once more. They took turns in choosing the songs, Lyle had picked Soundgarden's 'Rusty Cage' at the start of the drive, explaining that Johnny Cash had recorded a cover version of the song. Christie knew that she would be listening to that version at some point. Christie has chosen Blue Öyster Cult's '(Don't Fear) The Reaper'. Her classic rock knowledge and appreciation was rising at a level that Lyle found most impressive.

It seemed like the whole station was awaiting their arrival and when they walked in, the room erupted in shouts and applause. Hepburn was the first to congratulate them and even Montgomery was there. Although slighted muted, there was no doubt of his genuine feeling of gratitude that The Chain was in custody. Beer and wine bottles were laid out and Lyle had a crate of Irn-Bru on his desk. Hepburn, who had momentarily left the room, asked them to come to his office.

Standing at his desk was Assistant Chief Constable Gillian Campbell.

'Congratulations, I was very impressed when I got the news this evening that this monster in now once more in our custody. I have given the Chief Constable my own personal assurance that he will remain there for the rest of his days. He also asked me to pass on his own congratulations.'

'Thank you, ma'am,' Christie and Lyle said in unison.

'You deserve to enjoy this moment, trust me they do not come along too often. I must ask, however, that you do not overdo the celebrations as we still have another killer on the loose. The CC has offered additional resource, which will start tomorrow in here going over the case notes and all the information we have gathered thus far. DCS Hepburn will be keeping me abreast of all developments and I will be reporting back to the CC.' With that they were dismissed and stopped for a brief celebratory drink with Miles and Chowdhury.

The four of them were first to leave, they all had an early start in the morning.

Day 10 - 07:29 - Corstorphine Police Station, Edinburgh

The bottles had been cleared away and Christie and her three colleagues had arrived early for a case meeting. They knew that reinforcements were arriving today and they wanted to get a head start. They also wanted to make sure that they had not missed anything obvious. They were still awaiting results back from forensics on the hair sample, footprints and motorbike tyres, so they would have to start with old fashioned police work and their list of suspects.

'Right,' began Christie. 'Let's talk through a short list of suspects and potential motives. Firstly, we have Freddie Taylor. Freddie is local, knows the area and may have known all the victims. He was Samantha's boyfriend at the time of the disappearance and could be seeking revenge. Thoughts?'

'Well, it was a shock to discover the connection with Samantha,' Lyle commented. 'My main question is why wait all these years?'

'Perhaps he was waiting until he felt capable to complete the attack, or waiting to discover the identities of the whole group?' Chowdhury's point was well received.

'Second suspect, Nicholas Kerr or Nico as he is known. Samantha's brother who was young at the time of the disappearance. He has a clear motive and the time between the disappearance and the murders makes more sense. What do you think Lyle?'

'I've known him since he was a boy, I don't see it in him. That said, he probably has the biggest motive out of everyone and you can never really tell with someone.'

'Thirdly, we have Adam Robinson. Everyone who knew him has commented on how much he hated his father. Did he hate him enough to kill him? If so, why did he kill the others? Did he do it to hide the murder amongst the others or did he have another motive?'

'Seems unlikely that he would kill so many for the hatred of his father,' Miles answered. 'There may have been another motive that we do not know about.'

'Finally, and this may be slightly left field, Patrick Kerr. Motive clear, daughter murdered and also the breakdown of his marriage. I'm sure Lyle would agree that that seems to have affected him just as much as what happened to Samantha.'

'I'd agree ma'am. He may have a tough typical Scottish male exterior, but I saw how he was with Margaret and there is no doubt the feelings are still there. Revenge and the love of his ex-wife are equal motives.' Christie stood up, drawing the meeting to a close with a final statement.

'I think that we need to go and speak to these people again and try and establish who is hiding something and if any of these are the killer.

Keep thinking outside the box, because if the murder is not one of these four, we had better find others to investigate soon.'

Lyle headed back to his desk, mulling over the discussion and the four suspects. The fact that he had known two of them for such a long time sat uncomfortably with him, but in the case of murder and particularly multiple murders, sentiments went out the window. His thoughts were disturbed by his mobile phone ringing, the display confirming it was coming from a withheld number.

'Sorry to call so early DS Lyle,' said Dr Davis softly. 'I promised to keep you updated with Mr Mearns' progress and he was moved out of the High Dependency Unit late last night. His recovery has been remarkable and he could be getting discharged sooner than expected if there are no further complications. Had the bullet been an inch off, he may have entered a vegetative state, or died. He has been extremely lucky under the circumstances.'

'That's very positive news, Dr James. When can I see him, I really need to ask him some questions?'

'I see no reason why you can't speak to him again this morning. In fact he did say that he was keen to speak with you again, however, he wanted to ensure his solicitor would be in attendance also.'

Day 10 - 11:57 - St John's Hospital, Livingston, West Lothian

Lyle managed to get hold of Mearns' solicitor just after ten o'clock and hasty plans were made for a twelve o'clock meeting at the hospital. Mearns had been allocated a private room in the ward, so the solicitor was happy there would be enough privacy for the meeting to take place. The solicitor, to give him credit, had tried some stalling tactics, but Lyle was forceful on

214

how important the discussions were. He confirmed that he just wanted to conduct an interview of questions at this stage.

'So, are you going to tell me what is going round in your head yet?' Christie asked him as he pulled into the hospital car park.

'Nope,' he answered playfully. 'But I will say again that I think Mr Mearns knows who killed Samantha. In fact, I think all five of them knew who killed Samantha and they were too scared to speak out and tell the truth. I suspect that with his solicitor present, we may get an answer today. I also think I know what the answer is, but proving it is another matter. We may need a miracle, but knowing the truth may be enough for the Kerr family.'

The detectives were directed to the ward by the receptionist and then to the room by the kind nurse when they arrived. Inside the room Luca was sitting up and, despite the heavy bandaging, was looking so much better than at their last visit. Mrs Mearns was sitting beside him, holding tightly to a padded manilla envelope. His solicitor remained standing and introduced himself.

Jerry Layne was in his early thirties, with short hair that was waxed to precision. He wore an expensive, hand tailored suit with heavy cotton shirt and pink silk tie. His hand shake was firm without being uncomfortable but it also indicated that he liked to attend the gym. He appearance made him look more mature than his age, but Lyle had heard of him before and knew he had an excellent reputation in his field.

'Normally,' he began in his educated Edinburgh accent. 'I would discourage my client from undertaking such a meeting, especially so soon after such a traumatic experience. Mr Mearns, however, was as keen to speak with you and I surmise that you are as equally keen to speak with him. Before my client says one word, I want to ensure that everyone is clear that he does so of his own volition, and in a way to assist with your enquiries. Despite what he is about to tell you relates to a crime of over twenty five years ago, I understand that this may have an impact in a currently active case?'

'That is correct,' confirmed Christie.

'Thank you. I also want to confirm that my client speaks today as a witness and not a suspect of any crime and you have my assurance that what he will disclose to you will prove this.' Christie and Lyle excused themselves and headed outside the room for conference.

'This is a risky tactic, Lyle, and I'm not sure I'm entirely comfortable with it.' Lyle looked at her straight in the eyes, pleadingly.

'I need you to trust me on this one. We have already found Samantha and that may give the family closure, but unless we find out the truth, from someone who was there, they may never be at peace. I firmly believe that the answer lies in that envelope that Mrs Mearns is holding. Unless we agree to their conditions, we may never learn what is hidden inside.' Christie considered this for a moment, but she knew Lyle was right. Whenever he ask to be trusted, he had never let her down. She nodded agreement and they re-entered the room.

'Okay, Mr Mearns. At present this is an informal discussion, however, I must make you aware that we will want anything said today to be repeated and recorded as a formal statement should it prove vital for the case. We will also insist on any evidence presented today to be handed over to be used in our investigation. Do we have agreement?'

'Thank you DI Christie,' stated Layne. 'Mr Mearns?'

'I am happy with those conditions,' he replied. He took the envelope from his wife, peered inside and closed the flap over once more.

'Take your time,' Lyle said gently. 'Just tell us everything you know, from the start.' Mearns took a sip of water, a deep breath and began to tell the story he had kept with him for nearly three decades.

'The WMA started off as a bit of fun, young kids who were friends hanging around doing what young kids did in the 1980's. As we got older, especially living is a small village like Whitebank, we became more interested in booze, cigarettes and girls. By the early nineties were in our late twenties, but none of us had settled down and we had all agreed to meet up at New Year. Most of us were single and we had a massive blow out that year. Even David was drinking at Hogmanay, although he stopped drinking on the first whilst the rest of us continued.

'In the evening of New Years Day, we went out for a drive. David has recovered from the previous night's excesses and he owned this old Land Rover that he was working on, the type that had space for two passengers in the front and bench seats in the back. We were driving around West Lothian and we arrived in Kirknewton. We spotted a girl standing on her own, David and Dennis recognised her.'

'Samantha Kerr,' Lyle said.

'Yes. Dennis insisted that we pull over to chat to her. Samantha knew David to talk to and we pulled over to have a chat. I admit I felt pretty uncomfortable at this, she was a young girl and myself, Donald and Fraser all preferred girls of our own age. I think David and Dennis were different, but they never really spoke about it. As it turned out, Samantha was off to meet a friend, but he had not turned up and was over an hour late. She asked if she could get a lift to Whitebank, she knew that David lived there, and David was only too happy to accommodate. Dennis and Samantha sat in the front passenger seat chatting away and Donald, Fraser and I remained in the back, passing round a bottle or two. By the time we were approaching

Whitebank, I was pretty far gone, Donald and Fraser were passed out in the back. The next five minutes changed my life forever.'

At some point in the discussion, he had reach over and taken Tracy's hand. It was obvious that she knew this story, perhaps had known it for a long time, but it was still difficult for them both to hear in this setting. Layne had remained silent, taking down notes from time to time with his fancy fountain pen.

'Then Dennis killed her,' Lyle stated. Mearns looked up, there were tears in his eyes now. Christie knew that Lyle was right in his assumption of who the killer was.

'God forgive me for staying silent all these years, but the truth is that we were all frightened of him. It was an accident, of that I have no doubt, but he demanded that we cover our tracks and bury the body. He said no one would believe it was an accident and that we would all get charged with her murder. David was the most scared of Dennis and when Dennis suggested that we hide the body at his house, he was too petrified to say no. We drove to his house, and moved the body under the cover of darkness to his shed. Dennis agreed to help David bury the body, the other three of us were to have no further part in the proceedings and left. The two of them alone dealt with the body, they wouldn't even tell us where she was afterwards.'

'How exactly did she die?' Christie asked.

'I didn't witness it, I only found out after the event. Dennis had been resting his arm along the back of the twin passenger seat. He was drunk and started asking Samantha for a New Year's kiss. She refused his advances and then he put his arm around her neck to pull her towards him. You must understand that Dennis was an extremely powerful man. He worked out at the gym and had incredible strength in his arms. He was also very drunk and when Samantha turned away from him, and he pulled hard and sharply,

218

squeezing her as he fought to bring her closer to him. he must have crushed a bone in her neck.' At this point the tears came flooding and Layne suggested that they take a break.

Christie and Lyle headed down to the canteen to get coffee, neither having the urge to speak. It was a lot to process and there was still the question of the envelope. They gave Mearns fifteen minutes before returning to the room. Layne thanked them for their understanding.

'I have many questions to ask,' Christie began. 'But most of these can wait for a later time. The one thing that I am, however, keen to hear is what evidence that you can provide to prove that Dennis was the killer and that you had no part in the murder?' Mearns lifted up envelope and reached his hand inside. He pulled out a cassette tape and a piece of paper contained in a plastic folder.

'Before I asked Tracy to marry me, I wanted to have some form of security that should I ever be approached about this crime, I had the evidence to prove I was not involved. I met with Dennis, he had recently got married himself and was still living in Whitebank. I had already moved out of the village at the time and was living in Livingston. We met at his house alone, his wife was visiting her parents. I told him that I would remain silent about Samantha Kerr on the condition that he sign a letter confirming that he was solely responsible and that I had nothing to do with it. I swore that I would only use the letter as a last resort, if I was ever accused of the murder. He was not convinced and I said that if he did not sign the letter, I would do straight to the police and confess all, taking my chances in the process. I told him that Tracy knew everything, knew where I was and if anything happened to me she would know who was involved.'

He took a moment to compose himself, the memory of the meeting was obviously still painful.

219

'I was calling his bluff, of course, but it worked and he signed the letter. He believed everything I said and, until today, I kept my word. We both knew that a signed letter would not carry much weight, so I secretly recorded our conversation on my Walkman. The quality is not fantastic, but I am sure with modern day digital enhancement you will hear evidence that everything I have told you is the truth.'

Lyle took out an evidence bag and the letter and cassette tape were placed in it and sealed.

'Thank you for telling us the truth,' Lyle said genuinely, despite feeling an urge of anger at the man keeping this to himself for so long. 'At present, we will class you as a witness and take this evidence in for processing. I will do what I can for you in relation to your wishes and will let you know.'

Lyle stormed out the room without further comment and Christie followed him, struggling to keep up with him until they reached the car. Inside the car, Lyle just stared into space in front of him unable to speak. Christie just sat there, waiting until he was ready.

'Nearly thirty fucking years,' he said at last. 'How could anyone sit on that for all those years?' Christie didn't answer, there was no answer that she could give him.

'How did you know it was Dennis?' She eventually asked.

'Donald McIntyre told us.' Christie was none the wiser and Lyle knew it. 'He said that David was not responsible, but someone close to him knew what happened. He used the word knew, past tense, rather than knows, present tense. That meant the only person who he was referring to had to be Dennis. He was the only one, other that David, who was dead.'

Christie could not believe that she had missed such a crucial word in a witness statement and it just went to prove how much she could still learn from her sergeant.

CHAPTER TWENTY

Christie and Lyle updated Hepburn on the revelation in the Samantha Kerr case. They needed some guidance on how to proceed. In one way, pending proper examination of the evidence, they had finally found out the truth about what happened to Samantha. In the other way, they had an accessory to the murder who was wanting a deal of no prosecution in return for his statement and evidence. Hepburn reluctantly agreed to Mearns' terms, better to finally close the case and let the family try and finally come to terms with what happened was his opinion. Both Christie and Lyle were in agreement.

With The Chain back in custody and the Samantha Kerr case being closed, the team could all now come together and focus on the Whitebank murders. A team of five detectives had arrived from Glasgow and were buried in file notes and getting themselves up to speed with the case so far. Christie was more interested in the four suspects they had discussed early that morning.

'I don't want them ranked in order of most likely, Lyle, but I'm interested in talking to Freddie first. We could then have another chat with Patrick Kerr and get Chowdhury and Miles working on the other two. I want addresses and more background on them both.' Lyle went off to instruct them both and Christie took the chance to give Tom a quick call. It had been a few days since they had last spoken and she wanted some company this evening, it had been a traumatic couple of days. Plans made, she headed down to the car park and met Lyle at the GTI.

'Right ma'am, ask me any music question and I will give you an answer in song.' Christie had started to enjoy the little music games that they had recently started to play. It gave them both something to take their minds off things and helped ease the tension of the situations they invariably found themselves in.

'Ok, best cover version of all time?'

'Oh, that's a good one.' He thought about his answer carefully. 'I'm going to give you two answers and let me explain why. The first answer is the most obvious one. Jimi Hendrix's cover of Bob Dylan's 'All Along The Watchtower' is not only one of the greatest classic rock cover versions, it is one of *the* best cover versions of all time. My personal favourite, however, is Scotland's very own Gun with 'Word Up'. I can't think of any other rock band that would take a disco classic and turn it into a fantastic rock song.' Lyle played both songs as they made the trip once more into West Lothian.

Day 10 - 18:13 - The Whitebank Village Store, Whitebank Village, West Lothian

Christie and Lyle were surprised that Freddie was not at the store and Winifred was sat behind the counter flicking through a magazine. She was surprised to see the pair enter and rose, slowly and stiffly from her chair.

'Good Evening officers, is it not a bit late for you two to be still working?'

'I was about to say the same thing to you,' replied Christie, trying to keep the conversation friendly in the hope of gaining more information from her. Lyle would have used the same tactic and was pleased to see some of his tricks rubbing off.

'Aye, Freddie was meant to be taking over from me, but I guess he is running late. To think about it, I've not seen him since this morning.'

'We just wanted a chat with him, you may have heard of the latest attacks in Livingston?'

223

'Oh aye, terrible state of affairs that was. Another one dead and the other one in the hospital. Is he going to be okay?'

'It's early days,' Christie replied, careful to be non-committal but letting Winnie feel she got some information.

'I vaguely recall the names and I heard that the they grew up in Whitebank. It was a long time ago, and my memory is not what it once was.'

'Can you tell us anything about these men? Their names were Luca Mearns and Douglas McIntyre.'

'I can't recall the boy Douglas, but Luca rings a bell. Well, with a name like that you would get noticed in a place like Whitebank. He was a nice kid, always polite when in the shop but a bit of a tearaway with the other boys of his age. His mum was a lovely woman, but we lost touch when they moved from the village.'

'Thanks for your time, Mrs Taylor. So have you no idea where Freddie is?'

'No sorry. I seen him speaking to a man on a motorbike this morning, terrible machines those things, gives me the fear so they do. He might be over at The Arms, he's started going in there more often lately. To tell you the truth, I don't mind when he skips the odd shift. He's a great help to me and is the reason why we are still trading all these years later. He maybe nipped in for a quick pint and lost track of time.' Christie thanked her for her time and they left the shop.

'Well DS Lyle, why don't we go and make an appearance at the Mole Catchers and see if he's there.' Lyle raised his eyes brows, waiting for the punchline. 'And make a certain landlady's evening…'

Day 10 - 19:01 - The Mole Catchers Arms, Whitebank Village, West Lothian

The pub was relatively quiet at this time of the evening, four or five tables had diners and two older men sat at the bar debating politics. Freddie was no where in sight so they felt that their journey had been wasted. It had been a while since either had eaten, so they decided to stay for food, they had little choice in the matter when Andrea Wood appeared.

'DI Christie, you have brought back your handsome sergeant with you this time,' she exclaimed, much to Christie's amusement and Lyle's embarrassment. 'You will stay for some food, I hope. Unless you were just being polite the last time you were here. If you like fish, I've got some lovely fresh sea bass or salmon just off the boat today.'

They were escorted to a table in the corner, away from prying eyes and listening ears. Menus were placed in front of them.

'I'll have the halloumi burger again, if it's still available?' Christie asked in hope, realising how much she was craving it.

'I've got a couple spare, don't you worry. What about you Mike?' She was toying with him, using his first name to his obvious surprise, but a gentle hand on his arm and a warm smile confirmed she was just having some fun.

'I am partial to sea bass, so I will have that.'

'Great choice. Let me chat to the chef and make sure he gives you a decent sized portion, then I'll come back for a chat.' She headed off towards the kitchen and Christie couldn't keep the laughter in any more.

'Not a fucking word,' he looked directly as her. 'Ma'am,' he corrected himself. She raised her hands to indicate that she would say no more. Andrea arrived back soon afterwards. She took and delivered a drinks order before pulling up a chair to join them.

'Well,' she began with a more serious tone. 'This has all been rather horrible and I think the locals are in complete shock. They may look like they are going around their business as usual, but I can tell a big difference in the atmosphere lately. I hope you catch the person responsible soon as I can tell people as starting to worry about going out.'

'Does the letters WMA mean anything to you?' Lyle asked.

'No, should it?' She answered confidently and Lyle felt no reason to challenge her further.

'We wondered if you had any further information you could give us,' Christie was saying, moving the interview along. 'Any further word on Dennis or the people he mixes with?'

'Not really. Most folk are just in shock that something so terrible has happened on their doorstep, and twice. I think some people are missing him more than they expected. He could be an arse, but he was good banter most of the time. The locals feel as if they have lost one of their own. I know there was a whip round for the family, raised a few hundred pounds.'

'What about David Stafford? Has there been much spoken about him?' Andrea was shaking her head.

'Never really came in here and didn't go out much around the village. I think he was more of an enigma around these parts, his reputation preceded him and he didn't have the will to fight it. I think he just went into his shell and hoped people would forget over time. That's what most people think anyway.'

'Have you seen Freddie Taylor in the pub today? Lyle asked her.

'Not today, but he has been coming in more regularly. He's taken to having a few pints, mostly on his own. He's no trouble, but he seems to have the weight of the world on his shoulders.'

There was some commotion at the bar and Andrea excused herself. Christie and Lyle enjoyed their meal and contemplated heading back to Edinburgh. As they were saying their goodbyes, Lyle asked a further question.

'Do you know of anyone locally who rides a motorbike? Someone that Freddie knows perhaps?'

'Funny you should mention that, I seen him chatting to a motorcyclist this morning as I was opening up.'

'Who was it?' Christie asked a little too keenly.

'I don't know him personally, but his helmet had NICO painted on it.'

Christie and Lyle left hastily knowing that their return to Edinburgh was now being delayed.

Day 10 - 20:12 - A71 towards Kirknewton, West Lothian

Christie had called back to the station to both provide and receive an update. Miles was able to provide an address for Nico Kerr. He had a house on the outskirts of Kirknewton, choosing to remain in close proximity of his parents and an easy commute to his office in Livingston. There was not much more detail that Miles or Chowdhury could provide that had not already been shared, but they were continuing with their work. Christie told them both to head home and they would catch up in the morning.

Christie was surprised to learn that Montgomery was still at the station and keen to speak with her. He told her that he was studying the case notes and wanting to help if he could, but comfortable that Christie continue to lead the case. In normal circumstances she would have wallowed in the humble pie that Montgomery was eating, but in truth she was happy for any support. She thought he was maybe wanting to save some face, or show that a more senior officer was still involved in the case, especially with visiting officers in the building.

Montgomery was able to provide an update from the forensic team. The shoe print was a clear size 10 and the tyre tracks indicated that the motorbike was a moped style, rather than a bigger bike. DNA results were still outstanding, but Montgomery had pulled some strings and results were due before 10am. Christie thanked him and hung up the call.

'New Bestie ma'am?' Lyle asked with a smile.

'Piss off,' was the only reply he got.

Nico's house was a smaller semi-detached property in a new build development. The front lawn was kept neat and there was a large terracotta pot with red and yellow tulips. The BMW with the private number plate was parked proudly, cleaned to a sparkle, in the driveway.

If Nico was surprised by the visitors to his door, he failed to show it. He invited them in and offered the usual hospitality of tea or coffee. Both declining, he retreated to the living room and flung himself on the sofa. The house was filled with all the modern gadgets and the huge television overshadowed the rest of the room. A Playstation game was paused, some army based shooting game by the looks of it, but neither Christie nor Lyle were gamers and aware of such things.

Christie wasted no time and wanted to establish if Nico had an alibi for any of the attacks. He pulled out a blackberry from his pocket and scrolled down to his diary. He was saying that he had to keep his appointment calendar up to date so the office knew where he was at any time.

One by one Christie gave the dates with a two hour window either side of the estimated time of attack. To her shock, Nico was at home at each of the four occasions. Living alone, this meant that he had no alibi. He checked his phone for messages, to try and establish if anyone was with him at any of these times, but he drew a blank. He was now beginning to look more and more like the person they were after. The ultimate motive, the financial means, the opportunity and no alibi. She knew the answer to her next question could end in her first arrest in the case.

'What size of shoes do you take, Nico?'

He seemed somewhat confused by the question.

'Ten,' he said nonchalantly

Christie nodded to Lyle, who removed a pair of handcuffs from his pocket and arrested Nico on the suspicion of murder.

PART ELEVEN - LEASH

CHAPTER TWENTY ONE

Christie had spent the last three hours stuck at the station, waiting for Nico's solicitor to appear. He was refusing to answer any questions without him present and there was nothing that they could do. She called Tom, who had already headed over to her flat. He had taken a few days off work and said that he would stay over so he would be there when she got home. What ever time that might be…

Hepburn had made an appearance, looking like he hadn't slept in a few days. He confessed to having had a rough time of it from the ACC, however, The Chain result had her back on side. He was keen to see the Whitebank case reach a speedy and satisfying conclusion. Christie was feeling the pressure, she could not shake the notion that all her eggs were sitting in a one basket, a basket that Nicholas Kerr was currently keeping well hidden. Lyle was pacing up and down like a caged animal. They were going to go in together and they needed to get information. The clock was ticking and they needed answers before they were obliged to release him again.

A call came in that the solicitor had arrived and Christie and Lyle moved Nico to the interview room. They had already discussed tactics and were committed to sticking with them. Nico sat in his chair, staring forward at the wall behind Christie who sat directly opposite. Lyle reminded standing, leaning against the side wall, watching Nico intently. A few minutes passed before the solicitor arrived in the room.

'Morning, Nico. Don't worry, I'm sure we can get this all cleared up in no time.'

Gerard Scott was a large man, around six foot six and powerfully build. An ex-Scottish international rugby player, he stopped playing when the game became professional due to his commitment to his career. It had paid off, becoming a partner shortly afterward and was now one of only two senior partners in the firm. He had taken Nico under his wing early in his career, aware of his tragic background, and was keen to see him rise through the company before he was temped to sell himself to one of the larger firms. Gerard, when he got the news of the arrest, had no doubt that this was a big mistake, but had yet to hear the evidence against his colleague.

Christie and Lyle were asked to leave the room to allow him to consult with his client. They had arrested Nico around 9pm, and they only had twelve hours from then before they had to charge him. Christie had already asked Hepburn about arranging for this to be extended to 24 hours, as much may rely on the DNA coming through on time. Lyle remained silent during the period they were kept waiting. Christie often wondered what was going on in his head at these times, never more so than now. He had solved a cold case that had got under his skin, they had The Chain back in custody and now they had arrested one of the members of a family that they had just given closure to. She wondered if he wanted Nico to be guilty, thus solving the third case or innocent for the sake of a family that he had gotten to know over the last twenty five years.

Gerard opened the door to confirm that he was happy for the interview to proceed. Christie began by confirming the formalities covered at the start of each interview and made sure that Nico had everything he needed before they began. The last thing you wanted was a suspect to suddenly have an urge for a drink, food or a trip to the toilet just as the questioning was getting interesting. Nico confirmed that he was comfortable and ready to answer their questions.

Christie started by going over the times of the four attacks and getting Nico to confirm his whereabouts. At each incident, he claimed to be at home alone and had no one who could vouch for him. He said that he didn't speak much to his neighbours except to say hello in passing, although he had not long moved in. Christie decided to move onto the motive.

'Tell me about Samantha,' she asked. Nico didn't give much of a reaction, he had already worked out that this was a question that he was going to be asked.

'I was young when she went missing, but I do remember her well. She was a kind sibling and she looked after me. I think the age gap helped in that respect, she didn't feel threatened by me and we were a close family unit. Mum and dad would let us go off together as long as they knew where we were and that we would be back for dinner time. We would go off and play in the woods, sometimes Sammy's friends would appear but I liked them too. I became a wee brother to them also.'

'Do you remember when she went missing?'

'I don't remember much of the days when it was known that something had happened. I remember asking my mum when she would be home, I missed her and just wanted her back. There was always an excuse, she was staying at a friends, she was away for a few more days, etc. Eventually, I just knew she wasn't coming back and I stopped asking the question. I remember there being police in the house and being excited about that, but I was too young to appreciate what was happening.'

'What was it like growing up? It must have been difficult, especially with what was happening with your parents.' He conferred with his solicitor, who was happy for him to continue to talk. He knew the tougher questions were still to come.

'I was taken aside by my dad one day and he told me that I should forget about Sammy, she was never coming home and that I needed to focus on my own life and be the best I could be. I remember it clearly and I didn't think much more of it. He would have regular pep talks with me, getting me focused on improving myself. I guess looking back I could have gone off the rails, become a bit of a rebel, but I just wanted to make my parents happy. I knew they were heading for a divorce and thought if I did well in school, passed my exams and got good grades they would have less stress and maybe stay together. It worked for a while, but it was inevitable that they would separate. The best thing was that they stayed good friends, they still love each other of that I am certain. Unfortunately, they just can't live under the same roof.'

'What do you know about WMA?' It was now time to focus the questions on the case. Christie would proceed carefully, but needed answers. Again there was conference with solicitor and client. It seemed like the answering was going to stop at this point, but Nico got the approval to continue.

'I found out about it a few years ago about the Whitebank Male Association. At first I heard it was a club that David Stafford was in when he was a kid. I didn't link them to what happened to Sammy, but after I graduated I started to look into Sammy's disappearance more closely. I managed to get copies of the trial notes and started to do my own research. I just wanted to find out the truth, find out where Sammy was and give my family some closure.' He paused for a moment and then looked directly at Christie, a mixture of pain and anger in his eyes. 'The one thing I didn't want was to undertake some type of vigilante killing spree.'

It was the first denial from Nico and it was a powerful one. Christie paused to let Lyle ask the next question. He had taken a seat next to her, written a few notes in a pad and then looked at Nico.

'So you are telling us that you studied the case, with your newly acquired legal education, investigated the case, discovered WMA and possible links to Samantha's disappearance,' he looked at the notes in front of him, more for the dramatic pause than to read what was written. 'And done nothing?'

'What my client did, or does, in his spare time has no relevance to this case,' Gerard broke in. 'I suggest that the questions remain on the case.' Lyle was not fazed with the interruption.

'In his spare time he discovered the make up of a group of five individuals,' Lyle said, addressing Gerard directly. 'Three of those individuals are dead, and one very nearly died.' The reaction brought further discussions between the two across the table from him. Lyle knew he had won this particular battle. There was a request for a short break and the interview was suspended and Christie and Lyle were outside once more. It was too early to discuss opinions, there were more questions to be asked first, so they waited in silence.

Returning to the room, they recommended the interview and waited for Nico to answer Lyle's question.

'I did nothing with the information, but I did speak with David Stafford.' Neither Christie or Lyle expected this revelation, Nico was adding more suspicion rather than alleviating it. It was a risky strategy to admit this, it would have been discussed in the break. Perhaps it was agreed that it be better to confess this now, rather than for the information to come out later.

'What did he tell you?' Christie took over again.

'Better I tell you what I told him first. As you can imagine, he was not keen to meet me. He knew who I was and had been trying to put the whole episode behind him. I told him that I knew that he did not kidnap my sister and I just wanted to find out more about what was going on at that time. He eventually agreed to meet me at his house, but it took a few phone calls.' Nico took a drink of water before continuing.

'He told me about WMA and he told me that he knew Samantha, even admitting that he had a crush on her but knew it was not reciprocated. He said that he thought she had a boyfriend, but they would chat from time to time and he always enjoyed her company. The more I spoke to the guy, the more he opened up. After a while, he started to talk about the night Samantha went missing and the court case. He wasn't making much sense but he let slip something that stayed with me. He said that she should never have come across WMA.'

'What do you think he meant by that?' Christie probed.

'Well, I thought that he meant that she had trying to get into the group or she crossed them in some way. Whatever he meant, I knew that someone in the group was responsible. My plan was to try and find out who, but then someone started to bump them off.'

There was a knock at the door and the interview was suspended once more. A DC had a message that Hepburn wanted a word. Christie and Lyle headed to his office for the update.

'Word just in from forensics on the tyre tracks. Most likely model to have these tyre threads are that of a Lambretta scooter. What's more, Nicholas Kerr is the registered owner of such a model, purchased just six months ago.'

Christie and Lyle returned to the interview room with this information, but Christie had another question to ask before bringing up the Lambretta.

'Nico, you said that you are not involved in these murders and attacks. Are you willing to provide a sample for DNA comparison?'

'Happy to.' The reply was quick, quicker than Gerard liked going by his facial expression.

'Thank you, we appreciate your co-operation,' Christie replied genuinely. She made a point of flicking through the file she had in front of her, even though she knew the next question. 'You bought a Lambretta motorbike six months ago I believe?'

'Yes. My dad is a big fan of The Who and as a teenager I watched the movie Quadrophenia over and over. I've always wanted a Lambretta scooter, but it was only recently that I decided to splash out and buy one.' Lyle nodded to Christie an acknowledgement that he would explain the significance of the film later, she knew The Who were a band that Lyle listened to.

'Where is the motorbike now?'

'I lent it to somebody. They always wanted one too and I didn't get the chance to ride it much due to the hours I was working. I trusted them to look after it for a while until I had more time to take it out for a proper spin. I even let them borrow my helmet.'

'Who is this someone?' Christie asked.

'Why are you so interested in my scooter, it has nothing to do with any of this?' Nico's demeanour was starting to change, Lyle sensed it and took over the questioning knowing that the interview would be ending soon.

'We are the ones asking the question, who has the motorbike?' The question was demanding of an answer, it was a risky strategy but it had to be attempted. Nico was thrown by the sudden change in atmosphere.

'My partner, eh…' he tailed off answering the question but it gave them something. There was no mention of a partner in any of the background checks, no notable other half. Lyle asked the next question calmly.

'We would like to know your partner's name.' Nico whispered something into the ear of his solicitor who nodded his head.

'No comment,' he responded to Lyle's question. The interview was over, Nico was informed that he would remain in custody until at least 9am, however, they may extend that by a further twelve hours is they deemed it necessary. Nico's solicitor objected, but knew he had little power and after a short defending speech, he yielded. Nico had no objection and only asked if they had any books that he could read to help pass the time.

Arrangements were made to take the sample from him and Hepburn made some calls confirming that he wanted it run as priority. He was not willing to accept a result after the 24 hour deadline. Christie stood at her desk, her exhaustion showing.

'What do you think, Lyle?'

'Well a few things. Firstly, he was quick to agree to a DNA test. It could be a bluff, but that alone makes me question his guilt. Secondly, I believed him when he spoke about meeting David Stafford, just to find out more about his sister's disappearance. Finally, we need to track down this partner of his. They could be the key to the whole thing.' Christie agreed and then resigned herself that nothing would happen until the morning and asked Lyle to drop her off at the flat.

238

'Of course, Tom's been waiting long enough.' He gave her one of his cheeky smiles that actually made her laugh. Down at the car she turned to him.

'Right, you can tell me about The Who and the movie and an interesting fact on the way. Thank goodness it's a short journey.'

'Only one track from the album you need to hear.'

He put on 'Love, Reign o'er Me' with a return of the smile.

CHAPTER TWENTY TWO

Day 11 - 07:01 - Christie's Flat, Stockbridge, Edinburgh

Christie had enjoyed about half an hour of Tom's company before falling asleep in his arms. She woke up in the same position with her alarm going off at 7am. Despite the lack of sleep, she felt refreshed and ready for what could be a vitally important day on the Whitebank case. She got up, showered and made her way to the kitchen to make coffee and put the Swedish buns that Tom had brought in the oven. When the coffee was ready, Tom made his way to the kitchen.

'When this is over, however long it takes, let's get away for while,' she said to him. He reach over and took her hand, giving it a gentle reassuring squeeze. He poured the coffee and put the buns on the table.

'We could go to Sweden and try these out properly,' he said, mouth full of cardamon pastry.

After breakfast, Christie dried off her hair, finished getting ready and headed out to the Mini. Tom was planning a run later, but said he would stay at the flat over the next few days so that he was there when she got home each evening. It was a kind gesture, one that Christie appreciated greatly albeit she was unsure at what time she may get back.

Christie absentmindedly put on the playlist Lyle had given her and skipped through the tracks until she found something to help pick her up on the journey. AC/DC's 'Shoot To Thrill' seemed appropriate under the circumstances. She pulled into the car park in good spirits, ready to move the case towards a conclusion. She knew the evidence was mounting up and she was confident that she would get the killer soon.

Lyle was waiting at her desk when she arrived, looking annoyingly fresh.

'Do you not need any sleep, Lyle?'

'As the great Jon Bon Jovi said, I'll sleep when I'm dead. I'm sure someone said it before him, but it's a great song.' Christie rolled her eyes once more, before she spotted the coffee on her desk.

'Bless you,' she replied instead. 'Right, what do we have?'

'No update on the DNA as yet, but we are expecting that soon. Our guest is still sleeping, I think he read half of the paperback book he was given last night before giving up. No further news on the motorbike, but we have the licence plate and a description of the one Nico bought. Miles and Chowdhury have been going through Nico's background since six o'clock this morning and still no sign of a girlfriend or partner or any significant other on any of his social media profiles. Looks like he liked to keep his privacy.'

'MA,AM,' Chowdhury shouted from across the room, Christie and Lyle rushed over, he was animated as if he had found something.

'CCTV, ma'am, from the Livingston area. This was taken not long after the Luca Mearns attack. I can't get a clear picture of the licence plate, but it looks a similar model to the one we are looking for. I would ask the question, why would you use a brand new four grand scooter to deliver pizzas?'

Day 11 - 08:51 - Corstorphine Police Station, Edinburgh

Nico was woken up, but was refusing to answer any questions without his solicitor present. They needed to establish quickly who the mysterious partner was and if they had the motorbike at the time of the attacks. Again, it could be coincidence playing tricks on them but the threads were

241

connecting. The motorbike, the footprints, the lack of alibi and connection to WMA. Christie was reminded once more of The Chain and the various disguises he had used to get away with his crimes. She knew it was discussed at the trial so was public knowledge. Did this killer take a leaf out of The Chain's book and disguise as a delivery driver? It would explain their presence at that time of night and would also allow them to go relatively unnoticed.

'Shit,' she said aloud. She gathered the team around in the meeting room once more.

'Okay, we still have Nico as our number one suspect, but let's not lose sight of the others. He's clammed up now and I don't think we will get much out of him until the DNA results come back. Hepburn has confirmed that we have him for a further 12 hours so let's use the time to either rule in or out the others that are on the list. Also, we need to establish the name of his partner. Miles, you start to get a list of his friends and associates. Chowdhury, you go for family. I don't think there is any point in going for his colleagues, we are bound to get nothing out of them given their profession. Lyle, I think you and I need to go back to West Lothian and speak with Freddie again. I'm not convinced he is our man, but I want another shot at him to make sure.'

When the meeting concluded, Montgomery was waiting for her. She decided to be pro-active and leave personal differences to one side. Montgomery had been keeping up to date with the progress.

'Sir, I'm going back to Whitebank to speak with a witness. Nico is not speaking without his solicitor, who is on his way. Can you interview him and try and establish if he had the motorbike at any time during the last fortnight. We are also keen to find out the name of his partner, they could hold vital information.'

'I'll get her name if I have to squeeze it out him,' he replied with confidence. Christie thanked him and headed out with Lyle. She was more uncomfortable having Montgomery on her side that as her office enemy. Lyle summed it up perfectly as they walked out the door.

'Keep your friends close…'

Day 11 - 09:41 - Whitebank, West Lothian

They arrived at the Village Store to find Freddie restocking the shelves. The bored young girl was filing her nails behind the counter and chewing on gum. They were the only occupants of the shop. When Freddie turned round, he was sporting a nasty looking black eye.

'I walked into a cupboard,' he said in jest before leading them to the back of the shop to confess to the actual story. He sat at his late father's desk and told them what happened.

'Everything that has been happening over these last couple of weeks have brought back the pain of when Samantha went missing. We hadn't been going out that long but it felt different, you know? It could have just been that young love thing, but I really cared for her. Because our relationship was secret, when she went missing I just went into my shell, working all the hours mum and dad needed. Truth be told, I never got over it.' Tears were starting to form in his eyes, it was a different side to the cocky Freddie they had spoken to previously. It could be an act, but neither detective believed so.

'This last week, I started heading into The Arms for a pint before work. Then I started having a few pints after work. The last couple of days, they have merged and I didn't make work. Mum was great, she understood and I agreed to start doing more morning shifts and she would help the younger staff in the evenings. Last night, I went a bit too far. I had a few beers in the house, which is something I rarely do, and by the time I got to The Arms I was already mildly drunk. I've never been much of a whisky drinker, but last night I decided to embrace my Scottish heritage and try a few special single malts. I embraced the heritage a bit too much.' He smiled at the recollection.

'Anyway, nearing closing time this guy comes up to me and starts talking trash about Dennis to the guy next to me at the bar. I was too wasted to know who it was, I honestly can't remember. So, I go for the guy fuelled by alcohol and rage about what happened to Samantha. I just needed to take it out on someone, anyone, whoever was there at the time. There was only one problem, I'm useless in that situation. At school I was nicknamed Chippy Boy on the account that I couldn't batter a fish. Whoever it was, clocked me a good one in the eye and I fell over. He had legged it before I had been escorted from the premises. I'll need to pop over later and apologise to Andrea.'

The story sounded genuine and Christie knew that this was not their man. She decided to check his alibi and sure enough, he was at the shop during the time of some of the later attacks. In shop CCTV would prove it as would a number of customers and staff.

'We're going to pop over to The Arms now,' Christie told him. 'A few loose ends to tie up, but I will pass on your apologies for you. It will smooth the way before you go over.'

'Thanks, I will stick to the soft drinks for a while I think.' Christie and Lyle left the shop and started to walk in the direction of the pub. Christie was building up to the quip about the landlady as her phone rang, the display confirming it was Miles.'

'The first DNA sample is in, we are running it through the database pending Nico's results for a more direct comparison. It won't come as much as a shock, but we are looking for a male.'

'Well, it narrows down the suspects by around 50%,' Christie responded.

Day 11 - 10:22 - The Mole Catchers Arms, Whitebank Village, West Lothian

Andrea Wood was outside the pub watering the window boxes as they approached.

'Good Morning, handsome,' she welcomed Lyle. 'I assume that with your inspector joining us this is not a social visit?'

'Afraid not, Ms Wood,' Lyle replied, trying to remain professional and unsure if he was achieving it. Christie's smile defused the situation.

'Just a few questions, then we will be on our way,' she told her.

'Much the pity, in you come.' She locked the door behind them and they took a seat at one of the tables, refusing the offer of a drink. A classic rock radio station was playing in the background.

'Lyle may not be able to concentrate with this music on,' Christie teased.

'Yes, the locals prefer the modern rubbish during the day and it makes way for the sports television in the evening, but when I am setting up it's my time, my music.' Lyle did not know where to look, with both females enjoying the moment. Christie knew she better get back to the task soon or it would end up a social visit.

'Do you know Nicholas Kerr?' Christie asked.

'Nico? Paddy's son? Aye, I know him a bit. He comes in now and again, not too often. I think his dad wanted to try and get him onto the darts team, but he was rotten. To play darts properly, even for a lowly pub team like ours, takes hours of dedication and practice. He was too busy with his university work and Paddy says he's doing well as a lawyer now.'

'Do you know if Nico had a partner or girlfriend?' Andrea laughed.

'He kept his private life close to his chest, but being in this game for as long as I have been you learn to pick up the signal between who is just a friend and who is more than that. I think, unfortunately, that people in a village such as this don't always understand love like Nico's.' Christie gave a slightly puzzled look, Lyle had already worked out what she meant.'

'He had a secret boyfriend.' Lyle confirmed.

'A secret boyfriend who was in here last night, who left before I had the chance to throw him out.' They waited for Andrea to reveal the information that they so desperately sought.

'The man who threw a punch at Freddie Taylor, Adam Robinson.'

Day 11 - 11:01 - Whitebank Village, West Lothian

Christie called it in. She wanted to confirm if Adam still lived at his parent's house or if he had his own place. She and Lyle were already walking towards the family home. They reached the path leading to the property, the path that Dennis Robinson had been murdered on. Could it really have been his son that did this to him?

Their suspicions were raised further when they spotted Nico's Lambretta parked a few doors down from the house, his distinctive helmet chained to the back. They knocked on the front door, the sound of the dog barking was absent. Linda Robinson answered in her dressing gown.

'We were looking to have a quick word with Adam,' Lyle asked using all his experience to remain calm under the circumstances. 'Is he here at the moment?'

'He's just taken Bouncer out for a walk. I'm not feeling that well at the moment so he came over to see to the dog. You can come in and wait for him if you like.'

'That's alright, Mrs Robinson, where does he normally take the dog?'

'Whitebank Woods, just at the top of the path there. That stupid dog likes to chase the squirrels.' She laughed and Lyle thanked her and the two headed off in the direction of the woods. When they arrived they spotted the dog first, up on his hind legs front paws resting on a tree trunk, nose to the air sniffing for his prey. Adam was sitting on a fallen trunk, back to them swinging the dogs leash back and forth. Lyle approached him cautiously.

'POLICE. Drop the leash and put you hands on your head,' Lyle shouted. Startled, Adam had dropped the leash involuntarily and slowly raised his hands to his head, turning to face them. Lyle moved quickly to secure the handcuffs, before patting him down for a weapon.

'He's unarmed,' he confirmed. Bouncer had come over to see the commotion and Christie picked up his leash and secured it to his collar. They headed back to the house to drop off the dog in silence before escorting Adam back to Edinburgh.

Day 11 - 16:29 - Corstorphine Police Station, Edinburgh

It all happened quickly that day.

By the time they had arrived back at the station, Nico's DNA result was back and confirmed that it was not a match. Officers had been dispatched to Adam's flat just outside Livingston and discovered a sickening wall chart of the victims in his spare bedroom. They had also recovered a gun with silencer which matched the type of weapon used in the crimes.

Nico's DNA was taken, but it was just a formality. He had decided to confess to the three murders and the attempted murder.

Adam had met Nico at university, but the former had dropped out after a difficult second year. They had dated in secret on and off since then, Nico was too focused on his career to commit, Adam was scared of his homophobic father. The turning point came when Adam found out about WMA from Nico. Sickened that his father may be involved, sickened by the affect that it had had on Nico, he planned on revenge and justice. With the members of WMA gone, especially his father, he knew that Nico could be happy and they could finally live together in peace. He had even considered a holiday away with him when it was all over, to make the proposal. Adam knew, despite how careful he had been, that the evidence would prove his guilt.

Nico was released but asked to speak with Lyle before he left. Christie joined them the interview room to hear what was Nico has to say. He had been informed that his partner had been charged with the crimes, but was not allowed to see him at this time.

'It seems that my life is destined to tragedy,' he began. 'I've never quite managed to come from out of my sister's shadow and now I guess I never will. I promise I had no idea what he was doing or planning.' Adam's confession was already on the basis that he acted alone and that Nico had no part or knowledge of the crimes.   'The one positive that we can take out of this,' he continued, 'is that you found Sammy and we now get to give her a proper burial and my parents can finally have some sort of closure.' He stood up and shook Lyle's hand, holding on to it. 'I won't hold a grudge over what has happened in the last 24 hours. You will always be the person that brought my sister home and found out what happened.' With that, and tears falling down his cheek, he made his exit.

The two detectives remained in the interview after the door closed behind Nico. Lyle didn't ask for it, but Christie turned, put her arms around him and let him weep into her shoulder.

PART TWELVE - INDIFFERENCE

EPILOGUE

Two Weeks Later - The Classic Crock Cafe, Edinburgh

Christie was packed and ready for her cycling trip around Scandinavia with Tom. They had pulled out of their planned triathlon race in favour of the trip. She was meeting up with the team one last time before her long overdue and deserved three week's break.

'Seriously,' Lyle was saying. 'Could you not just lie on your arse for three weeks, soaking up the sun somewhere? You'll need a holiday when you come back.'

Miles and Chowdhury laughed and Christie tried, but failed, to explain the attraction of such a holiday.

'I'm off to Greece later in the year,' Miles told them. 'Two weeks with Songbird, beside the beach, with more cocktails than is good for us. What about you Chowdhury?'

'Paris. Never been, always fancied it.'

'Are you not a bit old for Disneyland?' Lyle quipped.

'Are you not a bit old for first dates?' Chowdhury retorted.

'Only someone as tee-total as you could go on a date with a landlady,' Christie chuckled, keen to join in.

They all laughed and enjoyed the rest of their night. For the first time in a long while, the thought of murder and abduction was the last thing on their mind.

The Next Day - Whitebank Village, West Lothian

This time would be different for Lyle.

He was heading to Whitebank on his own terms. The sickening feeling that he previously felt entering the small village was gone. The family may have had closure, but he too had experienced the same thing. At first he had felt indifference to the idea of closure, he thought it was something that was said to make people feel better about tragic events. Now, however, he fully understood.

He had been invited to Samantha's funeral and it was a celebration of her life rather than the expected somber affair. Lyle never got a moments piece, with all the family and friends wanting to come and thank him. It was an emotional day for him, but he had let his emotions go that day at the station with Christie. To her credit, she never mentioned it again, never brought it up. She knew what it meant and it was another link in the chain that bonded them together.

The Chain was back in prison now and increased security was in place. He would never have the opportunity to get out again and the whole police and prison system was subject to an enquiry. Lessons were to be learned, but that was for another day.

Lyle pulled up in front of the pub and killed the engine. It had been so long since he had been on a date and he was nervous. Ever since his wife left him, he had lost confidence in finding a relationship again. A few disastrous blind dates aside, he had just focused on his work and his cafe. He had a feeling that this one may be different.

Andrea bounced out of the pub. She was wearing jeans, black boots and a leather biker's jacket. Lyle recognised the faded AC/DC t-shirt under the jacket. It looked like an original. She jumped into the passenger seat and kissed him on the cheek.

'I can't believe you own The Classic Crock Cafe. I've been in a few times with friends after a gig, I don't get much time off, but you were never there.' She punched him playfully on the leg. 'Right let's get going and see what tunes we can put on this very impressive music system of yours.'

Lyle put the car into gear and sped off. They were heading into Edinburgh to an Italian restaurant that neither of them had been to. She had wanted to go to the cafe, but Lyle wanted that to happen on a later date.

'Oh here we go!' Andrea exclaimed. 'You have Whitesnake from before David Coverdale started to dye his hair and go all American glamorous.' She played the song 'Slide It In', singing the chorus loudly with that mischievous grin that Lyle had come to adore. Although she was singing in jest, she had a very good voice. He remembered that there was karaoke at the pub and wondered if she would get up herself to show off her talent. As the song played the final chorus, Andrea placed a hand gently on Lyle's thigh.

'Why don't we give the restaurant a miss and you can show me the size of your vinyl collection.' The mischievous grin was back and Lyle changed his route.

One Week Later - Corstorphine Police Station, Edinburgh

Lyle was completely pissed off and stormed out of Hepburn's office. He had managed to hold his tongue, but his facial expression would have given his feelings away. To his credit Hepburn was apologetic that he could not support Lyle's request, but the request was declined much to Lyle's dismay.

He headed back to his desk, Christie was somewhere between Western Sweden and Eastern Norway, so he couldn't even rant to her. He felt let down and betrayed by the system. He understood the importance of budgets and the senior management had to keep a tight control of the purse strings. Even so…

Lyle suddenly had an idea. There was a crime writer who lived locally who had consulted him on a number of police procedural matters. Perhaps they could come to the rescue. For what he did and for what he gave, Lyle never asked for anything other than his normal salary in return. Now was different, he needed more.

He picked up his phone and dialled.

The Next Day - Wester Hailes, Edinburgh

Bad Boy was sitting on the sofa watching a late night movie on the television, one he had seen before and it was nothing more than background noise. Maria was snuggled into him, cradling a well deserved glass of wine. Michael had taken an age to get to sleep, and the noisy bastard upstairs was obviously pissed and playing his music far too loudly. Bad Boy had challenged him before, but he was not the sort of person that you would challenge again.

Bad Boy's phoned pinged to inform him of a text message.

'Check Your Bank Account. ML'

Bad Boy, sat up on the sofa, immediately loading up the banking app on his smart phone.

'Who was it? Maria asked, wondered what had startled him. She was now more comfortable in his company, but there was always a niggling doubt that his old life would come back and haunt them. Bad Boy burst out laughing, dropped the phone and hugged Maria tightly. The glass of wine spilled to the floor, but he would worry about that later. He retrieved the phone and handed it to Maria. She took one glance and burst into tears.

They had just received a deposit of £20,000 into their account.

'Do you know what this means?' Bad Boy asked Maria. She nodded her head as she wiped away the tears.

'We have enough for the house deposit,' she mumbled before the tears flowed once more.

Four Weeks Later - HM Prison, Edinburgh

The Chain was eventually allowed the phone call he sought and had been asking for now for the last seven weeks. Contact had been made with the relevant authorities and permission had finally been given. He was allowed a three minute call, which was both being recorded and monitored. The call could be terminated at any time.

The phone rang three times before it was answered.

'DI Christie, thank you for agreeing to take my call. I promise you that I only have your best intentions at heart.' Christie asked him to go on and be mindful of his time limit.

'I'll cut to the chase then. You caught me fair and square and once more I find myself impressed by your talents. You have proven yourself to be an excellent detective and I am sure you will climb further up the ranks over time. That is where I come in.'

'What do you mean?' Christie asked.

'As well as earning the title of Scotland's Most Dangerous Serial Killer, I studied criminology at the Open University. I have a deep interest, a personal interest I am sure you will agree, but I have something that criminologists don't have. Experience. This is where I propose to support you. I can give you an insight to your next murder case, from the killer's perspective. After graduation, I spent a further four years studying serial killers from around the world before I claimed my first victim. That knowledge will help you. Please don't give me your answer now, I just wanted to give you my proposal to consider. Have a nice day, DI Christie.'

With that The Chain hung up the phone and was escorted back to his cell, leaving Christie staring at the phone on her desk.

Wondering…

THE END

ACKNOWLEDGEMENTS

As always, my first and highest level of appreciation goes to my wonderful wife, Amanda and by incredible daughters, Audra and Elisha.

Thanks also to my family and friends who have read my work, supported me and encouraged me to keep going.

Thank you to my colleagues, especially Alex for all the technical assistance he gives me (which will one day make it into a novel), Emma for reading my earlier efforts and encouraging me to finish this one quickly and to Sonja for the story about the fountain pen usage on the registers (which did make this novel).

To Dr David Cochran for the story about the mole catcher which I was able to sneak into the book also.

To retired police officer Scott Higgins, who has promised to help me get the police stuff right in the future with the help of his contacts in exchange for a character being named after him. I hope DI Higgins met your approval and he may very well appear in future novels.

To my fellow crime writers who have shared their knowledge and tips (mainly on Twitter) and replied to some of my mad requests and questions. Also my fellow independent crime writers who, like me, do it for the joy of the process and love of the genre.

A huge thanks to Sam McMillan for the coffee chats when things were a bit ropey and helping me set up my website when things were better.

Thanks again to Scott Liddell at Dark Edinburgh for another fine cover photograph.

This novel was written during the lockdown period of the COVID-19 pandemic of 2020 and I would like to personally thank all the wonderful staff of the NHS and all key workers who supported the country during this time.

Finally, my upmost gratitude to Craig 'Brodie' Simpson. He was there at the start of the journey and he is still here today. Your encouragement, support and friendship can not be put into words. We have both sailed in difficult waters and become better people when we reached dry land. It was a pleasure to finally finish our seven year collaboration and I can't wait to see the final result and share it with others.

To anyone I have forgotten, please accept my thanks and apologies - I'll get you in the next one.

Printed in Great Britain
by Amazon